KING OF THE FIRE DANCERS

Shift Happens, Book One

S.T. Sterlings

Published by
NineStar Press
PO Box 91792
Albuquerque, New Mexico, 87199
www.ninestarpress.com

Print ISBN # 978-1-947139-60-2
Cover by Natasha Snow
Edited by Sasha Vorun

When he's propositioned by a wealthy stranger, it seems Coy Conlin's impoverished life is about to be upgraded. But before he can share the news with his family, he comes home to find his grandmother murdered and his little brother missing. To make matters worse, he's thrown in prison along with every other shifter under the Sovereign's orders.

August Seaton left his laboratory job at the Asuda Registry to become a Registry officer. But after a mission with his partner goes horribly wrong, August ends up with Coy's dead grandmother on his hands, and Coy thinks he's the murderer. Worst of all, his partner discovers his secret.

August is a shifter. And now he's Coy's cellmate. Coy and August must survive each other, abusive guards, and a scientist hell-bent on forcing Coy into a breeding program.

Teamed up, the pair escape prison and journey across the country. With the Registry hot on their trail, they have enough things to worry about. Falling for each other wasn't supposed to be one of them.

Dedication

For Val, Sylvana, Becca, Kim, Rosie, and everyone else that has given me the courage to do what I love. And for Krystal who did it first, all those years ago.

Acknowledgments

A very special thank you to all the fans and friends of my past from y!Gallery and LiveJournal who motivated me to write my stories, no matter how silly they were. This goes the same for my friends on Tumblr and the crew on Twitter who make social media enjoyable. Sylvana, Becca, Kim, Rosie, and Val—having you all cheer me on means more to me than you will ever know. Val, sorry we couldn't go with *Furries of Love*, but it'll always be that in our hearts!

I would also like to give a huge thank you to NineStar Press who saw something in my writing that made them want to take a chance on this story. And last, but certainly not least, thank you to my amazing editor, Sasha Vorun, who helped make this story so much better than it could have ever been on its own. There are not enough words in the English language to express how thankful I am for you!

Chapter One

THERE WERE TWO things that Coy Conlin was exceptionally skilled at. The first was dancing. The second, and more unconventional, was turning into a dragon. Both were in his blood and took years of trial and error to perfect, but the former wasn't a danger to those around him. It wasn't easy maneuvering a dragon body, especially not one as big as his. Dragons had claws, scales, and fangs. He even had the misfortune of retaining his proneness to seasonal allergies, which sure as hell took explosive sneezing to a whole new level. Still, thanks to his grandmother—a dragon shifter like him—he'd mastered shifting and everything that it entailed from a young age.

Like hunting.

His prey was a slender boy with white skin and blue eyes. The boy raced past, auburn hair catching the wind and blowing about his head. He scurried through the dried grass, his pale, gangly legs kicking up dirt as he rushed to hide behind a large tree. Laughter disguised as a growl escaped Coy's mouth. As if a mere tree would provide the boy sanctuary.

Coy hated flying. Dragon or not, he preferred to keep his feet—and claws—securely grounded. But, humans were often smarter than they looked, and he knew that if he continued to creep along the ground, the boy would feel the vibrations caused by his heavy footsteps. And so, he pushed off, sharp talons grazing earth as he hovered above the coarse ground. His wings, as wide as sails on a cutter, pierced the air and sent forward a powerful gust of windblown, dusty dirt. He flapped them again, creating a mini dirt storm between himself and the tree and, most importantly, his prey.

A shower of prickly leaves and thin, brittle branches fell to the ground. Seconds later, the boy emerged from behind the tree, arms up and over his head, shielding himself from the downpour. Amidst the cascading debris, Coy caught the look of determination on the boy's face. Wedged tightly in the boy's grip was a rock, jagged and angled, the tip pointing toward the sky. A rock? Really? A puny, misshapen hunk of slate? What good would that do against a ninety-foot-long dragon with scales as black as onyx and five times as hard?

A *rock*.

The little idiot.

The boy let out a wail of a battle cry and charged forward, gripping the rock in his hand like a warrior wielding a sword. There were hundreds of ways Coy could have reacted, and most would have ended with the boy dead on his feet. Instead, he stood there, a beacon of massive power and pride, and allowed the boy to attack. He didn't feel the impact of the rock smashing against his leg, though he did see the resulting blood. It wasn't his. It would have taken much more than a rock to puncture his scales.

It was the boy's.

The force behind the thrust of his hand had caused the rock to ricochet off a section of scales and created a shallow cut in the center of his reddened palm.

Coy had been specific with the rules—no blacking out, no crying, and no bloodletting. If any of those happened, the game ended immediately. And, although the human tried to hide it, he was definitely bleeding.

"No, wait. I'm okay. I swear it. I'm fine. Look. It barely—"

The protest fell on deaf ears—literally. Coy couldn't hear—or see—anything during the transformation. It was as if he were alone in a black, soundproof room, nothing but darkness and depth and the feeling of endless falling. His heart rate quickened, slamming against his chest like a musician's calloused hands pounding against a hand drum. He inhaled through his nose, focusing on the rhythm and physically and mentally controlling the pace of his heartbeat. He calmed his mind, grasping at emotions pulsing like lightning, smoothing them out until his vision began to return. First, blurs of colors: reds and browns and a single blob of white standing directly in front of him.

Then, all at once, everything returned.

"It's barely a scratch," the boy muttered, folding his pale arms over his chest.

"Too bad," Coy replied, rubbing at his jaw. It felt good to use his vocal cords again. He was incapable of speech as a dragon, just limited to snarls and hisses...and fire breathing. That last one came in handy. "Rules are rules, Ari."

Ari—Coy's adopted brother—frowned. "You didn't even give me a chance."

"A chance to what?" Coy rolled his shoulders in an attempt to relax some of the tension in his muscles that came from shifting. "Find another rock? What was *that* supposed to do?"

He trudged away from his younger brother, crushing dead grass beneath his bare soles. He spotted his discarded sarong lying by a fragment of slate, the latter's golden-brown surface highlighted with speckles of fiery red. The color was reminiscent of his own skin, warm brown with red undertones—the exact opposite of Ari's. Even if Ari had somehow managed to slightly injure him with his dumb rock, the bruise would have been difficult to see. One of the many perks of having brown skin was that it didn't display bruises well. Growing up, that played to his advantage with the number of fights he got into.

Ari pouted. "It was the only thing I could think of."

"Yeah, well." Nude, Coy bent down to retrieve his sarong. "That type of thinking is going to get you killed. Or worse, you'll get your ass kicked."

Ari rubbed his bloody hand against his sweat-soaked tunic. "How can getting beat up be worse than *dying*?"

Coy watched as the blood stained the faded fabric. Ari had already outgrown most of his clothes. What he had left was either tainted or torn. Coy would have to take up private performances at this rate just to make sure he could afford to buy Ari clothes.

"If you're dead, you won't have me around to rub it in." He grinned at Ari and then motioned toward the open wound on his hand. "Better not let Dinina see that. You know how she gets."

He wrapped the thin, cobalt-colored sarong around his waist, securing the two ends into a knot. They'd spent half the morning outside, which meant he'd spent just as long in his dragon form. He'd be exhausted later, but it was worth it. He always had fun hanging out with his little brother. Still, he felt like he was forgetting something.

And then he remembered.

"Shit!" he shouted, the sound so loud and sudden that it startled an unkindness of ravens perched in a nearby tree.

"What is it? What's wrong?" Ari asked, blue eyes wide with concern.

There were several things wrong, and all of them could be summed up with two words.

"The Registry."

THE OFFICERS WERE late.

Luck wasn't a guest that visited him often, but today it had, as Coy had nearly been late himself.

The letter he and his grandmother had received lay on the chipped coffee table, its stark pallor contrasting with the wooden surface. The Registry's insignia—*AR*—stood out on the header, the text below it added as though in afterthought. He hated Registry visits. The tension and anxiety he felt before each one made his stomach ache. He thought he would have grown used to them by now. Then again, how could anyone get used to feeling like a prisoner in their own skin?

Sitting on the couch with his legs tucked beneath him, Ari glanced at the front door and bit at his fingernails.

"Hands out of your mouth. Feet off my couch," Dinina called from her spot in the kitchen, leaning against the countertop.

"How does she always know?" he whispered.

Coy propped his feet up on the scuffed table they'd found tossed away on a dusty sidewalk just a few weeks back. "Old dragons see everything." Dinina sent him an unimpressed look, but he suspected it may have been more to do with his disregard for their furniture, shabby as it was.

Ari continued to stare at the door. "Maybe something happened to them."

"One can only hope," Coy said.

He may not have liked their visits—nor the frustration he felt after each one—but at the very least, they could have cared enough to show up on time, even if he hadn't been.

Bastards.

Maybe something really had happened to them.

It was wishful thinking, of course. Only a moment later, the quiet of their living room was interrupted by a series of knocks on the front door.

"You do know you don't have to be here for these things, right? There are, like, a hundred other things you could be doing right now," Coy told Ari.

The knocking continued.

Ari shrugged. "I want to make sure they don't try anything."

"Two dragons protected by a scrawny, twelve-year-old human with noodle arms and skin like a cloud. That's a relief."

"Shut up. I don't have noodle arms. You have—"

"It's unlocked," Coy called, both interrupting and ignoring his brother.

The door creaked open, and in walked two male Registry officers. They moved like wooden boards, rigid and stiff, dressed from head to toe in black uniforms. They may as well have been on their way to a funeral.

Fate, the senior officer, was the first to speak, his voice like broken glass.

"Coy and Dinina Conlin, the Asuda Registry is here on this day of—"

"Yeah, yeah," Coy interjected. "Can't we just skip all this scripted bullshit? We've heard these same tired lines for years now. Just spare us, do the exam, and get lost."

"Fine," Fate said, interlacing his gloved fingers. "I'll take the female." He turned toward his partner. "Do you think you can handle the male?"

"We have names," Coy muttered, cleaning his teeth with his fingernail.

"Not as far as I'm concerned." Fate's monotone voice was nearly drowned out by the sound of his boots clicking against the linoleum floors. He stopped in front of Coy's grandmother, looked her up and down, and motioned for her to follow him farther into the kitchen. "Come, dragon."

The other officer stood in the middle of the living room, poised and polished. He looked more like a prince than an officer. Still, Coy could tell that he was a rookie. In the many Registry visits he'd been forced to endure over the years, he'd had his fair share of interacting with rookies. They all had a nervous look about them, as if they were trying—and failing—to be intimidating. Those types never lasted long—at least, not when they were assigned to him.

"I do not recall asking for an audience," the officer said, gloved hands on his hips.

Glancing over at his brother, Coy said, "Ari, go to your room."

"No way."

Shrugging, he turned his attention back to the officer. "You heard the kid." He met the officer's gaze, the intensity of his own mismatched irises working to unnerve the man standing a few feet away from him.

To the officer's credit, he didn't look away, though Coy could smell his fear like a subtle perfume.

"So, I'm guessing you're new, huh? Not surprised. Fate can never hold on to partners. Scares them away on the account of him being a piece of shit. Ain't that right, Fate?" He spoke loud enough for Fate to hear him.

"Seaton," Fate called from the kitchen. "If you'd please begin your examination."

"R-Right," Officer Seaton replied. "Coy Conlin, when was the last time you shifted?"

"About half an hour ago."

"I see..."

"But I'm sure you knew that already."

All shifters were monitored on how often they shifted. The chips embedded beneath their skin relayed this information. Unless they were in mortal danger or had the written consent of the Registry, shifters were limited to when and where they could transform. Registry law stated that Coy was only allowed to shift in Hamet, and only on his own land or a vacant lot. If a talon so much as touched property that wasn't his even with the landowner's permission, the Registry could—and *would*—fine him.

Coy observed Seaton, only half listening as he rambled off a bunch of annoying questions. He was a pretty, little thing. Lithe with perfect posture and eyes the color of maple syrup. His lips were rose petals, plump and pink, but wilted into a frown. His uniform did not blend well with his golden-brown skin, which gleamed like sand beneath sunlight. It muted it and made him look pale, especially when compared to Coy's darker complexion—which was a shame. Brown was his favorite color.

Even as a Registry officer, Seaton was too sleek, too elegant. Unlike his partner, his skin—at least that of his face since everything else was covered—was unmarred by scars or imperfections. Seaton was too beautiful to be an officer and too refined to be Hametian. He must have been from one of the northern provinces.

Other than his initial nervous stutter, he enunciated his words, spoke them slowly so that each one had a sense of finality to them.

"And your age is—"

"Twenty-five," Coy answered, growing aggravated with the endless round of questions. "Look, all of this is in my file, isn't it? You don't have to do everything by the Registry book, you know."

"I will," Seaton snapped, "follow protocol. Is that clear?"

Now they were getting to the fun part.

He'd seen officers just like Seaton come and go over the years. Whether they were rookies or veterans, high-strung or laid-back, they had one thing in common: fear. Coy knew the smell of fear. It lingered in the air around them, pungent and thick as smoke. He enjoyed it, especially when he was the cause of it—and he'd smelled Seaton's fear from the start. Still, there was something else about Seaton. Another smell that seemed familiar, but one he couldn't place. Whatever it was, it wasn't manufactured.

"Your file did not mention you were hard of hearing, so I can only assume that you heard my question. And yet, I am still waiting to receive an answer. Was the question too difficult? Shall I—" Seaton bent slightly at the hip, face the picture of false sincerity. "—dumb it down for you?"

"Oh, it's clear. Crystal clear, *Officer*," he answered, offering both a grin and a wink.

"Good." Seaton stood upright again. "A bit of advice. It would serve your best interest to not make things difficult."

A soft chuckle fell from Coy's lips. "My best interest? I'm supposed to believe that you have my best interest in mind?"

Seaton didn't reply.

"So, are we done here?" He already knew the answer, but he was quickly finding that he enjoyed getting under Seaton's skin. Maybe he'd make a hobby out of it—see if he could tease him without scaring him off like the others.

"Unfortunately, no," Seaton replied. "Your file states that you are a fire dancer at a circus. Is this correct?"

"More or less."

Seaton had further questions. Coy could tell just by looking at the curious expression on his face. He knew he wasn't going to ask them though. Too much pride.

"Right... If you would be so kind as to stand for the next part of this interview." His polite request sailed in on a sea of detectable resentment.

Coy stood—all six foot four inches of him—tall and broad in the small living room. He towered over Seaton, who was at least six or seven inches shorter, and held back a smirk at the widening of his eyes.

"Something wrong, Officer? Don't tell me a cat snatched that sharp tongue of yours."

Seaton would have to look up at him if he wanted to maintain eye contact as he answered, something that pleased Coy immensely. He couldn't stop his smirk when Seaton tilted his head so that he could stare right back.

"My tongue is exactly where it should be."

Coy's gaze dropped, lingering on his mouth. "I don't know about that. Could probably find a few places where it'd fit in just fine."

Seaton rolled his eyes and then slid a thin flashlight out of his pocket. He raised his hand, positioning the flashlight in front of Coy's lips. "Open your mouth."

"Never had someone say that to me without properly introducing themselves first." Coy spoke into the flashlight as if it were a microphone, the light beaming on his mouth.

"My name is Officer Augustus Seaton. You may refer to me as Officer Seaton."

"No problem, Auggie."

Seaton glared at him. Coy liked it. He found it endearing.

He stood still as Seaton moved closer, ordering him to bend down so that he could peer into his mouth without having to stand on his toes. To anyone else observing them—which was Ari, in this case—Seaton probably looked like a picture of confidence. He didn't fool Coy. He smelled Seaton's anxiety, saw the nervous tremble in his delicate-looking hand.

He waited until Seaton's hand was just an inch or so away from his mouth before exhaling, slow and deep. A small flame burst from his parted lips, red and orange swirling together and flickering.

Startled, Seaton snatched his hand away. The flame had missed him. Naturally. Coy knew better than to injure a Registry officer, but he was sure Seaton had felt the heat against his skin. He bet his fingers still tingled from it.

Coy licked his lips. "Oops. Sorry about that. Reflex." He grinned. "Please continue."

The scowl was back on Seaton's face. Eyes trained on Coy, he pointed the flashlight into his mouth again, briefly regarding his teeth.

"I am surprised."

"Oh, yeah? What about?"

"One would think that cavepeople would not bother with such trivial chores as proper dental care."

"Fuck you."

Fate must have completed his exam, because he and Dinina stepped into the living room. Fate's birdlike face was set in its permanent scowl, while his grandmother's expression was blank—her typical state whenever the Registry was around.

Fate kept his eyes on Seaton, like a father scrutinizing his son. There was pride behind that cracked, porcelain mask of a face. He must have caught some of the exchange between the two of them and was pleased by the way Seaton had handled himself.

Coy almost felt like laughing. Registry officers were elitist pricks with too much time on their hands, hell-bent on authority and ordering shifters about without so much as an inkling of human decency. Seaton's virulent tongue could spit out as many cutting words as he wanted, but it would not change the facts. Humans were afraid of shifters. They feared and—Coy knew—envied them. Shifters may have looked human, but they weren't. They were better than humans, superior in every aspect, and belonged at the top of the food chain. Intelligent, prideful, and fierce.

Unfortunately, in the Kingdom of Asuda, humans outnumbered shifters.

The humans' advantage in numbers had allowed the creation of the Registry in the first place. No living creature capable of intelligent thought wanted to be tagged and monitored, studied like some form of recently discovered species—especially given the legends. Shifters kept it to themselves, but there were stories, whispers of shifters being around long before humans populated the land. Sometimes, Coy wondered where *humans* must have come from, given their similarities.

Somewhere down the line, their shifter ancestors had let it get out of hand, had ensured their collective fate.

Chipped, logged, questioned, and observed. Locked in a system wherein they had to comply with rules set for them by people who despised them.

Of course, it hadn't always been this dire. The Registry's initial purpose had started out as protection for both shifters and humans. Throughout the years, the line between protect and punish became blurred. Shifters were no longer treated as equals, and they certainly weren't treated as the gods and goddesses his grandmother had told him about as a kid.

Not that they resembled gods, Coy thought with amusement. No one could identify a shifter in a room full of humans. They looked like everyone else, but most people refused to regard them as even mostly human. Some wouldn't even consider them animals. Humans valued their animals. Pets were treated like family members. Humans cared for them, loved them. Shifters were treated as wild, unwanted creatures, unworthy of love and respect. Yet, humans demanded the same from shifters. Expected them to be grateful for the scrutiny and humiliation. For the hands on the back of their necks.

And Seaton, with his full lips pressed into a thin line and his slender fingers tapping impatiently at his own arm, was no different. Coy never respected any of the officers he'd been forced to interact with, and Seaton's cold words and his bored eyes only guaranteed that.

"Where is the location of your chip?" Seaton asked.

Coy dropped his gaze from Seaton and focused on his fingernails, finding them more interesting than the man standing in front of him.

"You can do better than that. Ask nicely."

"Coy, that's enough. Just do what he says," his grandmother interjected from her spot where the living room bled into the kitchen.

He shot a glare at her, silently asking whose side she was really on. Yet, he knew that as fierce as she could be, she did not like unnecessary trouble. This went double when it had anything to do with the Registry. He loved his grandmother, and although he didn't agree with how easily she gave in to the Registry's foolish demands, she had taken care of him for most of his life. Listening to her every once in a while was the least he could do.

"It would be wise to listen to your grandmother," Seaton echoed. "She seems to be an intelligent woman."

Coy hated to concede in their battle of wills, especially after a comment like that. Unfortunately, one glance at Dinina told him that he'd suffer the consequences if he continued with this never-ending banter between himself and Seaton.

He huffed, smoke fanning out through his nostrils. His fingers, strong and calloused, gripped the hem of his sarong, raising the fabric to expose even more of his muscular thighs. He watched for Seaton's reaction, saw the way Seaton's lips parted just slightly before he retrieved a device from his belt. It was long and shaped like a pencil, except double the width. Its surface, smooth and black, was interrupted by a thin, rectangular screen.

Seaton was all business when he placed the device against Coy's thigh, just above the knee. Smirking down at him, Coy shrugged. He would have to venture farther north to find what he was looking for.

The perplexed expression on Seaton's face was almost worth the annoyance of having to interact with him. Coy felt the others' eyes on them as Seaton ran the device along his thigh, hand creeping toward dangerous territory. He saw the way Seaton gritted his teeth as he moved the device higher, followed by the slight exhale of his breath, shoulders sagging in relief, when the device emitted a series of beeps once it reached midthigh. The screen held a parade of letters and numbers, various codes that meant something to the Registry and nothing at all to Coy. Seemingly satisfied with the information from the device, Seaton attached it back to his belt.

"I have everything I need." He was looking at Coy but speaking to Fate, dark, elegant eyebrows shaped into perfect arches that sat evenly on his face.

"Same here," Fate said.

"Well, then. If there's nothing else we can do for you, let me be the first to invite you both to get the fuck out."

"Coy." Dinina dragged out his name in the same slow drawl all Hametians spoke in.

"Sorry, sorry. *Kindly* get the fuck out." He grinned at her.

Neither Seaton nor Fate bothered with a response. The two officers walked through the living room, past the shifters—and Ari, who had been seated on the couch, listening to the entire exchange—to the front door. Coy was right behind them, relieved that they were leaving and annoyed that they had shown up in the first place. He and Dinina had never broken a single Registry rule. All the monitoring and random checkups were pointless.

Seaton opened the door and was the first to step out. Fate followed him but paused, hand lingering on the doorframe. He turned around, ending up almost face-to-face with Coy. The shifter stood in the doorway, arms folded, waiting for the two of them to leave with all the patience of a cobra preparing to strike.

"Watch yourself, Conlin," Fate said. "Your mouth will land you in rough waters one day. Maybe much sooner than you think."

"Why should I worry about water when I can fly?" With a snort, he shoved the door with his elbow, receiving instant gratification the second it slammed in Fate's face.

"What do you think he meant?" Ari asked.

Thankfully, he'd been quiet throughout the entire interview. It was best if he didn't say much whenever the Registry came to visit. A human child living with dragon shifters wasn't something that was exactly celebrated in the Registry.

"Nothing," Coy said. "It's just a scare tactic. As long as we don't break the rules, there's nothing they can do to us."

His answer didn't seem to provide much comfort for Ari. "Are you sure?"

"Of course." He flicked away a strand of hair that had fallen into his face. "When am I ever wrong?"

Leaning back against the couch, Ari snorted. "More often than you think."

COY NEEDED TO protect her. He could no longer stand there, hidden behind a sycamore tree, watching as she was beaten by her own husband. He glared at his grandfather's broad back. The man hovered over her, his calloused hand raised in preparation for yet another slap.

If only Coy were bigger, stronger. He could stop him from hurting her.

The scars on her face blended into one another, layers of new tissue veiling the old. They were flat, like wood knots that had been rubbed down until smooth. The fresher slashes on her cheeks were vivid and pink, a constant reminder of what his grandfather had done to her, of what he was *still* doing to her.

She'd protected Coy from her husband's wrath, from his frightening drunken rages. Now more than ever, he wanted to do the same.

His body seemed to move on its own, luring him away from his spot behind the tree and into plain view. The air was crisp around him and smelled sweet, like fresh peppermint. The skies were bright and clear, but rain was coming. He could smell it. And yet...that wasn't all. He could smell the cherry pie cooling on the kitchen table indoors, the scent of honeydew carrying on a spring breeze, and even the blood that seeped from the corner of her mouth.

He could smell *everything*.

His anger spiked, growing into a rage, and settled in the pit of his stomach, bubbling—black and thick—like tar. It poured into his bloodstream, first as a trickle and then in a gush. He hated his grandfather. Hated how big he was. How robust and scary he could be. Violent and vicious to his own family, the people he was supposed to *love*.

The man slapped her again. His fingers curled in on themselves into a rock of a fist. Coy watched as the fingers unfurled, giving way to fur, to violence—shifting. A tiger, giant and merciless. He struck her hard across her face with razor-sharp claws, tearing apart the skin of her cheek and neck.

Coy was running before he even realized it. The weight of his own body surprised him. Sturdy, yet light, as if an anchor had been lifted from his very core. The backyard closed in around him and became a cage—one that was almost too small to contain him.

His grandfather's tight shirt strained against the muscles in his back. Coy could see the stretch of the fabric, pulling taut. It should have taken him longer to reach them. He was there within a second.

He screamed for his grandfather to leave her alone, to leave them both alone. To let them live in peace, to stop hurting them. But, the words did not come out that way. They weren't words at all. They were a melody of hisses and growls, deep and guttural, pulled from the center of his chest. Smoke seeped from his nostrils, gray and thick as ash, with licks of fire bleeding from his mouth.

There were claws where his fingers should have been, long and sharp. They dug into his grandfather's back, tearing into cotton, skin, and then muscle. His grandfather screamed, the sound piercing the air. It was a sound he'd heard before—one of pain, shock, and despair.

He wanted to hear it again.

Bits of orange fur fell around him like autumn leaves. Black scales with flecks of purple glimmered beneath the heavy sun. He could hear his grandmother's voice, calling him, pleading for him to stop. He wanted to listen to her, to give in to her cries, but he couldn't.

He didn't know how.

Fire poured from his mouth when he breathed. The air smelled of singed grass and burned flesh. He could not taste the blood, but he felt it on his tongue, saw it dripping from his teeth—his fangs—and onto the ground below him. His grandfather stopped screaming. The tiger was gone. In its place lay a man, curled against the ground. His skin was charred. Smoke rose from his body like steam from freshly doused steel.

He was dead.

Coy had killed him.

He stared down at his grandfather's body where it lay motionless on top of the scorched earth. He could taste the blood now. He moved to cover his mouth, to wipe the metallic taste off his tongue. There were claws where his hand should have been.

"Coy," his grandmother said. There was horror in her voice, as well as sadness and shame. Her face was streaked in crimson. "What have you done?"

He answered her in flames. He'd done what needed to be done. He'd slain the beast. He'd protected her, protected them both. He'd caused death, had tasted it on his tongue and swallowed it.

Like the gods she'd told him about, he had awakened his powers. He'd accepted his fate to be a god among men.

He had *shifted.*

Raindrops rolled down his grandmother's cheeks like tears.

Chapter Two

COY WOKE UP covered in sweat, feeling more irritated than afraid. It was only that annoying dream. Not a dream—a memory. One he'd already lived. He had no need—or desire—to relive it, especially not repeatedly for the last twelve years. The past was the past, and he couldn't do a thing about it. He didn't *want* to do anything about it. If his subconscious wanted him to feel guilty about his actions, it would need to try harder. His grandfather had been a piece of shit and deserved what he'd gotten. All tigers did.

He climbed out of bed with a yawn and cursed as he tripped, his foot catching on a block of wood. The result of his late-night whittling sat on the floor next to him. It was supposed to be an eagle. The damn thing didn't even look like a bird. Not one he'd ever seen, anyway. He'd been whittling for years and had never produced anything other than lumpy paperweights.

Bending down, he grabbed the eagle and brought it closer to his face for inspection. He could point out everything wrong with his creation. That didn't mean he knew how to fix it. Oh well. He tossed the blob of wood into a slowly growing pile of other failed projects. Whittling was just a hobby, and that meant he didn't have to be any good at it.

UNLIKE ARI AND Dinina, Coy didn't live inside the main house, as their small home could only accommodate two people. After they had found Ari as an abandoned infant—small and pink and wailing at the top of his lungs—and brought him home, Coy had converted their outdoor storage shack into a bedroom and gave Ari his room inside the house.

The space was too small for anything extravagant. He couldn't afford extravagant things anyway. He kept the essentials: a bed, a few items of clothing, a couple of shelves, and a pile of wood—for his attempts at whittling—which took up a quarter of the floor.

With a change of clothing in hand, Coy walked out of his shack. Patches of earth, warmed by the sun, felt not entirely unpleasant against his bare feet. He had shoes back in his room, but there was little point in wearing them at home. Hamet was almost always hot in the warmer seasons. Most people wore as little attire as possible, as the heat didn't leave much room for modesty. Besides, Hamet was poor, and thus fancy clothing was not wasted on Hametians. Men wore thin tunics or loincloths. Women wore chitons. Though, some citizens would occasionally save up enough money to purchase more modern skirts in varying lengths from Sago. Children, depending on their age, often wore nothing at all.

He stepped into the main house to find his grandmother bustling around in the kitchen. Ari lounged on the couch with a book in his hand. Coy glanced at the title—*How Humans Become Shifters*—and snorted. He didn't ask Ari where, or how, he'd gotten his hands on it. They didn't have money for books, especially for ones on such ridiculous topics. He'd probably stolen it. Something he most likely learned from watching Coy.

Ari was wasting his time. Humans couldn't become shifters merely because they wanted to. This was something he'd told him several times before. Shifting was, and would always be, hereditary. It wasn't something that humans could just tap into if they tried hard enough. Still, he understood Ari's desire to become one. As the only human in a family of shifters, Ari probably felt left out.

Only a small percentage of the population of Asuda were shifters. Due to the constant interference of the Registry and the overall public opinion on shifters, those numbers were likely to decline. No one wanted to have children with a shifter if it meant tying themselves to the rule of the Registry.

Even the shifters themselves absorbed this hate, turning it inwards. Shifting was a gift given to them by the gods, but many would have given anything to become human. To fit in.

To *belong*.

Coy wasn't one of them.

Making a mental note to burn Ari's book, Coy strolled to the back of the house. It felt weird to grin each time he stepped into the bathroom. In the past, he and Ari had bathed at the lake, which was located half a mile away from home. By the time they had finished washing and returned, they would be covered in sweat again. He'd worked hard at

Simone's Circus and had even taken on a few odd jobs to afford the luxury of installing their very own indoor shower. It was unlike the ones in Sago, where the water always ran hot and filled the room with steam, but that didn't matter.

He washed with lumpy, misshapen soap that smelled of lavender—a result of one of Dinina's and Ari's hobbies. It was nice knowing that he wasn't the only person bad at something he enjoyed doing.

He dressed in a tunic, its color the shade of a ripe plum, and joined Ari on the couch. His brother hardly acknowledged him. Being less interesting than a book wasn't something Coy was used to. He was, however, quite comfortable with picking on Ari. He snatched the book out of Ari's hands and held it high above his head.

"Give it back," Ari whined. He then stared up at him with a wide, toothy grin. "Your hair looks funny that way."

"What way?" Coy ran a hand through his damp hair.

"Wet." Ari stared at his hair, grin still plastered on his face. "It's too curly. It makes you look like a boy."

"I am a boy."

"A little boy."

"Ah—" He pointed a finger at Ari. "—so like you?"

"I'm not a little boy. I'm a man. I'll be thirteen in two weeks."

Coy smirked. "A man is not defined by his age."

"Then what defines him?" His expression changed from playful to curious.

"Do you really want to know?"

Ari nodded, his blue eyes glittering like sapphires.

Coy leaned down so that his lips were near Ari's ear. "It starts with a woman," he whispered, "or in some cases, another man."

"End your story there or suffer the consequences," Dinina called out from near the kitchen sink.

Coy snickered and ruffled Ari's hair. "I'll tell you later. Man-to-man." He brought his hand down as if to give Ari the book and then snatched it back again, laughing as Ari struggled to grab it, his fingers outstretched but not quite high enough to reach it.

Ari was indeed still a child, though there was some truth to his words. Year after year, Coy had watched him grow. He was braver than all the other Hametian boys. He was a dragon in spirit, and he would one day grow to become a great man. Coy felt pride in calling him his brother. They may not have shared the same blood, but that didn't matter.

He loved him all the same.

Unsuccessful in grabbing the book back from Coy, Ari stood up, gangly like a fawn.

"Oh, going to challenge me for the book, are you?" Coy teased. He shifted on the couch, raising his fist in the air as if he were preparing to fight with Ari.

"Nope. I'm tired of reading anyway. Kenneth said he and the others were sparring down by the lake today. I'm going to go challenge them instead."

"I thought you were tired of sparring with them because you always won?"

"Yes, but who ever really gets tired of winning?" Ari remarked, sliding his feet into his sandals.

Coy snickered. "You won't always be a winner, you know. Someone out there is always bigger than you. Stronger. Better. That's just the way life is, little brother."

Trotting to the front door, Ari dismissed his words with a wave of his hand. "So says the *dragon*." He gripped the doorknob, turned around, and stuck his tongue out at Coy before rushing off, leaving the door partially open.

SOMETHING WAS WRONG. He didn't know what it was, but he could feel it. It was like a sixth sense alerting him to a storm looming miles away. Coy wanted to ask his grandmother if she felt it too, but decided against it so that he wouldn't cause her any unnecessary stress. She was getting too old to be worrying about things that probably didn't even exist. Still, he couldn't shake the feeling that something was about to happen. That is, if it hadn't happened already.

At least he didn't have to worry about the Registry. Some officers would stop by eventually. Probably not for a couple of weeks though. They hadn't received a letter yet, but the bastards visited like clockwork, so they'd be getting one soon. He wondered if Seaton would still be around, or if Fate had already run him off.

Coy ate breakfast on the back porch, mixed fruit drizzled in brown sugar and honey sticking between his teeth. He stared at the lone tree in their yard, marveling at how much it had grown over the years. His grandmother had planted it as a sapling when he was still a boy. She had tended to it—much like she tended to Coy and Ari—and now it was well on its way to becoming something great. Maybe her green thumb wasn't just limited to vegetables, he thought with a smile.

After breakfast, he attempted to whittle while watching his grandmother tend to her garden. Both he and Ari had offered to help. She'd been quick to decline, however, claiming they'd do more harm than good. She was right. They both hated vegetables.

He leaned against the back porch, one hand clutching a knife, the other gripping a piece of wood. He furrowed his brows as he dragged the knife along the wood, bottom lip trapped between his teeth in concentration. Today's inspiration was a squirrel. Fun little creatures to watch, but they tasted like shit.

"Why do you keep doing it if you aren't any good at it?" Ari asked, snickering at the crude, colorful language that occasionally slipped from Coy's lips.

Coy continued to scrape at the wood, splinters falling to the ground below. "Because doing something you're shit at is how you get better at it. That's why." After a moment, he stopped and glanced over at Ari. "You wanna try?"

"Don't give that boy a knife," Dinina said. "He'll likely cut off all his fingers."

Coy wasn't surprised at her words. She was just as overprotective of Ari as she'd been of him when he was Ari's age, albeit more outspoken.

"He'll be fine, Nina. I'm sitting right here."

"Oh, and I should I find comfort in this, should I?" She tossed a handful of weeds behind her back.

"You missed," Coy said, a smirk tugging at his lips.

"Impossible. I was aiming for your pride. It's everywhere. Be careful, Ari."

Her back was to them, but he could hear the smile in her voice.

"Hey, I've been doing this for years. How come you've never told me to be careful?"

She tossed more weeds. They danced briefly in the wind, fluttering like butterfly wings before falling.

She scoffed. "As if you would listen."

HE WAS RELIEVED to find that Ari was just as bad as whittling as him. When they grew bored of sculpting wood, Coy stood in the middle of the backyard and blew fire from his mouth. He catered to Ari's demands—*bigger, higher, as high into the sky as it can go*. After a while, Dinina joined in. Her flames, although not as powerful as Coy's, were just as wondrous.

He lived for these moments, these ones shared with the two people he loved the most. They could have left Hamet years ago. Perhaps moved to Sago where it would have saved him an hour-long trip to and from work. He had tried to convince Dinina of this once before, but she was married to her old home and her garden full of vegetables. She wouldn't leave Hamet even if Coy begged her to, and he didn't have the heart to take Ari away from her. Maybe one day when Ari was older, the two of them would explore the world, leaving Hamet behind. Until then, Hamet was Coy's home, and as long he had his family, he wouldn't have it any other way.

The sun began to fade, the sky a landscape of oranges and pinks. Soon, Ari and Dinina would go inside to retire for the night. Coy had other plans.

"I'm going to Sago," he said, pushing himself up and off the porch. The disappointed look on Ari's face was expected, but Coy still humored him.

"What's with that look?"

"Can I come with you?" Ari asked.

Coy shook his head. "Not this time."

"You always say that." Ari folded his arms across his chest. "Not this time. Not this time. When will it *ever* be time?"

Sighing, Coy leaned down and grabbed his whittling knife from the ground. "Next time, I'll take you with me, okay?"

"You're lying."

"No, I swear it. If I don't—" He handed Ari the knife, who took it with a weak grip, eyes full of distrust. "—I'll let you stab me in the thigh with this knife."

"I don't want to stab you."

"No? Then what do you want?"

"You have to promise to fly me all around Asuda."

"What am I, a horse?"

"Horses don't fly."

"You know what I mean."

"Will you?"

"I'm not allowed to fly you around Asuda." He saw that Ari was about to protest, so he added, "*But*, I will fly you around Hamet."

"You promise?"

"I swear."

"Okay, but if you don't—" Ari looked down at the knife in his hands. "I *will* stab you."

Coy snickered. "I know you will."

HE WASN'T WORKING tonight, but he wore his costume anyway. A single gold-plated chain hung around his neck. From there, seven thinner chains of the same material extended down his chest and curved along his torso. They connected to a small ring that rested against his waist. Two other chains stretched along his back, joining the ring at the other end.

His sarong was black and trimmed in gold stitching—as were his sandals, leather straps winding up his legs in spirals. It was the costume he wore during his solo performances, when only he was the center of attention, glistening like the gold he wore.

The walk from Hamet to Sago took as long as it would during the day. Darkness surrounded him, but it did not hinder him. He pitied anyone forced to take the journey if they were not already familiar with the path. Uprooted trees, venomous snakes, jagged rocks, and dens inhabited by wild animals were only some of the obstacles one could encounter while walking along the path. Yet, he'd traveled it in both the warmth of morning and the eerie calmness of night and had grown to love it despite all its hidden dangers.

The cliffs along the outskirts of Sago became a little more treacherous as he neared the town. It wasn't anything he couldn't handle, but it did require concentration to make it through the area without stumbling. It wasn't long before he hit somewhat even ground and, subsequently, civilization. Amira's pub was just four buildings down from Simone's. Coy found the back door unlocked—it usually was—and slipped inside. The pub looked the same way it always did, dark and dreary like a dungeon. Amira was at the bar, towering over a group of people, her arms crossed. She was the picture of confidence and grace, her brown skin and cropped, dark hair immaculate. She stood like a goddess, both larger and taller than most of the men he knew.

For a moment, he watched her—her hands reaching for drinking glasses, heavily pierced ears listening to patrons' orders, red lips curling. Probably flirting for more tips. He admired her—had always enjoyed being in the presence of her company—even back when the two of them were teenagers, when she was known as Raul and hardly ever smiled. She'd changed a lot over the years, both physically and mentally. She was happier now, always smiling.

"How long are you going to stand there staring at me, Coy Conlin?" Amira asked from her spot behind the bar. "Don't think I didn't notice you slip in through the back door."

Coy smirked as he approached her, maneuvering himself past a couple of women entwined in each other's embrace.

"Back door's my favorite place to slip in," he said.

She rolled her eyes. "What are you doing in Sago? Simone said you weren't working tonight."

"She's right. I'm not, but I needed to get out of Hamet for a while. Thought I'd stop by and see my favorite bartender." He caught sight of a flyer on the counter advertising a party that would take place several months away. "Getting an early start, aren't you? Another one of your sex parties?"

"You stopped by because you wanted free drinks and—" She looked him up and down. "—from the looks of things, to get laid." She tapped the flyer with a grin, her red, painted lips stretched wide. "I want a good turnout this year. And it's not a party. It's an extravaganza."

Coy snorted. She got a great turnout every year.

"You mentioned getting laid. Are you offering?"

She threw a dishrag at him, wet and sticky with spilled beer. He dodged it.

"Not on your long, draconic life."

"That's not the only long thing of mine, Amira, my love."

"Save it and look over there." She nodded in the direction of a nearby table. Coy turned, following her gaze.

"Who is that?"

"I don't know his name. He's been coming in here a lot lately. Pretty, isn't he?"

"That's an understatement," he murmured.

The slim-hipped man made his way through the pub, sauntering through the crowd of people. All eyes were on him. Judging by his upturned nose, he was used to the attention.

"Interesting... Amira, can I borrow your office for an hour?"

Amira rolled her eyes and sighed. "Make sure you clean up afterward. I'm not running a brothel."

"I know," Coy said. "But, it's something to consider."

He winked at her, moving away from the bar and toward the pretty, blond man standing in the center of the pub. Diamonds in the shape of teardrops hung from his ears.

"Well, you certainly look out of place," Coy said. The man startled, his shoulders tensing from the sudden voice behind him. "Oh, sorry about that. I didn't mean to scare you."

Turning around to face him, the man seemingly recovered. "You didn't."

"Good to know. I'm Coy."

"I know who you are." He spoke slowly—enunciating every syllable of each word—not in the lazy drawl that Coy was most familiar with. It was similar to the way Seaton spoke. Coy mentally frowned at the stray thought. The Registry and its stuck-up officers should have been the last thing on his mind.

"Do you?"

"You are a performer at Simone's Circus. A fire dancer."

"You're right," Coy confirmed. "You didn't give me your name."

"Elias," he answered. "Simone said if I wanted to find you, this is where I should start. I have been coming here for a few nights now."

"All that for little ole me?"

Elias looked at him, eyes slowly roaming over his body. "You do not seem so little to me."

"I'm flattered," Coy said. "But, now that you've found me, is there something you needed?"

"Perhaps."

Elias brushed a stray hair, glinting like spun gold, away from his face. Coy watched as hands and wrists covered in jewelry shimmered even under the pub's dull lighting. Someone like that had no business in Sago.

"They say you are a dragon. Is it true?"

"Depends on who 'they' are."

"People."

"What kind of people?"

"Those who admire shifters," Elias said. "Are—" He licked his lips. "—*fascinated* by them."

"And are you one of those people?"

Again, Elias said, "Perhaps."

A groupie. That's what Elias was. It was not completely surprising. There were groupies for everything. Shifters were no exception. Coy wasn't unfamiliar with the type—in fact, he'd had his fair share of them. Most were limited to Sago and Hamet. Elias couldn't have been from either of those places.

"Let's talk someplace a little quieter," Coy said.

He led Elias over to a secluded section of the pub, away from the noise. Folding his arms over his chest, he leaned against the wall, feeling the chains from his outfit glide across his back.

"Where are you from, Elias?"

"Skiana."

"Skiana?" Coy repeated, hoping the shock in his voice wasn't noticeable. No Skianan would willingly travel to Sago just to watch a dragon shifter spit fire from his mouth. "Were you tricked into coming here?"

Elias looked confused for a moment, but he quickly rallied. "My birthday was a week ago. Visiting Sago is a gift to myself. I am of age now."

Coy raised a brow. "I see..."

Is Elias a virgin?

"Well, it's unfortunate that I've only just met you. Otherwise, I would have gotten you a gift to celebrate your becoming a man."

"Well—" Elias rested a hand against his own shoulder and brushed down the sheer fabric to expose his skin. "—you still can."

Coy followed the curve of his shoulder. It was without blemishes, smooth as cream and just as pale. Yet, knowing that Elias was rich—and most likely spoiled—left a sour taste in his mouth. He was probably used to getting what he wanted, and Coy wasn't sure if he should carry on with that trend. Maybe his gift to Elias would be to refuse him.

"I don't think—" Coy began. Elias cut him off.

"I am willing to pay for your time. Notes. Jewels... Whatever you would like. Money is no issue"

Coy tried to decline, but Elias continued. "I will leave for Skiana afterward. I will not—" He paused, as if trying to figure out the proper word to use. "—*cling.*"

Coy considered the proposition. Elias was easy on the eyes, and the fact that he wanted to pay Coy for sex was flattering.

"Do you have a place in mind? We can use Amira's office if you aren't looking for anything classy."

"That will not be necessary." He turned away from Coy and began to make a path between the sea of bodies grinding against each other. "Follow me."

COY HAD ONLY seen a few vehicles in his life, and none of them had ever been this massive.

"What is this thing?"

The huge machine parked in front of Amira's pub looked just as elegant as Elias. The jade exterior was so meticulously polished that it almost seemed to shine even in the dark.

"This is my travel home. Have you never seen one?"

"Pretty sure if I ever saw something like this, I'd remember it."

"Oh." Elias smiled. "Then I shall give you a tour."

He followed Elias up the three steps it took to reach the door of the vehicle, staring in both awe and confusion as Elias slid the door open and then stepped inside.

The interior was bigger than Coy's living room. Both sides were not only lined with comfortable-looking couches, but also had people sitting on top of them. They drank wine from spotless glasses and nibbled on cheese and strawberries.

"Look, Elias. I know we agreed on something back there, but..."

Elias looked around at the handful of people with a frown. "Do they make you uncomfortable?"

He moved farther into the vehicle until he was standing in between the parallel couches, staring down at the others like a prince atop a balcony surveying his kingdom. "Leave us." When the only response was a confused expression on every face, he added, "Now," in a voice that somehow managed to be light and airy yet full of authority.

The men and women scurried outside, bumping and brushing past him. "Er...sorry," Coy muttered, feeling guilty for bringing an end to their festivities.

"Shall we continue with the tour? There is something I'd like you to see."

Elias led him to a narrow door. Behind it stood a toilet, a sink, and a shower. The latter was bigger than his own back in Hamet. At least double, possibly triple, in size.

"Well, what do you think?" he asked.

Coy scratched at the back of his head, confused by the question. "Um, about what?"

"The bathroom. Do you not love it?"

"It's, uh...great, I guess."

Elias chuckled. "I'm joking." He flicked at the chain hanging from Coy's neck. "Follow me."

He brought Coy to another door at the very back of the vehicle. The jewels on his hand sparkled when he turned the doorknob.

It was a bedroom.

He motioned for Coy to enter first. Once inside, Coy stared down at the bed. The mattress was an ocean of blue satin. A curtain of white lace surrounded it. The fabric hung from a metal canopy, pulled open to reveal several pillows, of various sizes, made of the same fabric as the sheets. Moonlight spilled into the room through an oval-shaped window. The light caught on the gold stitching of the pillows, making them look as though they were twinkling.

There was a stand built into the wall next to the bed. Atop it sat a crystal bowl filled with an assortment of jewels: rings, necklaces, and bracelets. Probably others. He didn't want to be too obvious with his staring.

"Is this to your liking?"

Elias shut the bedroom door, enclosing the two of them within the room.

"It's...incredible," Coy said.

When he turned around to face Elias, he found him at the foot of the bed, smiling and unmistakably nude. His fancy clothing had pooled onto the floor around his feet.

Elias's skin was a canvas, as smooth and fresh as snow. He was hairless except for the tuft of blond curls between his legs, and even that was as trim and elegant as the hair atop his head.

His cock stood proud, pointing slightly upward. He had more length than girth. Still, a decent size overall.

He stepped forward, closing the distance between himself and Coy. "Then by all means. Do with me what you will," he insisted.

IT TOOK TWO hours. Elias may have been beautiful, confident, and rich, but he was also a virgin. Or rather, he'd *been* one.

Coy had taken care of that.

"What did you think?" he asked.

It was an unnecessary question. He knew exactly what Elias had thought. The scratches on his back gave him all the feedback he needed about his...*services.*

"Are all shifters as well-endowed as you?"

Coy smirked. Elias sure knew how to make a guy feel good about himself. "Doubt it. But, I haven't met many shifters, so I can't say so for sure."

Elias chuckled. "You are quite the handful, Coy." He smiled after he said this, and Coy could see the youthfulness in his manner. The way Elias carried himself made him seem older, more mature, but the face staring up at him now was definitely one of an eighteen-year-old. "Or perhaps 'mouthful' would be a more fitting term?"

Coy winked at him. "Why not both?"

"Well, then." Elias pushed himself up, and though it was slight, Coy hadn't missed the soft wince that followed.

"Try to take it easy for a bit."

Elias waved off his concern. Coy wondered if he were taught to ignore his pain, or if he was just trying to hide it in front of him.

"How much do I owe you?" he asked, leaning toward the stand next to the bed.

Coy tugged at a coil of hair dangling in front of his face and shrugged. "This isn't really something that I do often, so I don't really know. How about you just pay what you think I'm worth."

"I am afraid I did not bring enough notes for that."

Coy grinned.

Elias pulled open the stand's drawer, the inside lined with black velvet. Toward the back of the drawer were stacks upon stacks of notes. He reached in and pulled out ten stacks, turned to stare thoughtfully at

Coy, and then pulled out five more. He laid them on Coy's chest, whose eyes had grown wide with the amount of money being offered to him.

"Is this enough?"

"I-It's fine." Coy's voice trembled when he spoke as he held the papers in his hand. He did not know how much it was. A lot. Too much. More money than he'd ever held in his entire life.

"If you could be so kind as to send my people back inside on your way out."

"Of course." Keeping his voice from rising in pitch proved a challenge.

Coy set the money down, climbed off the bed, and dressed swiftly, fearful that Elias would change his mind and take back the money he'd given.

"Um...thanks."

He grabbed the money, cursing when he realized that his costume had no room for him to safely secure anything, let alone the stacks of notes Elias had given to him.

Elias laughed, sticking his hand back into the drawer. When he pulled it out again, he was holding a small, drawstring bag made of the same velvet material that lined the drawer. He tossed it to Coy with a smile.

"Thank you for an enjoyable night. It was a wonderful gift."

"My pleasure," Coy said.

He stuffed the notes into the bag and thanked Elias once more before opening the door and leaving. He slid through the space between the twin couches and—after a few seconds of confusion—figured out how to open the main door.

Trotting down the steps, he spoke to the small group of people standing near the vehicle. "He says you can come back in now." The amount of money in the bag he carried overpowered any feelings of embarrassment.

Elias's entourage climbed back into the vehicle and settled back into their previous seats. Startled, he jumped backward when the door slammed closed and the engine revved to life a few seconds later. Loud and snarling like a metal, roaring beast.

Coy stood in front of the pub, watching the slow spin of the tires as the vehicle began to move forward. When he looked up, he caught sight of delicate, blond hair through the oval window. Elias waved at him, green eyes glistening like emeralds.

He could only laugh at the sight and then waved back.

COY ARRIVED BACK in Hamet, tired, sweaty, and wealthy. His fingers ached from clutching the velvet bag filled with the money Elias had given him. He walked toward his shack, glancing up at the front window of the main house. The living room light was on. There was no way Ari was still awake this late. It must have been Dinina.

He entered his room, kicked the door shut behind him, and practically collapsed onto the bed. He lay there for a few seconds, face buried in the mattress, before turning around and sitting up. The velvet bag sat at his side. He caressed the material, feeling the smoothness against his skin. Flipping the bag over, he dumped out the contents, watching the notes spill onto his bed. So much money. He still couldn't believe it. He touched a few of them, as if allowing himself to fully accept that they were real.

There was a knock at his door. It didn't surprise him. He smelled her before she got there.

"Coy."

"It's open, Nina."

His grandmother stepped into his room. Her scarred face was bright, shining from whatever skin treatment she had used on it. Her hair was pulled up. A few flyaway strands had managed to escape the bun at the top of her head. She gasped when she saw the money.

"Where did you get this?" she asked. "What did you do?"

He smiled and scratched at his head. "I got it from a friend, and it's probably best if I don't answer your second question."

"Did you steal it?" She narrowed her eyes at him. Years ago, that look would have terrified him. Now, it just made him smile.

"I swear, I didn't. It was a gift. Or maybe, more like a business deal."

She folded her arms over her chest. "What *kind* of business, Coy?"

He wiggled his eyebrows at her. "A little of this—a little of that."

"Oh, Coy." She frowned. "You didn't."

"What?" He laughed. "It's quicker than making money at Simone's."

"What are you going to do with all of this?"

"Not me, Nina." He stood up. "*We.* This is *ours*. And we can do anything we want with it. Me, you, and Ari. We can finally have the lives we deserve."

She took her gaze away from the money and looked up at Coy. "My life is just fine."

He walked over to her and placed his hands on her shoulders. It was difficult to believe he used to be smaller than her at one point. He still remembered staring up at her, holding on to her as he learned to walk, crying for her to pick him up when he afraid. She had been his everything back then.

She still was.

He grinned at her, eager eyes full of excitement. "Then let me make it even better."

She rolled her eyes, but he saw the slight smirk on her face. She glanced back at the money on the bed before sighing.

"I suppose I could use a few new skirts."

"That's the spirit," he said, still grinning as he pulled her into a hug, wrapping his long arms around her. "I'll buy you all the skirts in Asuda. Every last one."

"Hush, you silly boy," she whispered, her frail arms squeezing against his sides.

HIS GRANDMOTHER STAYED in his bedroom for at least an hour, helping him plan what to do with his newfound wealth. He hid the money beneath a loose floorboard under his bed after she left and then climbed onto his mattress. He had to be at Simone's early the next morning. Fooling around with Elias had zapped most of his energy, and he knew he'd be tired when he woke up. He didn't care. None of that mattered. He had money now. He could do whatever he wanted. He could even quit Simone's if he felt like it. For once, everything in his life was perfect. He fell asleep a few moments later.

He dreamed about blue skies and clouds that tasted like honey. About dancing, singing, and warm, manicured fingers that caressed his skin.

For once, he didn't dream about tigers.

Chapter Three

THE SPACE SURROUNDING Coy was dark. The only source of illumination came in the form of a spotlight. It beamed down on him, casting an artificial glow on his skin. He felt his heart beating, as if each thump were counting down the seconds before he was to begin. The other dancers scattered from their set in a flurry of smoke and bronze-painted skin. He was a statue below the crowd, solid and unmoving except for the drumming of his heart.

Showtime.

A wordless song poured from speakers and resonated throughout the space, its captivating beat making the crowd sway. They stared down at him, an audience of far too many for him to count. He knew they were all watching him, waiting to be enticed and amazed.

After all, he was the main event.

The staff felt light in Coy's hand. His fingers pressed against the foam handle, each finding its own familiar groove. Fire clung to both ends, wicks dipped in paraffin so that the flames stayed lit even when he moved. He felt the heat from the blaze but did not fear it. He lacked the capacity to experience the pain of scorched flesh. His skin and hair never burned. One of the many perks of being a dragon.

The floor lit beneath his feet as he walked, large squares that glowed in bursts of white and purple with each step. He spun the staff above his head, weaving it between his fingers with swift flicks of his wrist. It slashed through the air, creating the illusion of fiery rings floating around him.

The other dancers stood on either side of him, heads bowed in a show of honor and respect. He was King of the Fire Dancers, teacher of everything they knew. His gaze shifted between them, counting the bandages wrapped around their limbs. A total of three between the six of them. He took pride in their improvement.

He moved the staff with practiced ease, guiding it through the air, around his shoulders, and beneath his legs. It became an extension of his body, a free-floating limb engulfed in flames demanding the eye of all who saw it. His body followed the staff's path, hips swinging in time with the music. It became his dance partner, the two of them twirling as if their movements were responsible for spinning the world on its axis.

He felt the audience's awe and their envy, heard their cheers, and saw their fists clenched in frustration. He knew some of them wanted to see him fumble, hoped that he would lose his grip and drop the staff. Their wish would not be granted. He would not give them the satisfaction of seeing him falter, of seeing him *fail*. He was better than all of them on his worst day and invincible on his best.

He continued to dance, heart racing from exhilaration. The floor became a blur of colors and flickering lights, the staff a golden ring of flames, spinning madly around him. The excitement in the air became a living thing—thick, intoxicating, and filling him to the point of inebriation.

He inhaled.

He took his time, letting the anticipation build around him. Their shouts expanded his ego, inflated it until it threatened to burst. Finally, when it seemed as though they would explode from their enthusiasm, he exhaled.

An eruption of fire flared from his mouth like from a flamethrower. It cut through the air, one steady projectile that cut off just a few feet short of the ceiling. The audience's cheers echoed off the walls, hundreds of people shouting his name in a frenzy of exhilaration and *fear*—that was the best part.

Coy felt no shame. He embraced his abilities, his power, and his strength. A danger to them all, he could kill them in an instant if he chose. Whether they lived or died rested solely on his shoulders. He was the gatekeeper of life and death. The dragon that could not, *would not,* be slain.

He would not kill them, of course. He had no desire for senseless killing. Nor would the Registry ever condone killing a human. Ugh, the Registry. The very thought of that organization made him grip the staff tighter than necessary. He would not let it distract him. This was *his* time, and for these few moments, as fire exploded from his lips and danced in the air in front of the audience's eyes, he was their god.

And he loved it.

UNFORTUNATELY, WHEN IT came to the early performance crowd, the line between a god and a piece of meat was as thin as dental floss. Early performances were awful, and Coy never managed to walk away from one of them unscathed. They were usually reserved for people with money. High-class humans who wanted entertainment, but were too old to stay awake long enough for the evening shows.

These guests were too aggressive, too demanding, and too *touchy*. Women leered at him, grabbed at him, and pulled and tugged at his costume until the chains fell loose.

And it wasn't just the women.

The men were just as bad. Begging him to take them backstage, asking him what he'd do to them if given the chance. He'd be punished if he answered, "Call the coroner," like he wanted to, so he'd have to play along. However, thanks to Elias and a hefty dose of irony, he could quit. Maybe even take up a new profession—but he couldn't imagine living his life without being a dancer. Besides, with the exception of early performances, his job wasn't a bad one, and he was good at it. In addition to the physical stamina required for dancing, the walk from Hamet to Sago and back again helped to keep him in shape.

The show was winding down. He and the other dancers maneuvered through the crowd—smiling, flirting, and picking up tips along the way.

"You. Come over here, boy," a woman with a raspy voice called over to him. He knew who she was without looking, could smell the scent of wine and heavy cigars drifting from her pores. She had a wrist full of golden bracelets, each of which tinkled when she pointed her crooked finger at him. Her lips were painted red, contrasting with the yellow of her teeth.

Madame Brethe was a horny corpse of a woman who would have ravished him if her weak bones could have withstood the act.

"Show me what you have under there." Her wrinkled fingers pointed at his sarong. "Let me see it."

"And what exactly do you mean by *it*?" Coy asked.

His words were playful. He knew what she meant, but he'd be damned if he did what she told him to do. Madame Brethe was no virgin to Simone's. She came to as many early performances as her schedule allowed, which seemed like almost all of them. She hung around like a ghost, and sometimes when her pale, sagging skin was cast in the glow of one of the many lights, he actually thought she was one.

"You *know*," she said, wiggling her drawn-on eyebrows at him. "Just let me wrap my hands around it."

She made a crude motion with her hand, and it reminded him of someone checking fruit for its ripeness.

Maybe quitting wasn't a bad idea after all.

AFTER HIS PERFORMANCES were over, Coy hung out backstage, making small talk with the other dancers. He was in the middle of adjusting the laces wrapped around his legs when Simone approached him. He watched her—full hips, jiggly waist, and large breasts. Her hair was dyed a fiery red, almost as red as the lipstick she wore. He prided himself on being able to hook up with almost anyone he attempted to seduce. And yet, Simone had never fallen for any of his charms. Too bad. He was certain he would have given her the time of her life.

"There's a rumor I heard about you, Conlin." She never called him by his first name.

"Is that so?" he asked, finished with the laces on one sandal and moving to the next. "And what rumor would that be, Boss?"

She put a pale hand on her hip. "That a pretty little thing got his money's worth from a night with you."

He held back a smirk. "With me? Nah. That can't be right. I'm a dragon of the utmost moral standards." He finished with his other sandal and stood upright.

"Bullshit," she said. "How much did you get?"

He snickered. "Enough to quit here if I wanted to. That's how much."

She moved until she was standing directly in front of him and flicked his bare chest with her fingers. "Who are you kidding? You're not going anywhere. Little boys like you love being the center of attention."

He raised a brow at her response. "I'm a lot of things, Simone. But I can promise you, I'm not a little boy. Give me an hour, and I'll prove it to you."

She rolled her eyes. "I don't sleep with my employees."

"Who said anything about sleeping?"

"Listen, *little boy*," she repeated, making sure to stress those two words. "Just keep in mind that I'm running a business here. A legit one."

He scoffed. "Everything in Sago is legit. You wouldn't believe some of the legit stuff I've seen happening in the parking lot of this place."

"All the same—" She flicked his chest again. "—don't go overboard with your little business, especially with those higher-ups. You know they can turn on you at any moment."

Higher-ups. That's what Simone always called Asudians who lived in places like Skiana. Places up north where the people were richer and the towns were cleaner—safer. Ever since he'd met her, Simone had seemed to have a grudge against anyone who lived a life of luxury. It wasn't as if she was broke, but the money she did have didn't come close to what someone in Skiana would have had. Someone like Elias.

"Whatever you say, Boss," he said.

He thought she was being paranoid. Sure, there were people in places like Skiana and Osin who were complete assholes. There were also assholes in Hamet and Sago. Tons of them. In fact, he was almost certain the ratio of assholes to decent people in Sago was at least ten to one. Besides, the sovereign was the richest man in Asuda, and he treated everyone equally. Coy had even heard a rumor that his late wife—the sovereign consort—had been a shifter. If the sovereign could treat everyone with respect, could treat *shifters* equally, then so could other people with wealth and power. Deep down, he doubted Simone really hated any of the higher-ups. If anything, she was probably just envious of what they had. It was also the reason why he held back on telling her exactly how much money Elias had given him.

With people like Simone, when it came to giving information, less was always more. The only thing she ran better than her circus was her mouth.

Chapter Four

THE WEATHER IN Osin was beautiful. Not that August would have noticed. He kept the windows in his apartment closed, the blinds drawn, and the curtains blocking any errant sunlight from seeping inside. He had been taught many things by his mother, the most important being privacy. Allowing anyone to get too close was, and would always be, unacceptable.

As a child, August never had birthday parties that surrounded him with classmates and friends. He hadn't been offered the luxury of being a typical teenager. No first date, no first kiss...no *anything*. He'd kept to himself as much as he could, and when he'd finished school—earning the highest marks of his class—he had followed in his mother's footsteps and began working in the Asuda Registry Laboratory.

There was no celebration.

His mother had not embraced him. Words of pride and encouragement had no place on her lips. A few months after working at the lab, he had moved into his own home. She hadn't been pleased, though she had made no move to stop him. A year after that, he bad left the lab and enlisted as a Registry officer. She had been even less pleased about that.

He'd thought that once he lived on his own, things would change. He'd have friends, a social life, *relationships*. It hadn't worked out that way. The years of being secluded—his thoughts, feelings, and personality hidden from everyone around him—had created a lasting effect.

The damage was done.

Well, at least he no longer had to deal with the constant headaches from hearing the endless construction of the new laboratory the Registry was adding to headquarters. Registry officers only had to check in every now and then—their work spanned Asuda, supervising the shifters under their care. Better than being locked away in a lab any day.

Sitting alone in the gloom, August scanned the computer monitor with wide eyes. Now, he almost wished he *had* gone into the office, even just to not feel useless. It couldn't have been true. An attack in Askia, the capital of Asuda. One that left Noralani, one of the sovereign's twin daughters, tragically injured and clinging to life. He could only imagine the turmoil the sovereign was in. His wife had died from illness less than a year ago.

Reports claimed that the attacker was a shifter. Normally, the media did not display graphic images of injured children, but the sovereign had demanded it. *Whoever did this shall be found and punished. You are not safe. You will not live.* That had been the quote floating beneath an image of Noralani's shredded body, her skin the color of pecans, split open like cut fruit.

The attacker had not yet been found. If it was a shifter, it wouldn't take long to locate the culprit. There were only three shifters fortunate enough to call Askia their home. Still, none of it added up. The Askian shifters were just as rich and prestigious as the humans who lived there. With so much to lose if they broke any of the Registry's rules, it was insane for them to attack *anyone*, let alone the sovereign's daughter.

Clicking away from the article, August sighed as he stared down at the stack of folders sitting on his desk. He may have no longer been a Registry laboratory employee, but he had helped conduct valuable research during his time there and still had access to most of the information he and his team had gathered. Now that he had some free time, he wanted to see if the lab knew anything about a couple of shifters in particular. Coy Conlin's file sat atop the pile. Beneath Conlin's file was Niami Tro's, Asuda's youngest shifter. Not only was Niami able to shift years earlier than most, but she had also somehow managed to master it.

August slid Niami's file out of the stack and read over the first few pages. He thought back to their first visit, when he and Fate had traveled to Nenzo to meet with her and her mother. She was a cute girl. Six years old, with skin the color of chestnuts and hair like a garnet-tinted cloud. She had been coloring the day he had met her—he still remembered the monochrome, yellow butterflies. Flipping back to the first page, he stared down at the photograph at the center of the file. She was smiling, and her two upper front teeth were missing. Periwinkles were wrapped around her head in the shape of a crown.

Niami was a special child, and August could only imagine how desperately the lab wanted to get its hands on her. Fortunately, there were policies set in place that prevented the head scientist from gaining access to her. He could only imagine how miserable she'd be if there weren't. The head scientist was far from a gentle person.

After setting down Niami's file, he fidgeted with the edges of Conlin's file, hesitating briefly before picking it up. He'd looked at Conlin's paperwork often enough to be able to recite every line of the document word for word. He knew Asuda was home to dragons, few though they were. Until Conlin, he hadn't actually met one. It was uncanny—Conlin could breathe fire even in his human form. It wasn't unheard of for shifters to retain some of their animal abilities while appearing human: powerful eyesight, a heightened sense of smell...things of that nature. Yet, none of the research August had ever conducted hinted that a dragon shifter could still manipulate his fire while in human form.

Coy was a unique shifter, and August wanted to know more about his abilities. Unfortunately, he was an unruly beast—rude, uncultured, and disrespectful. Clearly, whoever named him had no idea of what type of creature he'd grow into.

Just like Niami's file, Conlin's contained a photograph dated nearly six months ago. In the photo, he stared straight ahead, as if he were looking through the camera rather than at it. His eyes did not match. The left eye was hazel, while the right sparkled like a violet amethyst. The dragon shifter August had seen in person had had a layer of short scruff along his jawline, cheeks, and chin. The one in the picture was clean-shaven and had short hair not at all like the dark curls that bounced about his head when he'd stood up to tower over August. His skin was the type of brown that reminded August of peanut brittle, and the smile on his face gave him a certain youthful charm, but the sharp arch of his eyebrows combined with the uniqueness of his eyes made his appearance intimidating.

The fact that he was a dragon did not detract from that.

Looking at the photograph of Conlin, August couldn't help but compare their physical differences. They were both brown, but August's skin was lighter, like smooth pieces of pinewood. His dark hair spilled down his shoulders, the ends coming to rest just a few inches above his waist. With his brown, close-set eyes and long, dark eyelashes, he wasn't the stereotypical picture of masculinity. Although toned, he hadn't been able to develop a truly muscular physique. After months of grueling training, his stamina—combined with his luck in persuading the Registry—had resulted in him becoming an officer. However, this wasn't without its stipulations.

They treated him as they treated the female officers. He was not allowed to work alone, *ever*. The Registry had outdated biases when it came to women and their abilities. It was a disgusting insult to women and a form of ridicule to him—though not so much so that he refused to abide by their dictates.

The doorbell rang, the sound startling him enough to slam his knee against his desk. No one ever visited him. Not even his mother, who only lived a few short blocks away.

His steps were slow, feet dragging across plush carpeting. He wasn't sure who to expect. The only person he ever interacted with outside of work was the old woman who owned the shop a half a block away from his home. He opened the door with caution, just enough for him to peer out. Fate stood on the other side, greasy hair shimmering in the sunlight.

"Fate?" August pulled back the door, shocked to see his partner of all people staring back at him. He didn't remember ever giving him his address. "What are you doing here?"

"We've got work to do," Fate said. "Suit up."

"How did you know where I live?"

Fate shrugged. "It's in your file."

He said it as though employee files were not completely classified. Even veteran officers such as Fate should not have been allowed access.

Fate stepped inside August's home, brushing past him, and wandered over to the couch. He plopped down, folded his arms behind his head, and glanced up at him. August inwardly cringed, hoping that Fate hadn't managed to smear hair product on his furniture.

"I'll wait for you to get dressed. Oh, and bring supplies."

"Supplies?" August said. "What for?"

"We're heading to Hamet."

IT TOOK FIFTEEN minutes for him to put on his uniform and grab his Registry gear. Fate hadn't said much about why they were going to Hamet. August came to the conclusion that if he wanted to know what was going on, he would have to ask his partner outright. As a former scientist, he didn't mind probing for information, except his partner was a bit...intimidating. Even so, it hadn't been long ago that they'd left Hamet's unpleasant heat. If he was being forced to go back there, he at least wanted a reason.

"Which shifter is it?" August asked. It was one of those questions you asked for the sake of asking. He knew which shifter it was. Who else could it be? Conlin's smirking face made a home inside his head, and August scowled.

Instead, Fate said, "All of them."

Fate led him out of the house, only pausing long enough for August to lock the front door. Confused by Fate's words, August watched his partner's feet, the steps calculated as if he were being graded on their precision. Fate came to an abrupt halt, almost causing August to crash straight into his back.

"We'll be taking this."

"This" was a giant bus of a vehicle. It was painted black, much like everything else belonging to the Registry.

"Did something happen to the other car?" August stared apprehensively at the monster parked next to the curb in front of his house. He'd ridden in similar buses, but this one had a menacing feel to it. "Why is there a wall behind the driver's seat?"

"Other one's not big enough for this assignment. I'll brief you when we're on the road. Grab your bag. Time to head out."

August did as he was instructed. The bus didn't look as big on the inside as it had on the outside. The wall he'd thought he saw was actually a gate, its surface made out of a material that looked like black glass. It stretched from the bus's floor to its ceiling, like a dark veil. A duffle bag rested in front of it, black and blending in with the rest of the interior like a fresh pimple on an acne-riddled face.

A box the size of a calculator attached to the gate caught his attention. It contained a blank screen with three rows of numbered buttons ascending from one to nine: a digital lock.

Behind the glass were two columns of seats, twelve on each side. Where the seat belts should have been, there were chains.

Fate motioned for him to take a seat. "Buckle up."

August took the seat next to the gate, the only one—other than the driver's seat—situated up front. This one had a regular seat belt. No chains. Once he was strapped in, he spoke with all the caution of a man feeding a wild coyote, fingers tapping nervously at his thighs.

"You said you would brief me on the...situation?" He meant it as a statement. It came out like a question.

Fate started the engine. "You've been following the news?"

"Of what happened in Askia? Of course. It is terrible. I cannot believe that someone—"

"Some*thing*," Fate corrected him. "The thing that did that to Noralani wasn't a human being. It was a shifter. Don't humanize it."

"Right," August said after a pause.

"Anyway, there's been talk that the sovereign had already begun to mistrust shifters long before the attack. Not that anyone can blame him. It was a mistake, trusting them in the first place. Before anything else, a beast is a beast."

Human beings were also beasts, but August didn't voice this opinion. He had the feeling Fate wouldn't appreciate it.

"Is there a reason for such mistrust?"

Fate snorted. "There are plenty of them. What happened to Noralani was obviously the last straw. We have orders to bring in every shifter assigned to us."

"Bring them in? And do what with them?"

"What do you think? Lock them up."

"As in—" He hesitated. "—*prison*?"

"Absolutely."

August sat forward in his seat, fingers gripping his knees. Arresting shifters? Unheard of. How could they possibly accomplish something like that? Some of them could shift into animals that could *fly*. What was the sovereign thinking?

"But Asuda does not have a single prison that would be capable of containing high-level shifters."

"Asuda *didn't* have a prison that could hold shifters," Fate said, "but they do now. The Registry took care of it."

"You mean..."

"State-of-the-art. No shifter alive is ever going to get out of there. A couple of us got to tour the facility a couple of months ago."

"So the prison was already being constructed before Noralani's attack? Wait a minute. Was that... Was that the real reason for all that construction? They told us it was for a lab expansion. I helped write a grant for that."

Fate grew quiet for a moment, green eyes staring straight ahead. He glanced over at August, watching him with an expression that made August lean back in his seat. They were at a stop light. August wasn't certain whether Fate wouldn't have still looked at him that way if they weren't, even at the risk of driving straight into oncoming traffic. After a few uncomfortable seconds, he turned away from August just as the light turned green.

"It was inevitable. Shifters have no place among humans. It's just unfortunate that it took Noralani getting attacked by one before the sovereign finally acknowledged it. They're all the same. Maybe not on the surface, but inside, each and every one of them is exactly the same. All that power wasted on something so *worthless*. Their very existence disgusts me."

August said nothing during Fate's short rant. He didn't have anything to say. He knew there were people who worked for the Registry who were afraid of shifters, but he couldn't remember ever meeting someone who flat-out admitted to despising them—let alone declared their bias to a fellow officer. Fate was the only exception. One of the many documents a Registry officer signed confirmed that the enlistee held no bias toward shifters and viewed them as civilized members of society. He wondered if Fate had missed that document or had simply rolled his eyes and signed it anyway.

"Noralani seems like such a sweet girl. I hope she recovers," August said.

It seemed the safest thing to say without setting Fate off on another tangent. Fate was a veteran officer—if he hated shifters, he must have had his reasons. It wasn't August's business. His responsibility was to monitor the shifters assigned to him. Whom or what Fate hated had nothing to do with that.

THEY HAD SEVERAL shifters assigned to them. Three of them lived right there in Osin. Fate hadn't wanted to start there. He'd been adamant on starting in Hamet where they could get the most dangerous of all the shifters—Conlin.

"You don't like Hamet, do you?" Fate said. "Is it the heat?"

"It is many things," August answered. "You do not seem to dislike it."

"I'm from Hamet. Moved to Weren when I was fifteen."

"I am not surprised." The intense look on Fate's face made him want to clarify. "Your accent. You speak as a Hametian speaks." He was fond of the inflection. It was slow and inviting, like climbing into a warm bath after a stressful day.

From then on, the drive was long and silent. Fate said nothing more of Noralani's attack or how only the two of them were supposed to go about rounding up shifters. August stared out the window, watching the scenery go by in a mix of blurring colors. With a few stops in between to rest, it took hours to reach Sago, and once they had, apprehension began to creep in, settling at the center of August's stomach like a stone.

The streets were bare of people and littered with trash and empty wine bottles. It wouldn't be long until they reached the Conlins' house. He hadn't the slightest clue of how they were going to arrest one dragon. Arresting two seemed like a suicide mission.

"Do we have a plan?" August asked. A raven flew past, gliding through the air with its sharp beak pointed straight ahead. It reminded him of Fate.

"A plan?" August could hear the amusement in his partner's voice. He tried not to be insulted by it. "Do you have suggestions?"

"If we are to start in Hamet, it means that we will have to collect the dragons first. I find it hard to believe that either of them will be happy to come with us. Especially the male."

"He doesn't have a choice," Fate said. "Take a look inside that bag over there."

August looked over at the duffle bag he'd noticed when he first stepped onto the bus. He couldn't reach it with his hands, and his feet proved just as useless. After unfastening his seat belt, he slid down in his seat just enough to give him the length required to drag the bag closer to him with the toe end of his shoes. Once it was just below his seat, he reached down and picked it up with a surprised grunt. It was heavier than he'd expected.

He unzipped the bag and stared down at the contents in disbelief. Impossible.

"Know what those are?" Fate said.

Of course he did. He'd played a hand in their overall existence.

"Yes. These are..."

He pulled one of the items out of the bag and examined it. Smooth steel felt cool against his palm. He dragged his finger along the object's outer surface. It was a thick ring large enough to fit around one's neck, lined with an intricate design of integrated circuits.

A collar.

There were two tiny metal hooks at one open end of the collar that were designed to slide into the two small slots at the opposite end. When closed, the hooks fit perfectly into the slots. It was impossible to open without the use of a special key. He'd designed it that way.

August shook his head. "But, these haven't been tested on... If they fail to work—"

"They work just fine," Fate said. "Tried them on a few shifters already. They work perfectly."

August traced his fingers around the edge of the collar. "I am at a loss for words..."

"You have incredible talent, Seaton. I see why your mother was so upset about you leaving the lab."

His grip tightened around the collar. "You spoke to my mother?"

"Yeah. Had to see her to get the collars. Fascinating woman."

"Did she—" He cleared his throat. "—ask about me?"

"Can't say that she did."

He stared out the window. Of course she hadn't asked about him. What had he expected?

He held his breath when they took the final road that led them to Hamet. Conlin's house was just a few hundred feet down from the main road. He'd never admit it out loud, but he wasn't looking forward to what was to come. An officer was supposed to be in control of his emotions. Anger, excitement, fear—these were things that could interfere with an officer's ability to do his job.

He'd never been the type of person to have a complete handle on his emotions.

August tried talking himself into believing that everything would be fine. He exhaled, breath exiting his mouth in a soft puff just as Fate stopped the vehicle in front of the Conlin house.

"Grab a couple of collars and follow me," Fate ordered.

"Right." Digging back into the bag, he grabbed a second collar and then followed Fate off the bus. "So, how are we doing this?"

"Just follow my lead," Fate ordered.

FATE'S "LEAD" WAS to kick open the Conlins' front door. It swung from the frame, slamming against the wall hard enough to leave an impression in the plaster. Dinina and Ari sat in the living room, eyes widening in understandable fear. The woman slung a protective arm in front of Ari, guarding him from harm's way.

"Where's the ingrate?" Fate demanded.

"Have you gone mad, Fate? Look at what you did to my wall."

"Your wall?" Fate snickered, seizing the doorknob with a thick hand. He slammed the door back into the wall again, and plaster crumbled to the floor like heavy clumps of powdered sugar. "Do you think I give a shit about your wall? That bastard grandson of yours is in Sago, isn't he? When will he return?"

Dinina looked calm, but August could see she was barely containing her anger. Ari clung to her, his face partially hidden behind his grandmother's shoulder.

"What makes you think that I know? He's an adult. He comes and goes as he pleases."

August held his tracking device in his hand. Fate had ordered him to check on Conlin's whereabouts before they'd entered the house. The male dragon was still in Sago and didn't seem to be moving much. They had plenty of time to arrest Dinina without him interfering. Then they would just have to wait for him to arrive so they could arrest him, too.

"Why would I do that when I can just have you tell me?"

Fate moved further into the room, green eyes glaring down at her. "You're probably unaware, but there've been a few changes in Asuda. You see, the sovereign's daughter was attacked yesterday by a shifter. Do you know what that means for you?"

Dinina said nothing.

"It means," he continued, "that the few rights your disgusting kind had are no more. You're no longer protected." He reached and took one of the collars from August. "You're no longer free."

He moved toward Dinina, collar in hand, looming over her where she sat. His pale hand dangled the collar high above her head.

"Stand up, dragon," he ordered.

She still hadn't spoken, and she made no move to stand. August watched as she processed his words. Hamet was practically in the middle of nowhere. It was a poor town, and technology wasn't something that Hametians had access to. The Conlins didn't have a television, a computer, or even a phone. Unless someone had told them about the attack in Askia, they had no real way of knowing if what Fate said was truth or fiction.

"Are you deaf?" Fate asked, tone cold.

His words were like knives, sharp enough to pierce flesh. He reached down and wrenched Ari away with his free hand and then threw him to the floor. His fingers were around Dinina's neck before she could speak, yanking her upright with the ferocity of a lumberjack hoisting a log.

"Still not willing to talk, huh? That's fine. I'm just getting started. Seaton, locate Conlin. I'll deal with her."

Fate walked away, hand still wrapped around Dinina's throat, guiding her toward the kitchen. August was left in the family room with Ari, who had just begun to push himself up from off the floor.

"Why are you doing this?" Ari shouted. "What did we ever do to you?" Unshed tears filled his eyes. It wouldn't be long before they fell.

"Shifters are dangerous." August tried his best to speak with confidence, with the same authority that seemed to come so naturally to Fate. "We are trying to protect you."

"They're not dangerous. They're my family." Ari's voice cracked. "*They're* protecting me, and I'm gonna…" He looked at August, fear and determination apparent in his eyes. "I'm gonna do the same for them."

August made a move to intercept Ari when he rushed toward the kitchen, but he held back when the boy stopped at the entryway, watching. There was nothing Ari could do to save his family from being arrested. Ari was human. He didn't belong with shifters. They would find a nice human family for him. A good human home. One that would show Ari what it was like to live a normal, shifter-free life.

August glanced down at the tracking device again. Conlin was still in Sago, had barely moved. Who knew when he would actually arrive? It made more sense to simply retrieve him. He moved toward the kitchen, wanting to voice his suggestion to Fate, but he slowed his footsteps as he approached the entryway. Ari still stood in the doorway, glaring at Fate. His hands were balled into fists as he watched the scene before him, and August could see why.

Fate smacked Dinina with the back of his hand. His other hand gripped a knife, pressing it dangerously against her neck. Blood dripped from her lower lip and rolled down her chin.

Ari shouldn't have been seeing this. August could barely stand to look at it. He could only imagine things getting worse from here. He wanted to intervene, to calm down Fate long enough to rationally reevaluate the situation. Before he could say anything, Ari pulled something out of his pocket. His arm stretched out in front of him, hand gripping the handle of a knife. He ran forward, charging at Fate, the blade glinting in his hand.

"Leave my grandma alone!" he screamed.

The knife plunged into Fate's hip, piercing flesh until nothing but the handle protruded from his pants. Fate shouted, one hand gripping his hip, the other hurling forward to swipe at Ari's face. The blade of Fate's knife slit across Ari's cheek, blood spattering onto the table and kitchen floor. Ari crumbled to the linoleum, wailing, his hands cupping the wound on his cheek as blood seeped through his joined fingers.

"*You*," Dinina growled.

Her voice was deeper, animalistic, not the calm voice that August had heard her speak in before. He could do nothing but watch. It was as if he were frozen in place, stalled in voice and movement. A roar reverberated through the small house, low and filled with agony, loud enough to shake the walls. Dinina's hazel eyes seemed to glow as her arms stretched wide, slender fingers curled, clear nails yellowing and hardening into the shape of talons. Another roar. A few drinking glasses fell from a cabinet and shattered against the floor.

"She's shifting!" August cried, finally finding his voice.

Three shots rang out, bursting forth from the gun gripped tightly in Fate's hand. Both August and Ari screamed as the bullets pierced her skull.

"Grandma." Ari clambered to his feet, rushing over to where his grandmother lay.

She had fallen backward, talons smacking hard against the countertop as she went down. Ari dropped to his knees next to her, screaming for her to get up and be okay.

Fate's knife lay on the floor by his foot. Fate bent down and picked it up. Wiping the blood off the blade, he glared down at where Dinina lay. Ari sobbed, shaking his grandmother, and tried covering the wounds in her head while begging her to wake up.

It had all happened so quickly. One second, she was alive, and the next, Dinina Conlin was dead, her life snatched from her in front of her own grandson.

"Fate, you..." August felt bile rising in the back of his throat, burning its way up his esophagus. "Fate, what have you done?"

He rushed forward and then dropped to his knees next to Ari, desperately checking Dinina's neck for a pulse. She was dead. She must have been. How could anyone survive three bullets to the head? Still, he checked, hoping against hope that she was still clinging to life. His gloves prevented him from feeling anything, so he yanked them off, cursing and panicking as the seconds ticked by. If they called this in now, there was a chance that they could still save her.

"Seaton," Fate said.

"I have to get her heart going again. If I can just do that, then—"

"Augustus."

"Please help my grandma!" Ari cried.

"I need you to call it in. If we can get—"

"Seaton." Fate's voice boomed over him, loud and angry. "What are you doing? Why are you trying to save her? She was shifting in the proximity of known Registry officers without permission. She broke the law, and I did what was necessary. She would have killed us otherwise. Are you in disagreement with this?"

"I..." He shook his head. "I do not..." He looked at Ari, watched as the boy laid his head on his grandmother's chest and sobbed.

"Are you in disagreement?" Fate asked again.

August looked at the gun gripped in Fate's hand and shook his head once more. "N-No."

"Good. Now, find something to tie up the boy. And make sure you keep his mouth shut."

August stood up, only to lean down and grip Ari by the sides. Ari yelled, trying to fight August off of him. August felt like a robot, like a shell of a person, moving purely on autopilot. Dinina's lifeless body lay on the floor. He tried to pretend it wasn't there even as he grabbed Ari and hoisted him over his shoulder, feeling blood seep through his uniform shirt.

ARI MAY HAVE been a child, but he had the strength of a grown man. August finally managed to get him bound and gagged and onto the bus. Exhausted, he joined Fate back in the kitchen and watched as he nursed the knife wound in his hip.

They had come to Hamet to arrest two dragon shifters. Now, one of them was dead, and the other remained unfettered. August had worried about dealing with him before—now, he was downright terrified.

Fate turned and stared at August, eyes cold as stone. Blood seeped from his wound, leaving a dark, wet mark on his pants.

"You took care of the boy?"

August nodded.

Fate sighed. "It's a new day, Seaton. You've chosen your side. Now stick to it."

August held back tears. Dinina's body still lay there. Fate hadn't moved it. From the looks of things, he hadn't even called it in. August wished none of this had happened. He'd left the lab because he wanted excitement, but nothing like this. Not if it meant that people would die.

He hadn't killed her. Fate had. That didn't stop him from feeling just as responsible for her death.

He looked down at his hands. There were a few dried smears of blood on them from when he had lifted Ari. Letting out a shaky breath, he stepped over Dinina's body and walked over to the sink. The rush of cool water from the faucet physically washed the blood away, but he still felt it, imagined it seeping through his pores and mingling with his own. This moment would live with him for the rest of his days. A life, gone. A grandmother, a guardian, taken away from her grandson. He turned off the faucet. His hands were clean now. Why did they still feel so filthy?

"What do we do now?" he asked.

He turned to stare at Fate who stood next to Dinina's body, cursing as he snatched a rag hanging from the handle of the kitchen stove. He used it to apply pressure to the wound Ari had given him.

Fate said, "We wait."

Chapter Five

His preferred route from Simone's to his home was a path through a forest of trees with leaves that fluttered like eyelashes. The walk took an hour on a good day. Today, Coy was running.

He raced through the foliage, random, old memories coming to him in snapshots: stolen bottles of wine, lacquered lips, and muscular thighs. Too much drinking. Too much sex. He could never remember their names. Lydia? Laura? Avery? Alexander? Beautiful women and men of his past, whose names he couldn't remember, insignificant like raindrops falling into a puddle.

He didn't want to stop running until he reached Hamet.

The pleasant scent of honeysuckle lingered in the air, growing stronger as he moved farther out of the forest. Hamet was a small, secluded town with more people than available homes. Still, what it lacked in size, it made up for in hospitality. There were no guard gates stationed at the entrance, no men in stiff uniforms demanding to know who was coming or going. If someone were to complain about Hamet, it would not be because its inhabitants lacked kindliness. It would be because it was poor.

Hamet may have been poor, but Coy wasn't. Not anymore.

The excitement he felt in knowing that he would be able to spoil his family outweighed the overall exhaustion he felt from the day's early performances. No amount of annoying thigh squeezing or ass smacking could quell the joy bubbling up inside of him. He practically galloped down the road, his sandals kicking up dirt, coating his legs in a thin, grimy layer.

His neighborhood seemed quieter than usual. At this time of day, there would at least be a few kids hanging around outside, or the elderly couple a few houses down would be sitting on their front porch. The stillness of the road leading to his home made him a bit uncomfortable. This type of eerie silence wasn't something he was used to.

Several hundred feet away, there was a giant vehicle parked in front of an abandoned house. He wondered if someone was moving in, or maybe if they were planning to tear it down for good.

He couldn't smell dinner cooking as he approached his home, and he hoped the lack of aroma didn't mean that his grandmother was going to force one of her vegetable-centric meals on them. Yet, even if she did, he would grin and bear it. After all, he now had enough money to buy as much meat as he and Ari could consume.

He stepped into his shack and changed from his sarong into a tunic. It felt good to be home. As much as he loved hearing the crowd cheering for him, being the main event could be tiresome. Sometimes he had no desire to be the object of the fears and desires of the crowd. Sometimes he just wanted to be plain ole Coy—terrible whittler, cool big brother, and amazing grandson.

Leaving his little house, he walked to the front porch, hand reaching for the doorknob. It creaked open without him having to turn the knob. No doubt Ari had left it open by mistake. It was a habit of his.

"You left the door open again, kid," Coy said, stepping inside. He glanced around the living room, frowning at the large dent in the wall. "What the hell..."

Moving over to further inspect the damage, he traced the jagged outline with his finger, frown deepening. "Ari? Nina?"

No answer.

He moved away from the wall, still glancing back at it as he made his way through the living room.

"Hey, what happened to the wall?"

When he didn't receive a response, he started toward the hallway. Suddenly, something in his peripheral vision caught his attention—feet.

More specifically, his grandmother's feet. She was the only one out of the three of them who managed to keep her feet free from dirt even though she walked around just as barefoot as the rest of them.

"Nina!" he cried, rushing over to her. She must have fallen. Where the hell was Ari? He should have been there with her.

He froze, staring. He wanted to scream, except the sound wouldn't come out. He stood there, mouth open, eyes burning with tears. He needed to go to her, to help her. She was just lying there, face bloody. She wasn't moving. She wasn't talking, wasn't laughing or complaining about something he did or didn't do. She was just there, just...lying on the floor.

This wasn't real. It couldn't be. It was a joke. They were playing a cruel, horrible joke on him. His grandmother was fine. She was fine. She'd pop up any second now, laughing at the terrified look on Coy's face. Ari would jump from around the corner. He was in on it. He'd have to be. He'd tease Coy endlessly for falling for such a dumb prank. His grandmother wasn't dead. She *couldn't* be. She was the toughest woman in Hamet. She'd taught him everything he knew.

"Granny." He never called her that. She didn't like it. She'd yell at him whenever he did. It made her feel old. He waited for it, waited to hear her scold him for using that name.

She didn't respond.

"Nina, come on. Stop it. It's not funny." His legs felt too weak, and he fell to his knees next to his grandmother's body. "Nina, please." A sob tore its way out of him as he wrenched her off the floor and onto his lap. He screamed, tears streaming down his face. The holes in her skull didn't belong there, dark and bloody and ruining her sweet face.

"Who did this?" he shouted, cradling her against him and burying his face into her hair. It still smelled like lavender, like honeydew and sunshine. "Please," he whimpered. "Please wake up."

His grandmother's body was cold, pale, and lifeless.

"Nina," he whimpered, voice breaking with pure, unfiltered agony. He rocked back and forth, his back pressing against the cabinet behind him. Why had this happened? Why hadn't he been here? He should have been here. He could have protected her.

Sliding her body out from beneath him, he felt his heart splinter and then shatter into a billion pieces. She was gone. He wiped his eyes in vain. The tears kept coming back. He needed to mourn, to give himself over fully to his grief—but he couldn't.

His brother was missing.

He barely had the strength to move but forced himself to stand. A knife lay on the floor next to her body. His whittling knife. The one he'd given Ari just the day before. The blade was covered in blood. Was it Ari's?

"Ari!" he yelled. "Ari, where are you?" He ran upstairs, checking the two small bedrooms for his brother. He wasn't there. "Come on. Say something."

He ran back downstairs, opening doors, hoping that his brother had hidden himself away from whomever had attacked his grandmother. Every room was empty.

He wiped his eyes and sniffed to keep his nose from running—and then sniffed again. He knew that smell. Even through the overpowering, metallic scent of blood, he recognized it. The last time he'd encountered it was during the Registry's last visit. It was a smell he would never, *could never,* forget. It had kept him up on one or two occasions as he tried to figure out why it was both familiar yet so strange.

Officer Augustus Seaton.

That was his name. He remembered it. He also remembered the way Seaton had looked at him, had looked *down* on him. Had he been responsible for this? Sniffing again, he caught another whiff of Seaton's scent. He was nearby, hadn't left the scene of the crime. He'd killed Coy's grandmother and had the audacity to stick around.

It would be the biggest mistake of his life.

Coy bolted to the door, his legs propelling his body forward even when his heart lay dead on the kitchen floor. When he reached the threshold, he stopped running, feet skidding at the door's entrance and hands grasping at the doorframe.

Seaton.

He stood in front of Coy's house. Dressed in sleek black, Seaton had his arms folded across his chest as if he were bored, as if murdering Dinina had been as routine as brushing his teeth.

"You," Coy growled. "You did this."

Seaton put his hands out in front of him, as if they would keep Coy at bay. "I assure you, her death was not my intention."

Coy heard the fearful tremble in his voice even as he tried to offer false platitudes.

"I'll kill you!" Coy screamed.

Seaton took a single step back. "It's important that we both remain calm. If you shift—" He had the audacity to look pleadingly at Coy, like he hadn't just torn a piece of Coy's heart away. "—it won't end well for you."

Coy laughed, a dark and twisted sound. "You're worried that I'll *shift*?" He laughed again, agony, heartache, and despair twisting in his gut. "No." He shook his head, hands balled into fists, nails biting into his palms and drawing blood.

"Oh, no." A deep, demented growl rose from inside of him. "I'm not giving you over to the dragon." If he shifted now, he'd put the entire town in harm's way. Ari was missing, and Dinina was dead. There was no need for other senseless deaths. "I'm going to kill you as I am. Right here—right now. With my bare hands. And I'm going to enjoy every last second of it."

Coy lunged off the front porch, body a blur of solid, brown muscle. He would get his revenge. He would kill the man who killed his grandmother. He would avenge her death. He would tear out Seaton's cruel heart and offer it to the gods. He'd make him hurt, bleed, and scream.

Most importantly, he'd make him pay.

He stiffened just a foot away from Seaton, eyes wide, arms outstretched, and fingers just shy of the officer's neck.

"Why?" Coy asked, confusion etched across his angry face. A second later, he crumpled to the ground at Seaton's feet.

FATE STOOD NEAR the porch, gun drawn. It wasn't the gun from before. This one was bigger, longer. August hadn't heard a single shot being fired.

"Is he dead?" August asked.

Fate snorted. "Hell, I wish. They're tranquilizers." Moving to stand next to August, Fate pointed at the dart sticking out of the shifter's neck.

"You had tranquilizers the whole time? Why did you not use them on the female? We could have prevented her death."

Fate shrugged, snickering at Conlin's slumbering body. He used his foot to kick him onto his back, the shifter's long limbs spread out on either side of his body.

"I guess it slipped my mind."

August glared at Fate before bending down. He removed the tranquilizer dart out of Conlin's neck and placed the collar around him.

"What's with that look?" Fate asked.

"It is nothing."

He just didn't appreciate being lied to.

THE REST OF the day was as long as it was stressful. They traveled back north at a snail's pace, stopping and arresting the shifters assigned to them. The ones who didn't put up a fight were needlessly tranquilized for Fate's sick amusement. The ones who did were beaten, wounded, or worse. They'd originally had twenty-six living, breathing shifters assigned to their caseload.

Now, there were twenty-three of them.

Other than watching Fate abuse the shifters, the most difficult part of their mission was dragging each unconscious body onto the bus and strapping them into the chains. It was a necessary precaution. The collars may have impeded the shifters, but they did nothing to suppress their natural strength. If the tranquilizers wore off without the shifters being chained down, there would be nothing either of them could do. Fate only had so many bullets. He couldn't shoot *all* of their shifters—even if he may have wanted to. The chains were cruel and inhumane, but August was immensely grateful for them.

Pumped full of tranquilizers, the shifters slept. The only one Fate exhibited a bit of restraint for was Niami, the child whose file still sat on August's desk at home. He thought maybe it was because she was so young.

"What about the boy?" he asked.

"What about him?" Fate said.

"The man who picked him up—I have never seen him before."

"Don't worry about it. He's in good hands."

August couldn't bring himself to look at the back of the bus. The guilt was too much. He stared down at his hands, letting the entire day's events play inside his head like scenes from a movie. He hadn't been sure of what to expect when he had signed up to be a Registry officer, but it hadn't been this. To watch as shifters were beaten—or *killed.* He had regretted transferring out of the lab the moment that first bullet entered Dinina's head. Most of all, he regretted making those collars. This was *his* doing. He was responsible for this—*all of it.*

Maybe shifters were dangerous. Ari wasn't a shifter though. He was human and a *child.* At least he wasn't dead, but who knew what would happen to him? August really hadn't known the man who had come to retrieve Ari, and Fate was unlikely to ever bring up the subject again. If anything happened to the boy, he'd be just as responsible for it as Fate.

His mother was right. It took a special type of person to be a Registry officer, and he wasn't special. Not by a long shot. Just like she'd always said, he was too sensitive, too clueless, and too *weak.*

And now, worst of all—even though he hadn't pulled the trigger—a murderer.

Chapter Six

COY'S EYES FELT as if they'd been anchored down by sandbags. His mouth was full of cotton, thick and dry, and his tongue felt like sandpaper as it dragged across his parched lips. His head was a storm, memories flashing like lightning. Ari was missing.

And his grandmother was dead.

He'd held her against his chest, had sobbed his broken heart over her lifeless body. Someone had killed her. The Registry? No. Not the Registry—the pretty officer with the brown eyes and pink lips.

Augustus Seaton.

He was the murderer.

Coy had been prepared to return the favor. He remembered lunging at Seaton, remembered the startled look in his eyes just before he'd closed them, accepting his fate. He couldn't remember anything after that. Nothing but darkness. A single canoe drifting along the sea in the dead of night.

What happened? Why couldn't he remember anything?

A shiver worked its way through his body. He was cold.

The room spun when he tried to change his position. Not that he could do so, anyway. He could hardly move. Something was restraining him, pinning him back and only allowing superficial movements. The wiggling of his toes, the flexing of his fingers...not much more than that.

"Where am I?"

There were lights above him, bright and blinding. He struggled against the bindings—one leather band strapped across his ankles, another across his thighs. One at his torso, two at his wrists, and a final one pulled taut across his shoulders. The surface behind him was solid and unforgiving, frigid against the warmth of his back. His feet rested against the floor, which was meticulously polished to the point where he could see his distorted reflection in its surface.

"Is anyone there?"

"Oh, you are finally awake."

He turned his attention toward the voice and spotted a woman with short, dark hair and brown skin standing near a door.

"I was starting to think you would never wake up." Her thick, black-framed glasses slid down her nose, and she pushed them back up with her middle finger. She wore casual khaki pants, a dark green blouse, and a white jacket. The doctor who had once embedded the tracking chip into Coy's thigh had worn the same kind of jacket. "Perhaps those tranquilizers worked better than I thought."

"Who the hell are you?" Coy asked. "And where the fuck am I?"

"My name is Dr. Rowburg, and you are at the Asuda Registry."

"The Registry? Why am I at the Registry?" He closed his eyes and tried to remember anything after he'd attempted to attack Seaton. Nothing. "How did I even get here? I can't remember anything."

"Everything will be explained to you later, Mr. Conlin. Once you are secured in your cell, of course."

"My cell?"

"Yes," she said. "You have been confined here, at the best prison Asuda has to offer."

Prison? Why the hell was he in prison? He was the one with a murdered grandmother and a missing brother.

"Look. You people have the wrong person. It was Seaton. Officer Augustus Seaton. Get him. He's the one who did this. I wouldn't kill my own grandmother. And what about my brother? Where is he?"

Dr. Rowburg frowned. Doing so made her glasses slip down her face. She made her way farther into the room, shoes squeaking against the polished floor.

"You do not know, do you?"

"Know what? I told you, I can't remember anything."

"There was an attack in Askia. The sovereign's daughter was seriously injured. It is unknown if she will survive."

"Yeah, that's terrible and all," he said, "but what does *that* have to do with *me*?"

"The attack was carried out by a shifter. The sovereign is furious, so much so that he has decreed a countrywide arrest of all shifters. You are being detained here indefinitely. Or, at least until we hear further word from the sovereign."

"Look, lady. If any of that really happened, then it's fucked up, but I didn't have anything to do with it. I've never even been to Askia in my entire life. I shouldn't be here."

He looked around, trying to get a better view of his surroundings. There wasn't much to see. Just a few metal tables, some chairs, a couple of cabinets, and other contraptions that he'd never seen before. He shuddered at the coolness in the room. A second later, he realized why.

"Why the fuck am I *naked*?"

Dr. Rowburg chuckled, the sound managing to be both pleasant and frightening. "You are exactly where you should be, Mr. Conlin." She walked over to one of the cabinets. "And you are naked because I was curious."

"Curious about *what*?" he growled.

She chuckled again as she opened the cabinet and reached inside. When she pulled her arm out, her fingers were grasping a syringe. The needle, long and thin, gleamed beneath the obnoxious ceiling lighting.

"I know you just woke up a few moments ago, but you seem like you would be a problem for the guards. It will only have you down for an hour or so."

"Don't bring that fucking thing near me," he demanded.

He squirmed within his bindings, shoulders rocking against the solid surface behind him. It didn't do him any good. Dr. Rowburg moved closer, syringe in hand, and punctured his neck with the needle. He heard the slide of fabric rubbing against his skin as she pulled her hand away.

"What did you just do to me? What did you give me? Tell me, you evil—"

He blacked out before he could finish.

AUGUST DIDN'T KNOW how to respond to praise. He wasn't used to it. The number of officers, staffers, and administrators congratulating him and Fate on a job well-done was staggering. He didn't want to take credit for any of it. Fate was the entire brains behind the operation—August had just done what he had been told to do. It hardly seemed like something he should be proud of, especially since he had just stood by and let it all happen. He considered telling the Registry that Fate had practically goaded Dinina Conlin into shifting before he murdered her, but worried about the ramifications. He didn't want to overstep his boundaries, or make Fate and the other officers think that he couldn't be trusted. He didn't want others labeling him as the weak link in a chain. It was best to keep quiet.

He had a headache. The lights in the employee lounge only made it worse. He thought about resting his head on the table but decided against it. He wasn't the only person in there. Officers sat around him at separate tables, dressed in black uniforms just like his own. Some employees wore crisp white lab coats. None of them wore suits. Anyone who wore a suit at the Registry was either a visitor or had their own office where they could eat in private. Speaking of food, his lunch sat in front of him, growing cold. The events leading up to today repeated on a loop inside his head, and they all had the same theme—blood, chains, and death.

August wasn't very hungry.

He couldn't do this. He didn't *want* to do this. He'd signed up to be an officer because he had been tired of doing the same, dull thing over and over again at the lab. His work there had offered him comfort and security, but not excitement. Back then, he had seen the officers from time to time. They'd walked through the halls, bursting with confidence and pride. Respected by most and feared by all. He had envied them.

He'd spent days wondering what it would be like to have people notice him whenever he stepped into a room, wondering what it was like to be self-confident, to interact with shifters, and to enforce the rules. The day he had become an official officer, he'd assumed he would find out. Now he felt even worse about his already miserable existence. There was no other way around it.

He had to quit.

He knew the lab would welcome him back. The work wouldn't be exciting, but he would never have to watch anyone else die. It was a trade-off he could live with. Besides, now that the shifters were all imprisoned, he wouldn't have any of the excitement he'd initially wanted. There would be no more road trips across Asuda. Actually, that wasn't a bad thing considering how much he hated the southern climate. All officers would be reassigned to work at the prison as guards, monitoring the shifters on a daily basis.

August frowned inwardly, glancing at his coworkers. A *prison*. He should have known better. How could they have been building a new lab without ever inviting him to take a look? Why had he assumed that it was completely normal for all those laborers to move about the entire building, working on various floors? Most of the levels that had contained administrative staff had been revamped into cells, their personnel moved to other Registry office buildings. Between training and overseeing shifters, he admittedly hadn't spent much time at headquarters since his job at the lab, but he should have paid more attention. Something like this seemed like an impossible detail to miss. Maybe it was the lack of electric fences that failed to tip him off. He wondered when those would be installed.

"I thought I'd find you in here."

August inwardly cringed at the sound of Fate's voice. He was the last person he wanted to talk to or even *see,* for that matter. A cloud of death and destruction seemed to follow Fate wherever he went, and August wanted no part of it.

"What do you think of the upgraded facility?" Fate grabbed a chair next to him, sitting down with all the poise of a model, and patted August's knee. "Great, isn't it?"

"Yes, I suppose it is," August said. How could anyone define a prison as *great*?

"You don't sound impressed." Fate frowned, leaning in his seat so that he was hovering even closer to August. August could feel the heat from his body, could smell the flavor of his gum from such close proximity—spearmint.

"Look, if there's something on your mind, you can tell me. We're partners, aren't we?"

August sighed. He'd been hoping to save this awkward conversation until after he put in transfer papers to go back to the lab.

"There is nothing wrong. I just—" He hesitated, trying to figure out the proper choice of words that wouldn't make it sound like he was giving up. "—no longer feel that I am cut out for the duties required of an officer. I am planning to transfer back to the lab immediately."

He turned away from Fate, hoping that his confession would be enough to make Fate leave in anger or in disappointment. He didn't care which—he just wanted him gone.

"What?" Fate reached up, lightly gripped August's chin, and turned him around. He placed a hand on top of August's knee, invading his personal space, and squeezed carefully. "You can't quit, Augustus. Look, I know everything that happened was a bit intense, but we're just getting started. You're going to make a fine officer one day. You're destined for greatness."

"Fate—"

"Listen, Augustus. I'm going to tell you something. Something I've never told anyone ever before. Do you want to hear it?"

He didn't, really. He nodded anyway.

"The thing is," Fate began, "I hate having partners. In the past ten years, I've run off every partner I've ever had. I like working alone. I don't have time for someone getting in my way, messing things up. But there's something different about you. Something special. I know I can trust you." He stared at August, locking eyes with him, refusing to break eye contact. "I can, can't I?"

"Of course you can," August said. "But, it is not only the deaths of those people..." He noticed the pointed look on Fate's face and corrected himself. "Of those *shifters*. That dragon. Conlin. When I said those things. The things you told me to say. The look in his eyes... He could have killed me. He *wanted* to kill me. If you had missed your shot, I would be dead."

Fate gripped August's knee, fingers gently digging into muscle and bone. "You can't go around thinking horrible things like that, Augustus. I would never let anything happen to you. You have your entire life ahead of you. And, as long as we're partners, I'll always protect you. You have my back, and I have yours."

"Yes, but..."

He supposed Fate did have a point. While he hadn't appreciated being used as bait to make Conlin think that he'd been the one to murder his grandmother, he hadn't been injured at all. Not by Conlin, and not by anyone else. Fate had been stabbed, punched, kicked, attacked, and spit on. Yet, through each and every visit to their shifters' homes, August had come out completely unscathed.

"Give it some time," Fate urged. "At least a few more months. If I haven't fully convinced you that I'll always have your back by then, you can transfer out. We're still getting to know each other, but I want you to be able to trust me. And I want to know that I can trust you."

He slung his arm over August's shoulder, pulling him against his chest like the two of them had known each other for years instead of a few months.

Like they were friends.

"We have to be more than just partners, Augustus. You and me, we have to be friends."

Friends. August inspected the word like a gemstone. Fate was right—August was overreacting. Everything had been so intense and startling that his initial response was to flee. Fate was a veteran officer, and everyone at the Registry admired him. He could only imagine how many other officers would have given anything to be in August's shoes. To work with Daniel Fate, whose reputation preceded him. And yet, Fate had chosen *him*, wanted him to be the one person he could trust. It was humbling—flattering, even.

"It is August."

"What calendar have you been looking at? We're well into May," Fate said.

August chuckled. "No, I mean my name. My friends call me August." He didn't have any friends. If he did, he would have told them the same.

"I'll keep that in mind, August." Fate winked at him and smiled, showing off his perfectly white teeth.

August smiled back.

And, for the first time in years, it was authentic.

COY WOKE UP, no longer restrained, but still unable to leave. That was hours ago. Or, it felt like it, anyway.

His cell was a six-by-eight-foot room with bright, artificial lighting. A metal toilet sat a mere few feet away from his bed. A small sink was built into the top of it, and he couldn't help but be disgusted at the thought of washing his hands with toilet water, even if it was clean. At least, he *hoped* it was clean. The entire thing was bolted to the floor. Smart thinking on the Registry's end. Too bad. It would have made a great weapon. His bed, if one could refer to it as such, made him feel like he was lying on top of a slab of cement. To top it all off, the fourth cell wall—containing a single door—was made of impenetrable plastic. No amount of punching and kicking left more than a few sweaty smears along its clear surface. He knew that from experience.

They'd given him clothing—a uniform. White pants and white shirt, the fabric almost thin enough to see through. They hadn't given him underwear.

He couldn't shift. They'd done something to him, something that took away his abilities. Whenever he tried, his efforts were met with a shock that left him gasping for breath, as if he were being electrocuted from the inside out. He tried to breathe fire. That too was gone. Like a lighter empty of fluid. Not a single spark. Even his senses of smell and hearing had dulled. Was this what it felt like to be human? No wonder Ari hated being one so much.

He sighed.

It hurt to think about Ari. He didn't have a clue of where he was. Had the Registry taken him? Was he alone? All by himself with no one to take care of him? Maybe he had gone to a friend's house—someone who could keep him safe until Coy found a way out of prison.

And what about his grandmother? She was dead, but what about her body? Had the bastards that killed her even given her a proper funeral? Or, was she still just lying on the kitchen floor, rotting away?

"Fuck." He punched the thin mattress beneath him and felt the vibrations from steel platform below.

Maybe he could get some answers from Dr. Rowburg. He didn't know if she was the type to willingly hand over information, but right now, she was the only person he'd had some semblance of a conversation with. Plus, she sure as hell seemed friendlier than the asshole prison guards. The problem was, would she willingly answer his questions, or would he have to force them out of her? He supposed it didn't really matter. He'd be prepared for either scenario.

Coy had several plans of how he wanted to spend his life, and none of them involved rotting away in a prison cell. He hadn't yet come up with a plan, though he did have an outline—an itinerary he'd come up with while staring up at the ceiling.

First, someway, somehow, he would escape. Then, he would find Ari. After that, he'd track down Augustus Seaton and avenge his grandmother. Finally, he and Ari would go back to Hamet, grab his money—if it was even still where he left it—and flee Asuda altogether. They'd go someplace where the Registry would never find them. With his grandmother gone, what ties did either of them have to Asuda now anyway?

Fuck. Why had any of this have to happen?

He stared up at the bottom of the empty bed above his own, arms folded behind his head. So, first things first: an escape plan. He knew he was at the Registry's headquarters, but for the life of him, he couldn't remember *where* it was located. Osin? Perhaps Askia? Somewhere north of Hamet, that was for certain. He was racking up questions with no damn answers. One thing he knew for sure was that he wasn't the only prisoner. There were other shifters locked in the cells around him, one just across the hallway. He could hear them, shouting, crying, begging to be released. Occasionally, a guard would walk past, sometimes a woman, most often a man. They'd guide a shifter down the hall, chains hanging from the prisoner's wrists, ankle shackles dragging along the floor. Coy always waited for them to come back the other way so that he could guess what was being done to them in the interval. His first—and final—guess was torture. Their eyes were always startlingly vacant when they returned.

His stomach growled. He hadn't eaten for several hours.

"Are we going to get any food in here, or is the plan to just starve us to death?!" he shouted, banging his fist on the wall behind his head to grab the attention of one of the guards.

He wasn't calling to anyone specific. The few officers that walked past his cell had hardly interacted with him. Still, if he knew one thing about Registry officers, it was that they were easy to rile up.

"Shut the hell up, dragon," someone said. A man's voice. He hadn't yet stepped into view, but Coy heard the sound of his boots. "We'll feed you when we're good and ready."

He could tell from the accent that the other person was from the south, from Sago. Maybe even Hamet. He had the accent. No hiding that.

"A voice with no face," Coy said, raising his volume so the officer could hear him. "How mysterious."

The officer stepped into view. He was a huge man—about Coy's height and double his weight. His chubby face looked too young and soft for the rest of his body. Coy recognized him—he was the first officer Coy had seen when he had woken up, groggy and dizzy, in his cell. A brass nameplate on the officer's left breast pocket flashed beneath the harsh lights.

Officer R. Hickman.

"You're going to learn to keep that mouth shut, dragon," Hickman threatened.

"Oh? And I'm guessin' you're gonna teach me how, right?"

"Teach you?" Hickman snickered—a truly sinister sound. "Oh, I'm going to do a lot more than that. Just you wait."

"Oh, Officer." Coy batted his eyelashes and put a hand over his mouth, doing his best to imitate some of the more bashful women he'd flirted with in the past. "What if someone hears?" He raised the pitch of his voice, speaking as sweetly as he could muster without actually injuring his vocal cords.

"Don't worry." Hickman grinned, showing off a mouthful of coffee-stained teeth. "I'll make sure to muffle your screams."

"Likewise." He was back to speaking with his natural voice. "Say goodbye to your family while you still can. Consider making your funeral a closed-casket one."

"Considerate of you."

"I'm a considerate kind of guy."

"Did you get to say goodbye to yours?" The knowing smirk on Hickman's face told Coy that he was aware of the circumstances of Coy's arrest. His blood felt like lava pumping through his veins.

"Fuck you."

"In due time, dragon. In due time." Hickman winked and then walked away.

Coy debated whether he should add killing Hickman to his list.

AUGUST HAD AN hour and a half to burn before the employee bus arrived to take him back to Osin. The Registry headquarters—and now its prison—were both located in Weren, a mere thirty-minute drive from Osin. The differences in culture and community made it seem worlds away. Osin was a town of beauty. Its people, architecture, and even its animals were graceful and majestic. Weren gave off the cold, polished feel of steel, its people moving uniformly like robots, stiff and mechanical. If it weren't for the forest surrounding the prison, it would have seemed more like a town built indoors.

Technically, August was off duty, but he was still allowed to walk around the prison during his off-hours. He hadn't wanted to. Fate had convinced him otherwise, told him that it would be good for him. *You have too much compassion for creatures that don't deserve it. You're better than them.* That was what Fate had said to him. So far, everything Fate had told him—aside from the blatant lie back at the Conlin house—had been true. August wondered if it was time he started putting in more of an effort to believe him. Maybe he really was better than shifters.

What had they ever done to deserve his compassion, anyway?

Despite having the freedom to walk along the prison halls thanks to his newly issued Registry ID card, he still needed to wait for clearance from the top before he could access the cells of his assigned shifters. There were, understandably, some he wanted to avoid. It would be a while before he worked up the courage to be in the same proximity as Conlin, even if the dragon had been rendered harmless, collared and confined to a cell. He also had no desire to chance upon Niami. Knowing she was locked up with the rest of the shifters was a bit too much for him to deal with.

August chose the fourth floor to wander around in. Staring straight ahead, he moved down the hall, his footsteps echoing against the metal floors. He walked with his head held high, shoulders back, chin up, and eyes occasionally glancing from side to side, peering into each cell. He didn't recognize a single shifter. Relief washed over him like a light rain. It felt easier to believe he was better than people he'd never actually met.

The shifters stared back at him with hatred in their eyes. They had no reason to hate him. He hadn't put them in here. He'd acted under the order of the sovereign. Regardless, this wasn't worth explaining to them. They wouldn't comprehend. These people...these creatures were here because they'd been unfortunate enough to be born as shifters. If they wanted to hate someone, they had to start with themselves.

The cells were small and bright. The shifters wore white uniforms, but the latter didn't do much in the way of cover. He could see practically everything. For a second or two, he began to pity them, and then he reminded himself of Fate's words. This wasn't his fault. They didn't deserve his pity. He was an esteemed officer of the Asuda Registry.

August was just doing his job.

He rounded a corner and began heading down another hall. It contained just as many cells and just as many helpless shifters. They looked lost, weak, and pathetic. What was wrong with them? They just lay there on those tiny beds, doing nothing. Waiting. Waiting for what?

Someone to rescue them? For the sovereign to change his mind? The shifters in this hall didn't even look angry. Just tired and broken. If he'd been in their place, he wouldn't have accepted this as his life, as his fate. He wouldn't just lie around *waiting*. He'd be planning his escape. If they weren't going to even try to find justice for themselves, then they deserved to be where they were. These people... No. Not people. These *things* were exactly where they belonged.

Straight ahead, he finally saw the end of the hall. Thank goodness. August couldn't stomach another moment of this. It was too frustrating, too infuriating. He continued forward, quickening his pace and wanting nothing more than to free himself of the depression of seeing these damaged shifters. Two cells before the exit, just before he was almost free from the misery of the hall, he glanced to the side and saw Conlin.

He thought about rushing past, to get to the stairwell as quickly as possible. He should have pretended he never saw him. Once his eyes were locked on Conlin, he couldn't turn away, couldn't continue on as if he hadn't seen him. There was something about Conlin that demanded his attention. Something that forced him to stay put even when his mind told him he should flee.

He stared at the shifter through the glass, watching his solid body propped up against the wall behind his bed. Conlin stared back at him, narrowing his mismatched eyes, and August saw rage in its purest form.

Conlin wanted him dead. He hadn't said a single word, yet August could feel it. If it weren't for the barrier separating them, Conlin would have attacked him. It was in his eyes, in his expression, even in the way that he breathed. August thought he could feel Conlin's very soul battling to free itself just so it could put an end to his life.

August expected him to speak, to yell, to bolt off the bed, and to run over to the indestructible plastic separating them. He waited for the promises of beatings, the threats of torture, and the guarantees of death. However, Conlin didn't utter a single word. He just sat there, reclining against the wall, eyes unblinking as he looked back at August.

Conlin's reaction—or lack thereof—was both bewildering and unnerving. He remembered how quickly he'd been to taunt August during their first meeting. Now, he was just like the others, sitting there, broken and weak. Surely, he was more powerful than that. If anyone were to go down without a fight, it had to be a dragon.

"Is there a problem, dragon?" August asked. If he had to goad Conlin into a response, then so be it. He wasn't above petty childishness to get the things he wanted. He would make Conlin respond, make him react, make him show that even prison wasn't enough to silence and subdue him.

And yet, Conlin said nothing.

August watched, dark eyebrows furrowing in confusion when Conlin simply folded his arms behind his head and then closed his eyes.

Was that it? Had they drugged him? Did they erase his memory? Was that even possible? Could the lab have advanced so much in the short time he'd been gone?

No, that was preposterous. There had to be something else. Conlin believed that August murdered his grandmother. Wouldn't it have at least made sense to ask about his brother? There was no way Conlin could, upon seeing August's face, just take a nap. Where was his anger? What happened to his *rage*? August had felt it the moment he stared at him through that cell. He was certain of it. So, where was it? What had happened to him?

He didn't even know why he wanted Conlin to react so badly. Maybe he needed Conlin to express his hatred for him. To tell him how much of a monster he was, to insult and belittle him. He wanted it, *needed* it. Instead, Conlin pretended as though he didn't even exist. It left a feeling of emptiness inside of him, like a hollow shell of what he was supposed to be. The feeling frustrated him, enraged him. Who did Coy think he was to deny August a feeling he so desperately needed?

"I..." August bit at his lip, hands clenched into fists. "I did not think so."

He turned away and moved quickly down the hall, away from Conlin. Humans really were better than shifters. Even better—no—*especially* better than dragons.

IT HAD TAKEN every drop of Coy's willpower not to slam against the wall between him and Seaton. There was nothing he wanted more than to tear the life right out of the officer's body. However, he needed to think, and more importantly, he needed a well-constructed plan. One way or another, he would get his revenge, and he would forgo his typical response of brash brutality for something a little cleverer. Something that would make his grandmother proud.

Time passed either slowly or quickly. He didn't really know. He wasn't sure of the date, or whether it was night or day. He didn't even know what town he was in. He couldn't smell anything other than the dizzying odor of disinfectant. On the plus side—if such an outlook existed in this particular situation—the food they'd given him was delicious. Not exactly a silver lining, but it was better than nothing. He'd expected the Registry to feed them slop.

In short, prison was boring. Most of his time was spent waiting—waiting for a guard to come in, shackle him, and drag him to the lab. Said lab was run by Dr. Marian Rowburg, the same woman who had jabbed him with that long needle, rendering him unconscious. In whatever amount of time he'd been here, he'd come to hate her more than he hated anyone else at the prison.

"You are making this situation much more difficult than it needs to be, Mr. Conlin," Dr. Rowburg said, distracting Coy from his thoughts.

"What do you think they put in those potatoes they fed us earlier?" he asked. "I tasted garlic, but there was something else in there. Cayenne? Maybe paprika?"

"Mr. Conlin, please. I need you to focus."

"My grandmother made amazing mashed potatoes. Just a dash of oregano. You wouldn't think something like that would work, you know, but she knew what she was doing. It's funny. I hated all the rest of her vegetables. But potatoes are different. Everyone loves those. Crazy, right? A dragon loving vegetables. Still, that was her." He smiled. "She loved her vegetables."

"When you attempt to shift, you may feel—"

"You've probably noticed that I'm using past tense here. That's because she was murdered by one of your piece-of-shit Registry officers."

"Coy—"

"Anyway, how do you people sleep at night?"

"Soundly," she snapped, her chocolate eyes narrowed in annoyance, before visibly softening. "I am sorry about what happened to your grandmother."

"Thanks," Coy said. "You're not—but thanks."

"The quicker you follow my instructions, the quicker—"

"You'll release me?"

"You can go back to your cell."

"Great. Because I have plenty of things to do in there."

He let his head fall back against the metal table with a soft thud. He guessed he'd been in the lab for at least twenty minutes now. She was playing the role of a caring scientist by trying to convince him to shift out of his own free will rather than her having to resort to force. She wasn't very good at the role. Even if she had been, it wouldn't have mattered. If they wanted him to do anything, their only option was force. In prison, or out of it, he refused to make the Registry's job easier.

"I see we are going to have to do this the hard way," she said.

"That's my favorite way to do anything."

She muttered something under her breath that he couldn't quite make out.

"Are you sweet-talking me, Doc?"

"I said that you remind me of my son. You are both very stubborn."

He raised an eyebrow in disbelief. "*You* have a son?"

"What do you say it in that manner? As if you are surprised by this?"

"It's nothing. Nothing at all, Doc."

"Tell me," she ordered, leaning in as if he were about to share a secret with her.

He smirked. "Let me go, and I'll tell you anything you want to hear."

The slap was hard enough to make his cheek sting. She stared down at him, lips curled back in disgust and eyes narrowed into angry slits.

"You seem to have forgotten who's in charge here, Mr. Conlin." She slapped him a second time on the same cheek, the sudden force causing him to bite down on his tongue.

She pressed her finger against the electrode stuck to the center of his forehead for a second and then turned a dial on an unfamiliar-looking contraption. He'd been seconds from taunting her more when a shock burst through his body so painfully that it made him cry out.

Electrical pulses emitted from the collar around his neck and absorbed into his skin. It felt like thousands of tiny knives were stabbing him all over his body, piercing his sensitive flesh. His muscles stiffened, his nerves pulsing as though they were on fire.

Dr. Rowburg was an evil, sadistic bitch with extreme control issues.

THE BUS ARRIVED on schedule. August climbed inside along with a few other employees. Everyone looked tired. No one attempted to engage him in conversation, which he appreciated. The bus was similar to the same one he and Fate had used to capture their shifters. Except, of course, this one didn't have a wall separating the passengers from the driver. Also, no chains. Just a typical—though high-class—charter bus.

The air conditioner hummed as they pulled away from the parking lot. He'd managed to stay awake for ten minutes before the lull of cool, artificial air blowing throughout the bus made it difficult for him to keep his eyes open. Sleep came, and he welcomed it.

August woke up a few minutes before they stopped in front of his house. Thanking the driver for the ride, he stepped out and breathed in fresh air. He regretted that he'd been unable to stay awake during the trip. As a child, he'd always loved staring out of the window while his mother drove their car across the border between Osin and Weren.

About ten minutes after the border, right next to a bakery run by an old couple, stood the Valco Gardens, the largest rosebush maze Asuda had to offer. He'd only ever been able to convince his mother to stop there once. Its caretaker boasted that it took most visitors at least three hours to exit.

It had taken him twenty-three minutes.

Those twenty-three minutes were the most enjoyable minutes of his entire childhood. He remembered walking past the other visitors, surrounded by the smell of earth mixed with the subtle fragrance of roses. He'd ignored the others, paid no attention as they took wrong turns or turned down dead-end paths. He remembered how proud he'd been, even if he had completed it alone. His mother had stayed behind, deciding that working through some leftover lab calculations would be more enjoyable than exploring a maze with her son.

The owner of the gardens had waited at the exit, gray eyes smiling down at him. He still remembered her name—Rose. *Just like the flower*, he'd said. That was the most the two of them had interacted, but meeting her had made a lasting impact on him and instilled an appreciation for nature. It had happened over nine years ago, yet the memory was still so vivid in his mind. He liked to think about that day, to close his eyes and relive those twenty-three minutes wandering through that maze. Especially since the day that followed had been the worst one of his life. Still, ever since then, the sight and smell of roses always created a pleasant feeling inside of him. When he moved, planting them throughout his yard was inevitable.

He opened the cast-iron gate that led to the walkway and used his foot to shut it behind him. A gentle breeze blew past, rustling the bushes and fluttering the grass. He was dirty, sweaty, and exhausted, but he was smiling. The Registry had given him the week off to recuperate from his efforts. As he climbed the porch steps leading to his front door, he wondered what he would do with his free time. Socializing was out of the question, as he had no friends. It was probably best if he spent the week resting. And yet, lying around at home after the events he'd experienced seemed underwhelming.

Well, he didn't have to rush. He had the entire weekend to figure it out. He'd passed the Registry's boot camp and even arrested a dragon. Making a friend or two couldn't be as difficult as either of those. He just needed to be more confident in his abilities.

COY WAS DRAGGED back to his cell. It took two guards to move him. He was in too much pain to walk on his own. The guards dumped him onto the bed, not caring that his lower body hung off of it, limp and heavy against the floor, awkward and uncomfortable. Insult to injury.

Dr. Rowburg's torture was terrible, but he could handle it. What he couldn't handle was knowing she was doing this to other shifters as well. He wasn't a stranger to pain. He even got off on it sometimes. Still, many of the shifters he'd seen being dragged up and down the hallway were teenagers. He hadn't seen any elderly shifters, though he assumed they were there. There was no way that they would be able to withstand the abuse Dr. Rowburg had planned for them. Why was the Registry torturing them in the first place? What did they *want*?

It took effort to climb onto the bed. When he finally managed it, he flung himself onto his back and closed his eyes. Tomorrow, he would start off fresh. He needed the sympathy of at least one Registry employee. Maybe he could sweet-talk one of the female guards. One who didn't seem to hate him as much as the others. Someone who would be easy to manipulate. It would take a while to get that person on his side. Eventually, whoever it was would give him the vital information he needed to begin plotting his escape.

He also needed to figure out who some of the other shifters were. He could only get a good look into the cell across from his. The shifter inside was a tall, fair-skinned, middle-aged man who wore thick glasses and stuttered when he spoke. Coy didn't know his name, but he would find out. He wasn't sure how long it was going to take before he put his plan into action. Having a friend or two to keep him from going insane seemed like as good of an idea as any other.

In the meantime, it was best if he got some sleep. Who knew what the bastards in the lab had planned for him tomorrow. Or any other day, for that matter. He was going to need all the mental and physical rest he could get.

THE WEEKEND STRETCHED into the following week. August spent the next four days eating, sleeping, and reading articles about the public's reaction to the sovereign's decision. He may have mildly increased the excitement in his work life—even if it was short-lived—but his homelife was just as dull as ever. He wished he knew how to interact with people, wished he could socialize with others without worrying about the consequences. Most people called this social anxiety. He had a different name for it.

Sighing, he stood up from his desk and stretched. He couldn't just sit there wishing he knew how to befriend others. He had to put in an effort. The afternoon had just begun. There was plenty of time in the day left for him to shower, get dressed, go outside, and strike up a conversation with someone, *anyone*, willing to interact with him. Socializing wasn't as difficult as he was making it seem. He could do this. All he had to do was leave the house.

Or, maybe not.

Showered and dressed, he'd opened his door to discover Fate standing on the opposite side of it, his fist still raised, preparing to knock. After the initial shock—and the embarrassment of a startled scream—August calmed down enough to ask Fate why he was there.

"I assumed you were bored," Fate said. "I know I am."

"You could have called. You almost gave me a heart attack."

There was a warm flutter in his belly that increased with the realization that Fate had come to visit him. Not for work. Not for another round of arrest-the-shifters. Simply because he wanted to spend time with him.

"Sorry about that." Fate's grin did not add to his sincerity. "Were you headed out?"

August nodded. "I felt like exploring. I am sure there must be some parts of Osin I have yet to discover. I do not drive, and public transportation can be rather...complex."

Fate chuckled. "Two is always better than one. Mind if I tag along?"

The question surprised August. He wasn't used to anyone wanting to do *anything* with him.

"Of course not. But, I must warn you that I am not a very entertaining person." His mother had made sure to drill that tidbit of information into his head at a very young age.

"Let me be the judge of that." Fate flung his arm over August's shoulder, guiding him down the porch steps. Fate kept it there as they walked to his car. "All right, partner. Show me everything good ole Osin has to offer."

Leaning into Fate's embrace, August replied, "Gladly."

Chapter Seven

I T WAS IMPOSSIBLE to keep track of how many days passed. They refused to give him any writing utensils for a makeshift calendar. Not that it mattered. None of the officers liked him, so he hadn't been able to convince anyone to tell him what day it was. It was just him and his thoughts. No books, no music, no *anything*. There was nothing to do except sleep, and he'd grown bored with that weeks—or what felt like weeks—ago. He hadn't been to sleep in at least a day. Maybe longer.

A few hours ago, or a few minutes—it was all the same in prison—one of the guards had told him he was scheduled to see Dr. Rowburg. He was to be on his best behavior and do everything she said. He didn't give a damn about Dr. Rowburg, but the officer was someone he'd never seen before. She looked at him in the same way the audience once had at the circus whenever he did his solo performances. He knew that look all too well. *Lust.* If he was smart about this new development, he could find a way to use it to his advantage. He couldn't move too quickly. He would have to take his time, charming his way into getting what he wanted from her.

"Rise and shine, dragon. You got a date with the good doctor."

Coy cursed under his breath when he heard Hickman's booming voice echoing from down the hall. He could deal with Hickman with little sleep, but Dr. Rowburg's level of evil was more advanced. He wasn't in the mood for her poking and prodding. He'd found the first piece of the complex puzzle of getting the hell out of there, and he needed to focus on it.

Hickman laughed when he approached the barrier that separated Coy's cell from the hall.

"You look like shit."

"Whose shit?" he asked. "Your mother's?" He'd be punished for saying it, but it'd be worth it.

The amusement died on Hickman's face in an instant.

Definitely worth it.

"Real funny," Hickman said. "You have plenty of time to sit in here and think of jokes all day long, don't you? Unlike you, I've got a family to go home to."

"A bottle of lube, a pair of panties, and ole reliable righty hardly count as family, Hickman."

Hickman didn't reply. At least, not with words. Instead, he snatched a device from the wall next to Coy's cell door.

"You'd think by now you'd get tired of this." He pressed a single button on the device, his thick thumb pushing down on it so hard that his entire hand shook.

Coy screamed, hands clutching at the collar, trying in vain to pull it away from his body. Pain grasped at his nerves, squeezed at them until he fell to the floor, gasping and drooling on himself. He felt like he was suffocating, fingers clawing weakly at the floor as Hickman sent another round of shocks into him. Eventually, the pain blurred into numbness. He felt nothing, only pins and needles, the kind he'd experienced when a hand or foot fell asleep. Except, it was his whole body.

"You never know when to stop talking, do you, dragon? It's almost as if you want me to press this little button. You getting off on it?" He pressed it again.

The pins and needles sensation increased.

Hickman input a series of number into the keypad next to the cell door. It slid wide open a few seconds later, all the way across the cell, taunting Coy. He was too weak to stand up and race to freedom.

"This—" Coy sputtered out, saliva running down his lips and chin. It hurt to talk, hurt to breathe. His words came slowly, whispered, and filled with agony. "—is my favorite type of foreplay."

Hickman grabbed him by the shoulder, fingers digging into his skin, before wrenching him up and off the floor. "Shut up and move."

Coy dragged his feet as he was shoved toward the lab. He glanced into cells, staring at the other shifters who stared back at him. They were all in the same situation. Beaten, bruised, and experimented on. He felt sorry for them. He wondered how much longer some of them could last.

He hated his visits to the lab, but they didn't come without a specific perk. Because the officers assumed that the shifters would be there indefinitely, they never bothered to temporarily blind them while they were transported throughout the prison. This was at least his tenth time visiting Dr. Rowburg, and he'd already memorized the route to and from the lab.

For obvious reasons, he wasn't a fan of the lab, but inside—hanging on the wall next to the door—was a map of the inside of the prison. Removing it probably never crossed the doctor's mind. It was one of those things that most people didn't pay attention to. Coy did. And each and every visit to the lab gave him time to study it. He made mental notes of every twist and turn, every hallway, stairway, and exit sign.

They reached the laboratory. He didn't hear screaming, which either meant that there were no other shifters inside or that she had killed the last one to visit her.

"Get inside," Hickman ordered, pushing the door open with his meaty sausage fingers.

"Thanks for walking me. Gonna kiss me goodnight?"

"Anytime."

Hickman gripped him by the shoulders and slammed a knee into his stomach, sending him falling backward through the laboratory door. Coy hit the ground hard and groaned at the impact. When Hickman yanked him back to his feet, he could see the top of Dr. Rowburg's head through the rectangular glass window to her office.

Hickman strapped him onto one of the metal tables. He couldn't move, but he still took advantage of the situation by peeking at the prison map. He would have loved to snatch it off the wall and take it back to his cell so that he could make out even the smallest details. At least he knew he was on the fourth floor. Too high to jump from a window and live if he had to escape while still wearing that awful collar. If he wasn't able to get it off before escaping, he'd have to take one of the stairwells.

Coy blew a kiss at Hickman. The officer's finger hovered over the collar's controller, and Coy braced himself for the inevitable pain. It never arrived. Dr. Rowburg stepped out of her office, unknowingly saving him.

"He's all ready for you, Doc," Hickman said.

"Thank you, Hickman. You're dismissed."

Hickman took advantage of Coy's immobile state and gripped his chin, digging his nails into Coy's flesh.

"Have fun," he purred, smacking Coy, his hand as hard and coarse as a brick. A few seconds later, he was out the door, leaving him alone with Dr. Rowburg.

She looked tired. The whites of her eyes were pink. The skin beneath them was dark and puffy.

"Miss me, Doc?"

She didn't bother with the banter that he tried to draw her into.

"Are you," she said and then corrected herself, "*were* you sexually active?"

He raised an eyebrow at her. "Sorry, Doc. You're not my type."

"Likewise. However, we are in the middle of developing a program." He didn't like the way she said the word, "program." She whispered it, like it was something secretive, something taboo.

"It is—" She bit gently at her lip, and he was almost certain he could see a slight reddening creeping along her cheeks. "—for breeding."

"Breeding?" He thought back to her first question and put two and two together. "You want me to fuck other shifters?"

"The Registry is interested in monitoring shifters from conception to birth and beyond."

"There are plenty of male shifters here. Why me?" he asked, already knowing the reason.

"The decision was unanimous. We think it is best to use the essence of the most powerful shifter in Asuda."

"The essence."

"Your seed."

They'd murdered his grandmother—the woman who raised him—and he still didn't know what the hell had happened his brother. Then, they threw him in prison, along with a bunch of other shifters that didn't deserve to be there. Now, they wanted him to breed. To mate with women and produce children so that the sick bastards could run all sorts of experiments on them. Oh, no.

Hell no.

There was no way Coy was signing up for that. Ari was as far as his love for children went. He'd never wanted any kids, and the Registry sure as hell wasn't going to convince him to make any just so they could dissect them or whatever the fuck they would do to them.

"Not happening."

"You do not have a choice."

"I always have a choice."

She sighed. "It would be beneficial to you. We have already chosen the females. There are several of them. We maintained diversity and took age and build into account. The plan is to start with the youngest and work our way up. She is seventeen. We think that—"

"I'm not fucking a seventeen-year-old. I'm not fucking *anyone*."

"We are trying to learn more about the science behind shifting, Mr. Conlin. The nature of your abilities could—"

"Fuck science, and fuck you. If you think I'm going to be running around here sticking my dick into women just to please a bunch of scientists, and whoever else thinks they can get away with this shit, then you've got another—"

The rest of his sentence stalled in his throat. She grabbed him through his pants, her manicured fingers squeezing around him. His muscles tensed, and for a moment, he forgot how to breathe. Her hand was a vice, gripping him until he began to feel nauseous and light-headed.

"It is not *your* dick anymore, dragon. I am being generous by allowing you the opportunity to use it. And you will use it as you are instructed to. Do you understand?"

"Y-Yes," he gasped out, fingers clawing at the metal table beneath him.

"The program will start in a few weeks. In the meantime, I suggest that you make sure to get enough sleep. We will need you at your healthiest to maintain optimal seed."

His seed was always *optimal*, he wanted to say, but he knew better. She'd just released her grip on him. He didn't want to risk going through that again.

"Got it."

"I really wish you would not make things so difficult for yourself, Mr. Conlin. Regardless of what you may think about me, I do not enjoy hurting you."

That was bullshit, and he didn't believe a word of it. As far as he was concerned, the world contained three types of people—good, evil, and Dr. Rowburg. At one point, she'd mentioned that she had a son. Whoever the kid was, he felt sorry for him. Then again, whatever kid had grown up with her as a mother was probably just as sadistic. Either that, or he was mentally—and quite possibly physically—screwed up.

Chapter Eight

IT SEEMED RUDE to smile when he worked at a prison, but August couldn't keep the grin off his face. He'd spent most of the past week with Fate. The two of them had gotten to know each other during that time, and he was finally starting to feel like he belonged, like he'd found his place in the world. He had lost his desire to transfer back to the lab. This was where he needed to be. Working alongside with Fate. He'd been confused at first, but Fate had guided him. He'd shown August his true path.

It'd taken him so long to find a friend. Now, not only did he have one, but he also had a partner. Someone who would always have his back no matter what. He felt guilty for being upset with Fate after the disaster at the dragons' house. He understood now why it had been necessary. After spending time with Fate, everything came together. Everything made sense.

He rode the elevator to the tenth-floor meeting room. Today, he and many of his fellow officers would receive their new duties as Registry prison guards. They would all maintain their officer titles, naturally, but now each of them would receive a five percent pay raise to compensate for the change.

Stepping into the meeting room, August took the first vacant seat he saw. He watched as the other officers filed in, knowing some by name, and at least recognizing most. Once they were all settled in, the meeting was called to order. The debriefing was longer than he expected, but necessary. He was disappointed to learn that he would no longer be partnered with Fate. The prison needed Fate's expertise in various areas, and he couldn't dedicate himself to patrolling the cells exclusively.

He listened carefully when the prison director, Jonah Richards—a red-haired man with an equally red goatee—began calling out names and floor assignments. He hoped he wasn't assigned to the fourth floor. He may have been irritated by Conlin's weakness for not reacting when he saw him, but that didn't mean he wanted to give Conlin another chance. Dinina was dead, and he had no information on the boy's whereabouts. Even if he did, there wasn't anything he could do to change things. He had no desire to see Conlin's face every day as a constant reminder of what had happened.

August looked around the room, watching the expressions of the other officers as their names were called. Some of them looked pleased—others disappointed—most of them looked indifferent. As long as they received a paycheck, they didn't care what floors they were assigned to or what shifters they had to monitor.

"Monroe, levels nine through eleven," Director Richards called, his gruff voice booming throughout the room.

August hadn't been officially introduced to Monroe, but he'd held the door open for him when they began filing into the room. Monroe was a quiet, mysterious man who hadn't stopped taking notes since the moment he'd sat down.

"Page, levels one through three."

Page was one of the few women in the room—an intimidating officer with brown eyes and spiky, blonde hair. She looked disappointed with her floor levels, muttering something about "weak shifters" and folding her arms across her chest.

As he continued to listen, August began to realize that their method of assigning shifters to floors was flawed. The logical layout should have been to keep the most powerful shifters at the higher levels, with the weaker ones on the lower levels. The prison had followed some of this reasoning, but it wasn't consistent. Conlin was on the fourth floor, and he was a dragon. He should have been on the highest level the prison had to offer. The lab must have wanted immediate access to their most powerful shifter. Still, it felt like asking for trouble. August thought about voicing his concern with the room but decided to speak to Richards in private, if he ever worked up the nerve. He didn't want to overstep his boundaries.

"Seaton," Richards said. August held his breath. "Levels one through three."

He resisted the urge to let out a sigh of relief. He'd walked along the first and second levels when he arrived earlier that morning. It seemed like most of the shifters on the lower floors wouldn't be much trouble. If the Registry had assigned him to these floors because they didn't trust his ability to handle more powerful shifters, he didn't care. As long as he didn't have to work on Conlin's floor, he was happy. Then again, he supposed even if he had been assigned to his floor, it wouldn't have mattered. With the way he'd designed the collars, none of the prisoners posed a threat.

AFTER THE DEBRIEFING, the time came for his first official day as a prison guard. Knowing that he would be doing it all without Fate was disheartening, but Fate had assured him that if a job entailed the efforts of two men, he would call on him before anyone else.

August walked down one of the third-floor halls, glancing into various cells. He wondered what it would have been like if the shifters had still been allowed to use their powers. The prison would have looked more like a zoo. That would have at least been better than looking at these downtrodden creatures stuck in their human forms.

He continued down the hall, listening to his own footsteps. Coming upon another hallway, he found two guards harassing a female shifter. She looked terrified, her wide blue gaze pleading for help. The whites of her eyes were red from crying, and her hands were balled into fists—not that she could actually hit anyone. One of the guards had her wrists pinned against the wall, while the other one slid his hands beneath her uniform top. Oh, no. That was *not* happening. Not if he had anything to say about it. He moved to intervene, but someone else beat him to it.

"Hey!" a voice shouted from the other end of the hall. "Knock it off. You two assholes have work to do."

The two ceased their abuse of the shifter immediately, offering their apologies to the man who'd spoken. They grabbed the woman by the wrist, revealing Fate as they moved aside, and dragged her down the hallway toward an open cell.

"It looks like you showed up just in time," August said.

Fate shook his head, staring back at him with an exasperated expression.

"I don't understand it, August." He put his hand on August's shoulder. "There are thousands of gorgeous women in Weren looking for suitors, and those two idiots decide to molest a disgusting shifter."

"Suitors?" August snickered awkwardly. "You are showing your age." He rolled his shoulders where Fate pressed into his muscles, releasing some of the tension that always seemed to linger there. "Some people have questionable taste, I suppose." He couldn't bring himself to look at Fate as he spoke. Just speaking those words made him feel ill. Were the guards making a habit of harassing the shifters? It wasn't even a question of taste. This was...wrong. Still, he imagined it was what Fate would want him to say.

"Oh? And what about you? How's your taste?"

August smirked. "My taste is...*refined*."

Fate winked at him, giving his shoulder another squeeze. "Lunch today? My treat."

"If you insist."

"I do."

He winked again before heading down the hall in the same direction the other two officers had gone.

THERE WAS A certain amount of a confidence that came along with telling shifters what to do. Confidence wasn't something August had much of, but he did a good job at pretending around the right people. For so many years, he'd been insecure. The seclusion his mother forced on him had taken its toll, but thanks to Fate, he was finally working on breaking free of his insecurity. He had a friend and a role model. Now, the real Augustus Seaton was shining through, the one that others would learn to respect, to admire.

Working at the prison was less exciting than traveling across Asuda to monitor shifters in their natural habitats, but the pay was incredible. If he stayed at this job for at least ten years, he could retire in his thirties. Maybe he'd move to Askia. He'd be able to afford it by then. He bet Fate could afford it too. Still, his former partner chose to live in Weren, as close to the Registry's headquarters as possible. *Weren is home*, Fate had told him. August didn't have anything, or anyone, keeping him in Osin. Maybe he'd forgo moving to Askia altogether and move to Weren.

Each level of the prison was like a never-ending hallway that branched off into other endless hallways. He could just about remember the cubicles that used to occupy this space. As they no doubt had been when the building was still an office, levels one through three of the prison were uneventful. The shifters here were harmless, and not just because of the collars. The most dangerous of the shifters on his floors had the ability to shift into a wolverine—somewhat dangerous in the right situation—but even if he could transform, a swift kick to the snout would take care of him.

August sighed to himself as he patrolled. The shifters were like creatures in an animal shelter, sad and unfulfilled. Scared of what would happen to them, or simply resolved to their fate and waiting for death. At least at the shelter, there were a few animals that still had some fight left in them, even at the expense of being euthanized. He didn't know what was in store for the shifters. Most of them were already dead inside. Putting them out of their misery seemed humane at this point.

He turned down a hall and almost gagged at the smell. He was on the first floor, where the weakest of all the shifters were located—the elderly, in other words. From the smell of things, one of them, a male with white hair and large eyebrows, had soiled himself. He lay there as if he were on his deathbed, which may as well have been the case. He looked too weak and frail to move, let alone shift.

August sped up his footsteps, hurrying past the elderly shifter. As he moved farther down the hall, he caught an officer standing in front of a female shifter's cell. The guard was exposing himself. The woman huddled in a corner, her wrinkled hands shielding her face. The guard laughed. He hadn't noticed August.

August thought back to Fate's interactions with the other two guards from before.

"Do you not have work to do?" He tried to say it with confidence, in a way that Fate would have. "Or perhaps you have completed all of your duties for today and need more?"

The other officer looked at him for a few seconds, as if sizing him up. His penis still hung out of his pants. It was unnerving, to say the least. August held his ground, maintaining their staring match. A few seconds later, Calder cursed and stuffed himself back into his pants.

"Whatever." He walked away, only stopping once to glance back at August before stepping through the exit door.

August patrolled the rest of the hall without incident, head held so high that his shoulders ached.

AUGUST HAD TO bring a female shifter to the lab after lunch. It was his first time, and he had to do it alone. He didn't know what to expect, but he was promised that he wouldn't have any problems. Besides, if a shifter tried to escape, all he had to do was shock them with the controller that hung next to their cell door.

He did as he'd been instructed to do during one of the many demonstrations carried out by Director Richards. He pulled the device from the wall and input his personal code to open her cell door. The moment it opened, she rushed out, crying and dropping to her knees in front of him.

"Please," she begged. Her hair, almost as long and dark as his own, looked like it hadn't been washed in weeks. "You have to help me."

"Help you?" He wanted to ask how. He *almost* asked how. Just before he opened his mouth, he thought about Fate. What would he have done in this situation? "That is not in my job description."

"But, my children," she sobbed, tears clinging to her long eyelashes. "They have no one else. They're so young. They need me."

"Are they shifters?" he asked.

The woman shook her head, wiping her tears away on the back of her hand. "It is too soon to tell. Only five and seven."

"Well, if they are, I can assure you that you will be seeing them soon enough. Now, get up."

He pulled her to her feet and felt a spike of power when she cried out and scrambled to stand upright.

"Start walking."

He wished Fate had been around to see him in action. He would have been proud.

The lab was on the fourth floor. He could get to it without having to pass Conlin's cell, but the trip would take longer. Also, he was becoming distressed from hearing the woman cry. If it kept up, he might even begin to take pity on her. At this point, the longer route wasn't logical. He'd have to walk past the dragon's cell.

He stared at the back of the woman's head as he guided her down the hall past the cell. He didn't look to see if Conlin was in there. He knew he was. He felt his presence, like a shadow looming over him in the dead of night. He felt Conlin's eyes on him, watching him, and was tempted to do the same. He knew better than to cave into his curiosity. Conlin would try to make him feel guilty. He wouldn't even speak. He wouldn't need to. All he would have to do was stare at him with those mismatched eyes filled with rage and churning sadness.

August had nothing to feel guilty about. Conlin's grandmother was dead because of her actions. Dinina had attempted to shift within the vicinity of Registry officers without express written consent. She'd broken Registry law. The boy had assaulted Fate, had stabbed him. A crime according to Asudian law. They'd both broken the rules set forth before them. They were criminals, and the resulting actions were a consequence of that.

Against his better judgment, he chanced a glance inside Conlin's cell just before they passed it. Conlin was there, just as August knew he would be. Staring straight ahead, he sat on the bottom bunk, back against the wall, unmoving and unblinking like a statue. As August predicted, he didn't speak.

"Keep moving," August ordered. The woman had slowed down to look at Conlin, and he didn't have to guess why. Even with a busted, swollen lip, he was still breathtakingly handsome.

THEY REACHED THE lab. August was ordered to strap the woman into an upright table. Dr. Rowburg stood next to her office door, waiting for him to finish securing the woman's restraints. He straightened, expecting further orders.

"Dismissed," Dr. Rowburg said.

He left the lab in a worse mood than he'd been in when he'd arrived. Dr. Rowburg had that type of effect on people.

Now that he'd transported the shifter, he needed to focus on doing his second-floor rounds, but another officer stopped him before he reached the stairwell.

"Seaton, a favor."

Keona—a short, stubby man whose puffy cheeks turned red whenever he exerted himself—jogged up to him. There was a large envelope in his hands. A giant letter *A* was printed on the outside of the envelope in gold, glittery lettering. Whatever it was, it was something official from Askia.

"Keona, is there something wrong?"

"Could you deliver this to Fate? I think he's on this floor somewhere. I'd do it myself, but I'm kind of in a rush. I have to bring one of the shifters to Dr. Rowburg, and she doesn't like when people are—"

"Late," August finished for him. "I know. I will take it to him."

"Thanks, Seaton," Keona said, placing the envelope in August's hand. "You're a life saver."

"Do not mention it." He wondered what business Fate had with Askia.

Keona rushed off, his rounded shoulders slumped forward in what must have been caused by years of bad posture. Once he was sure Keona was gone, August read the name of the sender: *Callas Fate*. Callas Fate was the Ambassador of Asuda, and the sovereign's right-hand man. The envelope was addressed to Daniel Fate. August had always prided himself on noticing slight details that went unnoticed by most, and yet somehow, he'd never realized that the Ambassador of Asuda and Fate shared the same last name.

August wandered along the fourth floor looking for Fate. It was a decision he regretted the moment he caught sight of a familiar little girl huddled in a corner and softly weeping. It couldn't have been...

"N-Niami?"

She looked up at him.

Seeing her without flowers decorating her fluffy hair or the pastel-blue dress covering her tiny body was a shock. When he'd met her, the dress had made her look like a flower, its subtle blue fabric bringing out the warmth of her brown skin. Now, she looked like a lost child wearing clothing that was too big for her.

Her cheeks were wet from crying, and her eyes were so sad, so empty, that it made his heart ache. She was already so small. Now, she looked even smaller. Her collar didn't even fit well around her neck, August realized with a wince. Of course—he hadn't designed them for children. This wasn't right. She didn't belong here. This was *wrong*.

"Where's my mommy?" she asked.

"I do not know."

He tried to keep walking, wanted nothing more than to rush off without having to hear the sadness in her voice, but he couldn't. His feet were lead, forcing him to stay there, to witness the fear in her eyes.

"I'm scared. I want to go home."

He stopped at the edge of her cell and sighed. She was a shifter. However, she was also a child. He knew far too well what it felt like to be a sad, scared, and lonely kid.

"They will not hurt you." He wanted to assure her, wanted to reassure himself.

"They won't let me color."

August bit nervously at his lip, glancing around before leaning down closer to her cell door. He was out of his mind. He needed to end their conversation right then and there. Still, he couldn't just walk away from a child in need. Niami had never done anything worthy of imprisonment. She was smart and special. The Registry had to recognize that, didn't they? She wasn't like all the other shifters. She was different.

"If I find a way to let you color, will that make you happy?"

She nodded, her tiny hands wiping slowly at her eyes.

"Then, that is what I will do. Until then, try to stop crying. You do not want to upset the officers. You must do everything they say. Can you do that for me?"

She nodded again.

"And the scientist in the lab. Have you met her yet?"

She shook her head, her fluffy coils bouncing around like metal springs.

Good. If she had, there was no amount of coloring that would make her feel better.

"I will see what I can do."

"You promise?"

It was his turn to nod now.

"I promise," he whispered.

IT DID NOT take him long to find Fate after his exchange with Niami. He nearly crashed into him after turning the corner.

"Just the man I wanted to see," August said.

"Am I?"

Fate looked annoyed and not exactly happy to see him. He wondered if it had anything to do with the envelope in his hand.

"I have something for you." He held out the envelope. Fate stared down at it for a few seconds before taking it out of his hands.

"Thanks."

He turned and left before August could ask if they were still on for lunch. August had the sinking suspicion that he already knew the answer.

FATE WAS NOWHERE to be found around lunchtime. August ate alone, poking at his food with his fork and wondering what happened to Fate. He'd been looking forward to telling him all about his day. Whatever was inside that envelope must have been serious for Fate to skip out on him. He hoped nothing bad had happened.

After lunch, August asked permission from Director Richards to provide Niami with a coloring book and crayons. Richards wasn't sold on the idea. He did not say yes, but he also did not say no. Whatever August decided to do was on him, as were any ramifications. August accepted this without a second thought. He'd made a promise to Niami, and he intended to keep it. It was the least he could do. Besides, what harm could come from coloring?

THE NEXT DAY, August woke up earlier than normal. There was a shop a block away from his house where he typically made most of his purchases. Living in Osin meant that he could afford either a house or a car. This was the main reason he never bothered to learn how to drive. Why learn to drive when he couldn't afford a car and a shop was within walking distance from his home? Granted, he could have moved to another town, one where he could afford both the luxury of a home and car, but he wouldn't give up the beauty of Osin, not even for convenience.

The walk to the shop didn't take long. He didn't know his neighbors, so no one stopped him on his journey. He knew the owner of the shop by face, but not by name. She was a middle-aged woman, fair-skinned and freckled, who wore thick glasses that magnified her eyes. Sometimes, she gave him recipes that she promised were easy to make, even for "handsome bachelors." Unfortunately, these recipes usually included lots of vegetables.

He ate a lot of red meat.

She was there when he arrived at the shop. She stood behind the counter, busying herself with getting a line of customers checked out and on their way. He was thankful for that. He wasn't in the mood for small talk. The news of the Registry imprisoning shifters was still making headlines. Her eldest son was a shifter—a gorilla. He had made a decent amount of money shifting for local crowds in the back of their shop. Him being snatched up by the Registry had probably caused a significant loss of income to her family.

August hadn't worn his uniform for that very reason.

He walked up and down the aisles, searching for what he was looking for and finding it a few minutes later. The stationery aisle contained a few shelves full of coloring books and crayons. He didn't know which to get. His mother had never let him color as a child, and he'd never had a reason to buy these things as an adult. He grabbed a coloring book with a princess holding a bouquet of flowers on the cover and then grabbed another with a little pirate boy holding a sword. He'd get them both. Niami may have been a child in prison, but that didn't mean she had to follow outdated gender norms. He got crayons, too. A twenty-four pack. He didn't know if this was what she wanted, but it would have to do.

The woman smiled when he stepped up to the counter. However, the smile didn't reach her eyes. It didn't even come close. She looked like she'd aged ten years in the past few weeks.

"This is new," she remarked, scanning the items. "Trying out a new hobby?"

"They are for a friend."

"You know, I have heard coloring can be therapeutic when someone is under a lot of stress." She gave him another tired smile. "I should probably give it a try."

August paid for the items, thanked her, and left. He felt bad. She'd always been kind to him. Even so, it wasn't like *he* had arrested her son. Still, realizing how many lives had been destroyed by the Registry in such a short amount of time was staggering.

THE EMPLOYEE BUS arrived in front of his house on time. August had stashed away the coloring books and crayons inside his lunch bag. He couldn't wait to see the look on Niami's face when he gave them to her.

It was business as usual when he stepped inside of the prison. He did his rounds for four hours, watching each shifter lie on their bed, listless and defeated. When he was allowed to take his lunch break, he rushed up to the fourth floor to deliver Niami her gifts. Her eyes lit up like lanterns when he slid them through the food slot in her door. He was pleased that she was happy, but he didn't stick around to watch her enjoy them. His plan was to find Fate and to see whether or not he was in a better mood today than he'd been in yesterday.

He searched for Fate for at least twenty minutes before giving up. After lunch, he went back to his rounds. As usual, the shifters had no life in them. They lazed around, staring at the ceiling or crying. Some of them begged to be released. Others prayed for death.

He thought about Conlin.

He still remembered the look in Conlin's eyes when he'd lunged at August. Fate had told him not to fight back. They'd rehearsed what he would do and say to make Conlin think that August had murdered his grandmother. Fate said it wouldn't have worked the other way around. To take the shot, they needed someone with perfect aim. August's aim wasn't terrible, but it wasn't perfect.

August hadn't doubted for a moment that Conlin would have killed him if Fate had missed his shot. For a few short seconds, he'd stared death in the face. And, the most frightening thing about it was that Conlin had been in his human form the entire time. He could have easily shifted. In a morbid sense, August had *wanted* him to shift. He'd never seen a dragon before. He'd seen Conlin's grandmother in the midst of shifting, but Fate had killed her before she could finish the transformation.

He felt cheated...in more ways than one. On one hand, he'd gotten exactly what he'd wanted. Excitement and adventure. Yet, it had only lasted a few weeks. Now, he was back at the Registry. Back in the very building he'd wanted to escape. The excitement of being a Registry officer had been stripped away from him. Fate had told him to stick it out for a few months, to give these new duties a chance.

August wanted more. He wanted to be thrust into the world of the unknown. He wanted the thrill of an adventure. He wanted to be excited and maybe, just a little bit, *scared*.

He wanted to feel the same way he'd felt when Conlin had tried to kill him.

"August!"

August jumped, startled at Fate shouting his name from across the hall. Fate stormed over to him, his boots smashing against the floor like he was stomping bugs along the way.

"Do you want to explain this?" He shoved the coloring books and a few broken crayons into August's hands.

"I..." August stared back at him with wide eyes. "Richards gave me permission. I did not think—"

"That's right," Fate cut him off. "You didn't think, did you? Did you forget all the things I've told you about shifters? How they're manipulative. How you can't trust them. How you can't just...*give* them things because you feel sorry for them. You shouldn't feel sorry for them. You shouldn't feel *anything* for them but disgust."

August shook his head, trying and failing to come up with the right words. "She is just a child," he spoke softly. "I couldn't just let her—"

Fate grabbed him by the front of his shirt and jerked him forward. The tips of August's boots skidded against the hard floor.

"You listen to me, *Augustus*. If I ever find out you've pulled another stunt like this, you'll be back in the lab working as Dr. Rowburg's slave for the rest of your life. Do you understand me?"

"Daniel..." He'd never called Fate by his first name before. Fate had given him permission to, but it had seemed too intimate, too familiar.

Fate growled, switched his grip to August's collar, and shoved him against a shifter's cell door. August's head smacked against the plastic, causing spots to flicker in his vision.

"I said, do you fucking understand?"

"Y-Yes," he answered. "It will not happen again. I swear." He was terrified of what Fate would do to him if he said anything else.

"Good." Fate released his hold on August's collar and pushed him backward. "Now, get rid of those things. I never want to see them in here again."

August rushed off, legs racing just as quickly as his heart. He felt embarrassed, humiliated. Having Fate scold him like that in front of the shifters was heartrending. He thought they were friends. He may not have had any to compare Fate to, but he was sure good ones weren't supposed to behave like that.

Fate had told him that he would always have his back, told him that he wanted August to trust him. What had just happened didn't make him feel that way. August didn't see anything wrong with letting a kid in a bad situation enjoy herself. How else was she supposed to cope?

Maybe he should have run things by Fate first. Maybe he should have gotten his opinion. Did he feel like August had gone behind his back? Is that why he was so angry? Maybe if he just apologized... Yes, that was exactly what he'd do. He'd apologize to Fate for not asking him first. He couldn't afford to burn bridges, not with someone as respected as Fate. Still, he'd have to give him a day or so to cool down first. After that, he'd keep things short and simple. He'd apologize and then he would get away from Fate as quickly as he could. He knew what hatred was. He'd witnessed unadulterated rage. He saw it in Fate's eyes, just like he'd seen it in Conlin's, and even in his own mother's. His former partner had wanted to do more than just yell at him or rough him up a bit. He had wanted to hit August, to *hurt* him.

Disappointment overcame him all at once. It hung heavy on his shoulders, weighed him down so that even walking took effort. Fate had once told him that he had potential, but August was starting to realize that the only real potential he had was for messing everything up.

He should have just stayed at the lab.

Chapter Nine

THE DAYS BLED into one another. Had he been there for a month? Three months? A year? Every second felt like a minute. Every minute felt like an hour. Every hour felt like a day.

And every day felt like an eternity.

Coy had learned that the shifter across the hall from him was named Samuel. He was forty-three and spoke with a lisp. He wanted to go home to his wife and son. His plan was to do everything the officers said. When they saw how obedient he was, they would realize their mistake and let him go.

Samuel was delusional and unhelpful. He couldn't be a part of Coy's plan. He'd be a liability.

So far, his interactions with the female guard had been unsuccessful. He was starting to get impatient. If this remained the case, he'd have to try to sweet-talk one of the men, and all of them despised him. Not that the feeling wasn't mutual, but an easily manipulated guard was his only access point to vital information. If he didn't have that, he didn't have anything.

"Lab time, dragon. You know the drill."

Coy sighed. His visits to the lab were becoming exhaustingly frequent. He was certain that he took more trips to the lab than anyone else. Maybe that was for the best.

He behaved himself when he was released from his cell. He wasn't in the mood to be beaten or shocked. Knowing Hickman, he'd do it anyway.

"You're a lucky fuck. You know that?" Hickman said.

"Must have a screwed-up life to consider having your family murdered and being thrown in prison as lucky."

Hickman shrugged. "Heh. Guess you haven't seen the piece of ass waiting for you yet, huh?"

"What?"

"Nothing. Shut up and walk." He hit Coy in the back of his head with his elbow.

When they reached the lab, Hickman shoved him inside. Coy assumed the position against the upright table, waiting for Hickman to strap him down. Hickman just snorted at him. A moment later, the door burst open and a woman was flung inside, kicking and screaming. Three guards quickly followed, reaching for her.

Blood dripped from a cut on one of her legs. Her hair hung around her shoulders like silk. Her eyes were large and wide, and Coy saw the fire behind them. Her lips were small, pink, and somehow still managed to curve subtly into a heart shape even though she was snarling. She elbowed one of the guards in the crotch. It must have been the last straw, as one of them pressed the button for her collar, forcing a scream from her lips. She fell to the ground as if she'd been shot. There were tears in her eyes when she looked up. Tears and defiance.

She was beautiful.

"Strap her in," Dr. Rowburg said.

"I hope you like them feisty." Hickman snickered, handing Dr. Rowburg the controller to Coy's collar. He waited while the other guards strapped the woman to the horizontal table. When they were done, the officers left the lab, two of them chatting while the other one rubbed at his groin.

Coy looked at Dr. Rowburg, the girl, and then at the door.

"Do not try anything funny, Mr. Conlin. I have your controller right here." She raised the device in her hand. "I believe it is best to start our mating program a bit early. Don't you?"

He looked at the shifter. She was the type of woman he'd treat as a conquest. Wild and untamed, just like him. He could have agreed to it. It would have at least put him on Dr. Rowburg's good side for a little while. Under different circumstances, he wouldn't have had a problem fucking her, but he couldn't. Not now. Not in this situation.

He was many things, but a rapist wasn't one of them.

"I'll pass. Thanks, though."

"She is not the seventeen-year-old, if that is your worry."

"Good to know. But I'm still not doing it."

"Do you remember our talk during your last visit?" Dr. Rowburg asked.

"How could I forget it?"

"Then you will do as I say."

"I'm not doing shit."

Dr. Rowburg narrowed her eyes at him. "Is this truly the route you wish to take, Mr. Conlin?"

"Sure is. Guess you better call those guards back in here, Doc."

"As you wish."

He leaned back against the wall, glancing over at the woman. She stared at him with an expression he couldn't figure out. Was she relieved? Did she think he was an idiot? If it were the latter, she wasn't the only one. He didn't have a lot of morals, but the ones he did have, he stuck to them faithfully.

Oh, well.

Sighing, he closed his eyes and mentally prepared himself for the beating of a lifetime.

AUGUST ARRIVED AT work the next morning with two goals: first, he'd apologize to Fate; second, he'd keep his distance from him. He'd spent the majority of the night researching social behaviors and had come to the conclusion that he should keep his interactions with Fate to a minimum. Admittedly, he wasn't looking forward to becoming friendless once more. Then again, Fate hadn't really been a friend in the first place, had he? Someone who would attack you over something so trivial couldn't be a friend. August imagined that the only thing worse than having no friends was having bad ones.

He found Fate in the cafeteria chatting with a bunch of their fellow officers. He waited, watching as the other officers hung on to each and every word that dripped from Fate's mouth. They threw themselves at him. It was a competition to see who could gain his attention the fastest, who could laugh the loudest at his jokes. August pitied them. They hadn't seen the real Fate, the one who'd gripped August by the collar, the one who'd threatened and humiliated him. Just a day ago, he would have been just like them, admiring everything Fate did, believing everything he said.

Fate noticed him—his gaze sought out August just on the tail end of his anecdote. He stared at August, and August stared back, uncomfortable with the attention. Fate was an intimidating man with a temper as unstable as quicksand, but August wouldn't back down. He couldn't. Not when he'd spent the past hour convincing himself to seek him out just so that he could get this over with.

It was now or never.

Fate offered him a small smile, and it took everything for August not to roll his eyes at the false gesture. He knew better. His mother always smiled at him after she wronged him, too. He may have fallen for it as a child, but he wasn't a little boy anymore.

Once the crowd around Fate dispersed, August took a deep breath, relaxed his shoulders, and began the short journey across the lounge toward him. Even though his confidence wasn't present, he'd fake it. He was great at faking things.

Fate opened his mouth to speak. August cut him off—hand raised, palm facing forward—silently asking him to hold whatever it was he was about to say.

"I wanted to apologize for yesterday," he said. "The crayons... I should have run it by you first."

Fate sighed and shook his head. "That should be my line. I didn't mean to react that way yesterday. I'm sorry. You're a good officer, August. I just don't want those dirty shifters to manipulate you. You're special."

So, now he was August again. Yesterday, Fate had called him *Augustus*.

"It is fine." It wasn't fine, not in the least bit, but there wasn't anything else he wanted to say. Their partnership ended weeks ago, and their friendship ended yesterday. There was nothing left to do but part ways. "I need to start my rounds." He'd just begun to turn away when Fate grabbed him by the wrist.

"Hey, August. Wait."

He looked at Fate and then down at where Fate's hand held him. When he lifted his head, he could see the challenge in Fate's eyes, as though daring August to pull away or ask him to let go. Fate slid his thumb back and forth against the skin on the inside of August's wrist, caressing it.

"Do you want to see something?"

"I really need to start my rounds, *sir*." The only time he'd ever called Fate "sir" was upon first meeting him. By the look of his face, Fate was definitely surprised to hear him say it now. August didn't want to be on a name basis with him. No first name—no last name. No name at all. He didn't even want to talk to him. He just wanted to leave. After he was finished with this pointless conversation, his plan was to submit his transfer papers, and Fate was holding him up.

"Then, what about lunch today? My treat."

He almost snorted. He'd heard those lines before, word for word. Fate hadn't even bothered showing up the last time he had offered to buy August lunch.

"I brought my lunch today. Sorry."

"Then, I'll sit with you," Fate insisted.

"Unfortunately," August said, "I will be using my lunch period to study. I would like to brush up on my training."

"Oh, is that what you'll be doing?"

"Yes."

"Because it sounds like you're trying to avoid me."

The playful way Fate said it made it seem like it was meant to be a tease. August knew better now. He didn't reply.

Fate still hadn't let go of his wrist.

"Just let me show you one thing. It'll be quick. You'll like it."

"My rounds."

"Screw your rounds. Come with me."

Fate pulled him out of the cafeteria and down the hall. August expected him to release his wrist once they began walking down the prison halls, but he didn't. Even when they passed other officers, Fate kept his grip tight. August felt yesterday's humiliation all over again. He wanted to hold his head down, to avoid eye contact with anyone they passed, but he stayed upright. He wouldn't give Fate the satisfaction.

"Hey," Fate said, glancing down at him. He pulled August toward an elevator, rough fingers digging into his skin. "You've got pretty eyes. Anyone ever told you that?"

"No," August said.

It was true. Never in his life had anyone ever told him that, and as far as he was concerned, he still hadn't heard it. It didn't count coming from Fate. Compliments given by people who wanted to hurt him held no weight.

"Well, you do." Fate pressed the elevator call button. Already on their floor, it slid open almost instantly. Fate stood back, offering August the opportunity to enter first.

August hesitated.

Seeing that August was reluctant to go inside, Fate stepped in, pulling him along. August prepared himself. He couldn't win in a fight against Fate, and all he had was pepper spray and a stun gun. Neither of which he wanted to use in the confined space.

"I know you're still upset with me," Fate conceded, "but I'm going to make it up to you. You'll see. What I'm about to show you will change everything."

"You can let go of my wrist now."

Fate grinned. "How do I know you won't run away if I do?"

Was he...*flirting*? August held back a disgusted groan. "We are in an elevator."

"We won't be forever."

Yes, and August was quite thankful for that. "I am not going to run away."

"Well..." Fate took a step closer, and August braced himself, back pressed firmly against the wall. "Maybe I just like holding you like this."

He leaned forward, lips just a few inches away from August's own. The elevator doors slid open, and August pushed past him and wrenched away from his grip, escaping as his heart raced from what had *almost* happened.

They were on the fourth floor.

Fate was no longer holding on to his wrist, but he might as well have been. He kept close to August, as if the two of them were glued at the hip. He told him how amazed he'd be. How what he was going to show him would make everything worth it. August didn't believe that for a second.

Still, he was curious.

For both their sakes, he didn't bring up what Fate had tried to do to him back in the elevator.

August half listened to Fate ramble on as they walked. He gazed out of the corner of his eye, knowing they were approaching Conlin's cell. When they reached it, he spotted Conlin lying on the floor and staring up at the ceiling. His lip was still busted. It should have healed by now, which meant that it was a new wound. The top of his head was covered with a blood-soaked bandage. A purplish bruise decorated his right cheek.

"What are those? Love taps, dragon?" Fate called to him as they passed. "I see you're getting along with everyone."

"Where are we going?" August asked.

Fate grinned at him.

"To the lab."

AUGUST HEARD THE screams before he saw who was making them. It was the sound of agony in its truest form. Someone was being tortured.

Fate opened the door with a smile.

When they stepped inside, August saw a man on the table being electrocuted. From the looks of things, it wasn't enough to kill him—just enough to make him wish he were dead. He was bleeding from the corner of his mouth and just below his hairline. One of his eyes was swollen shut. His lips no longer looked like lips, but like bloated pieces of bruised flesh slapped haphazardly onto his face.

He was naked and unable to protect his modesty. His thighs reminded August of flowers, colors of blues and purples—like violets and tulips—decorating his pale skin.

"Why did you bring me here?" August asked. He wanted to leave.

"Do you have any clue of who this man is?"

August shook his head. Whoever he was, he felt sorry for him.

Fate walked over to file holder on a nearby wall and snatched a folder out of it. The smile remained on his face even after he tapped the folder with his hand and handed it over to him.

August opened it and read the name printed at the top of the first document: *Stanley Patton.* Useless information. It didn't explain why August was here. He didn't have any connection to this man. More importantly, he had no interest in watching him be tortured.

"Stanley Patton. Should I know this person?"

"Take a look at where he's from."

August scanned the file until he found the former address of the shifter. Askia. He still didn't get it. Why was any of this relevant to him? He didn't want to be here watching Dr. Rowburg and her sadistic assistants abuse this man. Moreover, she didn't seem to care that he was there. She hadn't even acknowledged him.

"I do not understand."

"There are only three shifters that had been rich enough to live in Askia," Fate said. "Two of them are on levels assigned to you."

"Yes. And?"

"This is the third one."

"I know how to count," August replied, raising his voice so that he could be heard over Stanley's screaming. He needed to get out of there. He was starting to feel sick.

"This is the shifter responsible for attacking the sovereign's daughter."

August's eyes widened. Was this shifter really the one responsible for hurting such a sweet and gentle girl? Stanley looked barely capable of moving, let alone maiming a child.

"How can you be certain?"

"He admitted to it. Got his confession a couple of hours ago. We've been questioning all three Askian shifters since we hauled their sorry asses in here. But ole Stanley finally broke today. We're making him nice and pretty for the sovereign."

August remembered the news. He remembered the photographs. Noralani's once flawless skin torn apart, like something had tried to rip her in two. It had left her in a coma. No one knew whether she was going to recover, and the sovereign—the great ruler of Asuda—didn't know if he was going to have to bury his daughter just a year after burying his wife. What kind of monster could do something like that? How depraved did Stanley have to be to harm a little girl? What kind of sick animal was he?

"What is his animal?" August asked.

He was holding the file and could have looked himself, but the knowledge that the creature responsible for injuring Noralani was just a few feet away from him disrupted his thinking process. He couldn't believe it. The sovereign and his daughters, especially Noralani—with her sweet smile and cheerful laugh—were loved by all.

"Bottom of the page," Fate said without looking at him. He was too busy watching Dr. Rowburg and the others unleash a series of shocks to Stanley's testicles.

August was starting to feel a lot less pity for Stanley. He scanned the file, his eyes reading over trivial information until he found what he was looking for. Next to a line marked *Type* was a word printed in bold, capital letters.

TIGER.

Chapter Ten

AFTER TWO HOURS of alternating between the guards beating him up and Dr. Rowburg trying—and failing—to get him aroused, they finally gave up and threw Coy back into his cell.

Controlling himself hadn't been an easy feat. She was evil, but she had certain... talents. The only thing that kept him from getting erect was the fact that she was a sadistic bitch and had tried to force him against his will. Well, that and also the guards had beaten him to the point where even thinking about sex made every muscle in his body ache. He wasn't looking forward to any of that happening again, but he knew it was just a matter of time. He just worried that, in the next round, she might figure out a way to make things work in her favor. His plan was taking too long to come together.

Coy needed to move quicker.

His back ached. Lying on the floor was not helping, but he didn't have the energy to crawl onto his bed. Besides, he needed the guard he was trying to seduce to notice him. More importantly, he needed her to take pity on him. He was wearing her down. Or at least, he hoped he was. She had started to linger whenever she came by to deliver his food. He didn't know how much longer it would take for her to break. Maybe a few weeks—time he did not have. He needed something to actually go the way he'd planned, at least just this once.

He used to believe in gods and goddesses. Now, he wasn't so sure. If there were any supreme beings watching him, whoever or whatever they were owed at least one thing going right for him. His grandmother was dead, and his brother was missing. And, he was locked in a cell for something he couldn't control. Where was the fairness in that? What gods would let something like that happen?

"Time to eat, Conlin." Ah. He knew that voice. That was the voice that would lead him to freedom. "You look like you could use a decent meal." There was an awkward pause before the voice added, "And a shower."

He shifted his gaze from the ceiling to the cell door. There she was. Officer K. Fair. She wouldn't tell him what the K stood for. She wouldn't tell him *anything* useful. They'd trained her well. One way or another, he'd get it out of her.

"Aren't you a sight for sore eyes," he remarked. "You're already taking care of the meal. Don't suppose I could have you help me when it's time to shower?"

"Just take your food."

She slid his meal tray through the slot in the door. He crawled over to her, slower than necessary, wincing and cringing, gripping at parts of his body that didn't actually ache. It was all a show, and before anything else, he was a performer. He needed her sympathy, and she was close to giving it to him. The look on her face—eyes lowered, teeth worrying her bottom lip—gave him hope.

"If you didn't give them such a hard time, none of this would happen to you. You do know that, right?"

Maybe there was a god or goddess up there listening to him after all.

He nodded. He took the tray with a shaky hand, exaggerating his pain. His hands were fine. They were always strapped down when the guards—and Dr. Rowburg—kicked his ass. She didn't need to know that.

"It's hard for a man to turn off his pride."

"You're not a man. You're a shifter. A...*dragon*." She said it like it was a secret, like she couldn't believe it herself.

"Yes, but I'm a very gentle, sensual dragon." She rolled her eyes. Even so, he saw the smile creeping its way onto her face. Couldn't hide that. "You've changed your hair. It's shorter."

Her eyes widened at his comment, and although it was slight, he saw the reddening of her cheeks. He'd watched her every day, silently taking in her physical appearance. While the collar may have suppressed all of his shifting abilities, he could still use the ones he'd developed from years of charming others.

She reached up and touched her hair, smoothing it down against her neck.

"Barely," she said. "Just a trim."

"It looks good."

"Thanks. You're actually the first person to notice it."

A few seconds ago he was a shifter. Now, he was a person. He was making progress.

"I always notice when a woman makes a change to herself that somehow manages to enhance her natural beauty."

"I know what you're trying to do," she warned, face red, arms crossed.

He chuckled. It was immediately followed by a wince. This wasn't a ploy to tug at her heartstrings. One of the guards hadn't been easy on his ribs.

"I enjoy talking to you, and I'm in no rush to see you leave."

"You'll see me tomorrow."

"Will you stay and chat with me again?"

She looked around, checking to make sure there were no other guards nearby. She bent down, leaning so that her mouth was as close to the food slot as it could get without actually touching it.

"What exactly do you want from me, Conlin?"

"A lot of things." He let his eyes roam over her body, slow and seductive, and knew what she would assume from it. He didn't want sex from her—still, needs must. "But, I'll settle for a few minutes of conversation. This is a lonely place. Having someone to talk to makes it a bit less depressing. Especially when that person is as beautiful as you."

He offered her a smile—something he shouldn't have done. The bruised and battered skin on his lip broke open, causing a small stream of blood to trickle down his chin. He hadn't planned that, though it was a nice touch.

"Sorry." He wiped the blood away with his hand.

"I'll try to find some time to talk to you tomorrow," she whispered.

"You've brightened up my day. Or night. It's hard to tell in this place."

"It's day." She looked down at her watch. "Noon. I just brought you lunch, remember?"

"It all feels the same to me."

"I have to go, Conlin." She paused, hesitating just briefly before speaking again. "*Coy.*"

"Talk to you soon, Officer." He smiled again.

"Katherine. My name's Katherine."

"A beautiful name."

"See you tomorrow." She left with red cheeks and a swish in her hips.

Coy smirked. He'd laid down the first piece of his puzzle.

Finally.

AUGUST FELT SICK.

The nausea was sudden. It snuck up on him as he listened to Stanley's screams of agony. He rushed out of the lab, leaving Fate and the others behind to enjoy the show. His body felt weak and shaky, like something had zapped all of his energy. He couldn't finish the rest of the workday like this.

He caught the next employee bus home.

The sick feeling subsided on the ride back to Osin, but he still couldn't shake off the jitters. Maybe he was just overwhelmed. So many things had happened in such a short period of time. Seeing Stanley being tortured must have set something off in him. He just needed a few hours. Just some time to rest and relax and gather his thoughts together. Just a little bit of rest. That was all he needed. He'd be fine by tomorrow.

August arrived at his house much sooner than he'd expected. There were fewer vehicles on the road at this hour—fewer people in a rush to get home to their loved ones. Not to mention that a percentage of the population was now rotting away inside the Registry prison. It wasn't a large number, but it was a number all the same.

His roses' scent was strong today, stronger than it'd been in months. They had already been in bloom. There was no logical reason for their fragrance to be stronger.

Unless...

The nausea came back to him in full force. He knew what was happening.

He rushed into his house, kicking the front door shut. He needed to calm down. If he could just get ahold of himself, he could prevent it. It'd been almost two years. He just needed to focus. Or, maybe he could distract himself. Yes, that was it. He needed a distraction. He couldn't think about it. He needed to pretend everything was the same. Nothing was happening. He'd just gotten off work, and his day had been uneventful. He was home now. He was in his beautiful house, surrounded by roses outside and cool, lemon-scented air inside. Everything was fine. Nothing was wrong. He was going to be okay.

He wiped his forehead with the back of his hand, and sweat dripped from his fingers. A shower. He could take a shower. He would keep the temperature low, let the cool water run down his skin. It would calm him, help him relax. Yes, a shower was just what he needed.

He took a step and his body lurched, jerked forward like someone had shoved him. For a second, he thought he was going to vomit. Had that been all this was, he would have gladly welcomed it. This was much worse than gastrointestinal distress.

August had to get outside. *Now.*

And clothes. He needed to take off his clothes.

He rushed through the living room and into the kitchen, yanking off pieces of his uniform and throwing them onto the floor. He'd never been a messy person. He preferred everything neat and in its proper place, just like his mother had drilled into him. Cleanliness may have been next to godliness, but he didn't have time for cleaning, gods, or clean gods. His only goal was to get outside and control himself while he still could.

The backyard was engulfed in daylight. Much too risky under normal circumstances. Luckily, the fence had high walls and thick vines. He'd have privacy. He'd be secluded. The neighbors wouldn't see him. It wouldn't take long. A few minutes, maybe? An hour at the most? Hopefully. He'd just have to wait it out. He'd be quiet, he'd be patient, and he'd wait. He didn't really have a choice. There were no other options.

He was still wearing his socks, black like the rest of his discarded uniform lying on the kitchen floor. He didn't have time to remove them. He hadn't been quick enough.

It was happening.

He ran outside, feet pounding against the ground. His socks grew wet, stained with mud and bits of dead grass. His heart slammed against his chest, racing, beating so fast that he was certain he could hear it. He tried to remember what to do. What had he done the first time? The last time? It'd been so long—he could barely remember.

Crouch down. Deep breaths. Don't struggle. Don't fight it. Put his body on autopilot and let instinct take over. He didn't know if any of it would help. No one had ever taught him.

He didn't want this.

He thought about Niami alone in her cell, sad and lonely and afraid.

He was scared.

It only took a few seconds. Blinding lights and a whirlpool of vibrant colors. He lost his sense of the world around him. He couldn't see. Couldn't hear. Couldn't think.

And then, he could sense *everything.*

The world around him seemed brighter, looked crisper, *smelled* better. The earth felt cool against his feet, massaging them as he padded along the soft grass. There wasn't much to do. The space was small, but it was his. His and no one else's. Good. He liked that. It was in his nature, in his blood, and in his genes.

He didn't like to share.

He used a tree to scratch the itch in his back that he couldn't reach on his own. He noticed a flock of birds and watched them curiously as they stared back at him before flying away, wings flapping, air currents carrying their little bodies even higher into the sky.

They were out of his reach. He swatted at them anyway, claws striking at nothing but air. He wandered around the backyard, scratching, sniffing, and exploring. When he didn't find anything of interest, he moved back to the tree and plopped down below it, the leaves providing him with a decent amount of shade. Maybe one of those birds would come back.

He hadn't eaten since morning.

NOW THAT THE first part of his plan had been put into action, Coy needed to work on the next part—and it would be much harder than sweet-talking. He needed a way to keep track of what guards would be on his floor and where they would be. Like at any other job, there were officers who slacked off. Some of them had to be assigned to his floor. When he made his move, it would have to happen when one of the slackers was scheduled to patrol.

He also needed a way to figure out the time. Breaking out only to realize there was daylight on the other side of the prison walls would bring trouble. When he escaped, it would have to be after nightfall. He would have an easier time avoiding anyone the Registry sent after him in the dark.

His tray lay empty next to him. The food was good, but nowhere near as delicious as Dinina's. He tried not to think about her and Ari. It always hurt when he did.

He'd make it out of here alive. He was sure of that, yet it didn't stop him from feeling like the walls were closing in on him. He wanted to know the truth—even if it wouldn't make him feel any better. Knowing his grandmother, she must have died fighting. Or, at least trying to. Ari had probably tried to protect her. She must have sent him away to hide. Otherwise, he would have been right there with her. That was just the type of kid he was.

He just wished he could have been there to protect them—to die for them, if he had to. It wasn't fair that he was alive while Dinina had her life taken away from her. He'd been performing—dancing for a crowd of strangers while his family was attacked for who knew what reason. He felt guilty. Didn't he have enough of that already?

It should have been him.

Maybe it would have been best if he just admitted defeat and gave Dr. Rowburg and the guards a cause to kill him. Everything he'd ever done in life was to improve the quality of life for his family. Now that his grandmother was gone and his brother was missing, what was the point? He didn't even know if Ari was alive.

No. He couldn't think like that. They wouldn't want him to think like that. They'd want him to carry on. Augustus Seaton deserved to die for what he did, even if it went against Coy's grandmother's wishes. Coy hadn't been able to protect her in life, but he could avenge her death.

He'd break out of prison. He'd find his brother. And then, he'd kill the man who'd murdered her.

AUGUST DIDN'T KNOW how many hours had passed, but he was aware of the change. He remembered seeing and hearing things through eyes and ears that weren't his own. Most people called this shifting.

August called it a curse.

He was still in his backyard—naked, shivering, and waiting for the Registry to burst through his back door and discover his secret. When it didn't happen, he exhaled and silently thanked the gods for his fortune.

His secret was safe.

The entire ordeal was just as terrifying as it'd been when he was a teenager. The only difference was that he didn't have his mother standing over him asking him what he'd done and who he'd done it with to make him this way. He still remembered the look on her face, appalled and disgusted that her son, someone born of her very blood, was inflicted with such a curse. She'd slapped him when he had changed back, hand striking against his face so hard that he bit the inside of his cheek. She had told him never to do it again, made him promise. Made him *swear*. And he'd tried so hard to fulfill the vow, except he couldn't.

He had no control over it.

She didn't help him, nor did she try to get him any help. Shifters were supposed to learn from other shifters, but he wasn't one. He was *human*. She'd made him live his life as one. He was a shut-in, shielded away from everyone and everything. Shifters mingled with other shifters, interacted with them, learned from them. He didn't do any of those things. He wasn't one of them. He wasn't like the creatures locked away at the Registry prison, and he refused to think of himself as such. He was different.

Just...different.

Save for his mother, he'd managed to hide his curse from everyone else. How long could he hide it, he wondered. What if it happened while he was at work? He'd had so many close calls at high school. August closed his eyes, trying to remember. Two years had gone by since he last transformed. Two years. He thought he was cured. He thought he didn't have to worry about this anymore. How could he possibly explain it to anyone? Would they understand that he wasn't a shifter? That he was merely a human who occasionally changed outside of his control? It was clear how much the other officers hated shifters. What if they found out and grouped him in with the others? No, that wouldn't happen. *Couldn't* happen. He couldn't survive with those people...those *animals*. He'd just have to be careful. He'd make sure no one ever found out. He'd come up with a cure to rid himself of this disease once and for all. Even if it meant having to ask Dr. Rowburg for help.

With a sigh, he stood up from where he was huddled beneath the tree and made his way back to the house. The worst part was over, for now. If he was lucky, maybe he could go a few more years without it happening again. He just wanted to go inside, take a shower, and pretend none of this had ever happened.

Once inside, he shut the back door behind him. Realizing he'd forgotten to lock it, August turned around, shaky fingers fumbling with the latch. Too busy fighting with the lock, he failed to notice the figure leaning against the kitchen entryway, watching him.

"I've got to hand it to you."

August startled. It was the last voice he wanted to hear. Slowly, he turned around.

"You're a great actor, August."

"Fate..." He reached down, shielding himself with his hands. "How long have you—"

"Long enough." He held August's pants in his hand.

"Fate, I swear. It is not what you think. Please, just... Just let me explain." He felt the walls closing in on him. Fate knew his secret. It could have been anyone else. Why did it have to be him? August needed to run. To escape. No. Fate was too quick for that. Maybe he could talk his way out of it—say it was something he was testing for the lab. He'd tell him it wasn't permanent. It was just temporary.

Fate gave him a small smile. "It's fine, August. Relax. Your secret's safe with me."

"Really?"

He had to be lying. There was no way Fate wasn't angry. He hated shifters—and August had pretended to be solely human around him. He'd fooled Fate. Fooled everyone. And yet...Fate didn't look angry at all. Maybe he had misjudged Fate. Still, he needed to be cautious. Just in case.

"Of course."

He walked over to August slowly, as if showing him that he meant no harm. The pants were draped over his hand in a strange way, not quite resting inside of his palm. He offered them to August.

"Besides—" He placed his free hand on August's shoulder. "You've kept mine."

Fate raised his opposite hand, and the pants fell to the floor, revealing a gun. The same one he'd used to kill Dinina. Before August could even think to react, Fate drove the butt of the gun into August's head with a hard thrust.

The last image August saw was of Fate's green eyes glaring down at him, and then he was submerged in darkness.

Chapter Eleven

AUGUST AWOKE TO find himself upright. A few confused moments passed before he recognized the lab. He was strapped to the vertical table—just like the shifters he'd once escorted here. His head ached, and his mouth tasted like blood. His forehead felt wet, and he couldn't quite open his right eye—not because it was injured, but because something sticky was keeping it partially closed. The room spun around him. He had to close his remaining eye to keep from getting dizzier, but the throbbing in his head only made him nauseous. He tried to move his hands, but to no avail.

"And you're certain he's never told you about this?" Director Richards asked. "He's your son. Surely, you would have known about this."

Curious despite himself, August opened his uninhibited eye.

"I swear I had no idea," Dr. Rowburg answered. "I cannot believe this." She walked over to August. Her lips were pursed into a tight line that caused the corners of her mouth to wrinkle. She stared at him for several seconds, not speaking. She didn't need to. The slap she doled out spoke volumes.

"How could you?" she demanded.

August blinked back tears. He knew what she was doing. She was trying to protect herself. He was supposed to go along with the lie, to tell everyone else in the room that he'd been keeping this secret to himself all of his life.

"Is this true?" Director Richards asked him. "Was the doctor unaware of your condition? Did she not know?"

Yes, she knew. He wanted to scream that she had known about it since the beginning. That she was a horrible mother, and that she had ruined his life. She was supposed to protect him. She was supposed to care about him. It wasn't his fault he was...a shifter. It wasn't his fault that any of this had happened.

"No one knew," he replied. "I was too ashamed to tell her."

She slapped him again.

Richards looked like he didn't believe him, but he didn't push the issue. "It's a shame. I had high hopes that you'd become an exceptional officer. Especially with Fate's guidance. Now, we'll have to put you in a cell just like all the others."

"I understand."

He didn't understand. He didn't understand anything. He thought about all the other shifters, the ones he'd looked down on with disgust and contempt. He remembered how weak and scared they'd all looked, remembered hating them because he had felt the same way every day for as long as he could remember.

August was scared. He wanted to scream and yell and cry. He wanted to break free from the straps constraining him. Run away from Asuda and never return.

He felt a tickle against his sides and realized his hair was down. He hardly ever wore it down around other people.

"We still have a few cells with only one shifter in them," Richards said. "We won't put you on any of the levels that you worked on. Maybe we could—"

"Don't reason with him," Fate growled. Shocked, August jerked his head toward the voice. He hadn't even noticed Fate lurking in the background. His heart lurched from betrayal. "He's a useless shifter just like all the others. He doesn't have a say in what cell he's put in. What does it matter? For all I care, we could put him in—" He smirked, green eyes shining with sadistic amusement. "—put him in the cell with the dragon."

August's eyes widened, and Fate's smirk morphed into a full-on grin.

"No, please," August implored. He knew begging would only make everyone despise him more, but they couldn't put him in a cell with Conlin. Conlin wanted him *dead*. "You do not understand. You cannot—"

"We can do whatever we want," Fate snapped, his normally pale face flush with anger. In the back of his mind, August wondered if he felt betrayed, too.

"*Mother.*"

It was his last resort. One last plea for a mother to help her child. To show him that deep down, somewhere in her heart, she at least loved him a little bit—that she wouldn't put him in a situation where he may end up dead by morning.

His mother looked at him, and he saw nothing in her eyes. No compassion, no love, no empathy. Nothing.

"I have no son." And, if that wasn't bad enough, she added, "Give him to the dragon."

August fought.

He struggled hard, kicking and scratching until Fate got both of his hands behind his back, pinning them together. Fate pressed the button on a controller, emitting a series of painful shocks via August's collar. He almost fell from the sheer intensity of them, but Fate forced him back on his feet. Through the pain, August wondered how Fate avoided the shock—his gloves had to have been nonconductive.

In the confusion of the lab, August hadn't even realized they'd put one on him.

"It really is a shame," Fate said. "A pretty thing like you doesn't belong in prison, but that's where you'll spend the rest of your disgusting shifter life." He pressed the button again, and August cried out. "A pity. I'd been so ready to fuck you."

August panted, felt drool running from the corner of his mouth and down his chin. "As if I would have given you the chance."

"I don't need your permission to fuck you. Not then, and not now. Maybe I'll come pay you a visit when Dr. Rowburg has you strapped onto one of her tables." He snickered. "Normally, I wouldn't even think about putting my dick in a shifter, but..." He pressed the button again and then pulled August by the hair to prevent him from falling over. "I'd make an exception for you."

He let August's hands go, likely knowing that August wouldn't run. He couldn't run. He could barely stand.

"You'd like that, wouldn't you? Your little shifter ass impaled on my cock."

August knew better than to answer.

"Or, maybe we'll start with your mouth first. I guess we have time to figure it out, don't we?" He laughed again. "Especially you."

Fate kept shoving him forward until both their steps began to slow. They were getting closer to Conlin's cell.

"Wake up, dragon," Fate called out a few feet before they'd even reached the cell. "I have a surprise for you."

They stopped walking. August felt every one of his muscles tense up. Fate held him by the neck, fingers just above his collar. He rocked August from side to side, waving him around like a piece of raw meat in front of an animal on the brink of starvation.

Conlin's cell door slowly opened. August made one last attempt to run. Only, Fate was quicker, *stronger*. He threw August inside and then laughed when he fell onto the floor.

"Now, you two play nice."

He whistled as he walked away, not even bothering to look back.

THE GODS HAD answered him.

They'd heard his cries of frustration and promises of revenge, and they'd delivered the beast on a silver platter.

Coy smiled. It was his first genuine smile in weeks.

"Well, look at what the Registry cat dragged in. Officer Augustus Seaton." His smile was still in place, even as he climbed off the bed. "You have no idea how much I've been thinking about you."

This was some type of test. It had to be. Probably Dr. Rowburg's doing. Seaton was an officer. They wouldn't just throw him into a cell with Coy—not without a catch. He wouldn't fall for it.

"Your grandmother," Seaton began. He was still on the floor, having scurried away as soon as Coy stood. He was pressed so close to the wall that he could have become a permanent fixture. "I did not kill her. I swear."

"You know," Coy said. "If I had killed a guy's grandma and was then locked into a tiny room with them, I'd say the same thing. Funny how that works."

"I swear." Seaton held his hands out in front of him, as if shielding himself. "It was not me. It was Fate."

"You expect me to believe that?" Coy took a step forward.

"Please." Seaton scrambled against the floor, trying to push himself even farther back. "I am telling you the truth."

Coy laughed. "Fate had years to kill all three of us if he wanted to." He took another step, slowly closing the distance between himself and Seaton.

"It's true." Coy watched as Seaton became more frantic as the gap between them diminished. "The boy, your brother. He said he would protect you and your grandmother. He came at Fate with a knife. I watched him push the blade in and..."

Coy paused. "And what?" he demanded. "Tell me."

"Fate retaliated. Your grandmother, when she saw what Fate had done. She began to shift, but Fate shot her."

"And you did what? Just stood there?" he whispered, words coming out rough and gritty. His eyes stung, burning with unshed tears.

"I..."

"So, yes, you just stood there and let her die. Just watched her be murdered? And Ari? I don't even know if he's dead or alive."

"He is alive," Seaton assured. "At least, he was the last time I saw him."

"This whole story is bullshit," Coy growled. "Why are you even in here?"

He charged forward and snatched Seaton up from the ground. Seaton cried out for help as he shoved him against the wall. His dangling feet kicked at Coy's shins.

"What game is the Registry playing putting you in here with me, huh?"

Seaton moved his lips, eyes widening when no words came out.

"Fucking tell me!" Coy rammed him against the wall.

Seaton cried out when his head hit the tiles. Coy's long fingers pulsed where they were wrapped around his neck, just above the collar.

"Please..."

"Answer my question, or I swear I'll rip your fucking head off."

"It is no game. I am a—" He hesitated. "—a shifter. Fate found out, and they put me in here."

Coy looked into Seaton's eyes and then at his face. Spotting the wound on his head, he jabbed his thumb into it. Seaton screamed, blood dribbling down his face, hands clawing at Coy's wrist.

So, the wound was real after all.

"You expect me to believe that?" Coy asked, voice low.

"No, but it's the truth. I did not kill your family. I have never killed anyone in my life."

"So, you didn't kill my family, and now, surprise. You're a shifter."

Seaton didn't say anything.

"Augustus."

They both turned their heads to see Dr. Rowburg standing in front of the cell door.

"Mother."

"Mother?" Coy repeated, eyes narrowing in confusion.

"Mr. Conlin, if you could be so kind."

Coy released his hold on Seaton, who fell weakly to his feet and then walked the few steps it took for him to end up before Dr. Rowburg, the plastic wall between them.

"You know why I'm here?" she asked.

"Please forgive me. I could not... I did not know how—"

"You will not get any special treatment. Do you understand? You will be treated like every other shifter inside these walls. Do not expect me to be lenient on you simply because I gave birth to you."

Seaton nodded.

"You are no different from the beasts. You are nothing more than something for us to study."

"Yes," Seaton said.

"You will address me as Dr. Rowburg, just as the others do. Do not consider me your mother. I have no desire to hold such a title. Understood?"

He nodded again.

"Good." She looked up at Coy. "Carry on, Mr. Conlin."

She strode off, having said her piece, leaving Seaton staring at the empty spot where she had once stood.

"ROWBURG'S YOUR FUCKING mother?"

August did not trust himself to speak. There was a lump in his throat, one in danger of crawling up and spilling out of his mouth.

It hurt.

He had expected it. He had expected all of it. It still hurt. He did not know why he continued to imagine that his mother would one day wake up and admit that she loved him. She did not love him. She never had. All those years of shielding him away had not been to protect him from the Registry. It had been to protect herself from the shame and embarrassment of giving birth to a shifter. She hated him, *despised* him. Her own son. Her own flesh and blood.

August felt sick.

The feeling hit him again. The same feeling as before. He clutched at the collar around his neck, his breath coming out in gasps.

"What the fuck is wrong with you?" he heard Conlin say. It sounded distant, so far away.

His body lurched forward—just like it had done last time—but the collar stopped anything from happening. He felt the shock throughout his nervous system, electricity beaming through his very core. Another jerk of his body—another shock. It happened like this, over and over again, tearing screams from him until he lay sprawled on the floor, an aching and drooling mess.

Conlin hadn't done anything to help him. He had just stood there, watching. If August could have laughed without causing himself more pain, he would have over how ironic that was.

"What was that? Some kind of panic attack?" Conlin asked with a snort. "Everyone has problems. No need to act like a drama queen about them."

"They were not panic attacks," August protested. It took effort to get the words out loudly enough for Conlin to hear them.

"Then what were they?"

"It was my body trying to shift. I don't... I never learned how. I don't know how to control it."

He felt ashamed admitting that. The only boy in the locker room who hadn't grown pubic hair.

"A shifter who doesn't have control of his shifting? That hardly ever happens."

August wanted to explain that he wasn't a shifter, not really. Only, it wouldn't do him any good. He was imprisoned with all the other shifters, and his former colleagues had treated him like one. If it looked like a duck and quacked like a duck, people would assume it was a duck.

August closed his eyes. Exhaustion had finally caught up with him. If Conlin was going to kill him, at least he would be asleep for it.

"I suppose I am the exception," he murmured just before sleep claimed him.

COY WATCHED SEATON sleeping on the floor next to the bed. He wasn't sure if he believed anything his new cellmate had said, and he sure as hell didn't trust him. Still, what if he were telling the truth? If he killed Seaton, he would be killing a—mostly—innocent man. Moreover, there was still the possibility of all of this being an elaborate setup. Seaton could be a part of some larger trick of Dr. Rowburg's to get him exactly where they wanted him. The collar seemed a little ruthless though, even for Rowburg. He would have to be smart about whatever move he made next.

He would have to wait things out just a bit longer. He needed to find out the truth. He had already put his plan into action, but he hadn't expected the person he wanted to kill to just fall into his lap. Too many variables were coming into play.

Coy would let Seaton live for now—at least until he found out whether or not he was lying—but he wouldn't give him an easy time. He wasn't about to let the man who may have killed his grandmother trick him into feeling any sympathy for him.

He would milk every drop of information Seaton had right out of him. If he found out he was lying about anything, he would end him without a second thought. However, if Fate really *had* killed his family, then he was going to have to redirect his attention to killing him instead, and that was bound to be a bit more difficult. He doubted he would be lucky enough to have Fate turn out to be a shifter as well.

Whatever. He would figure it out later. Now that Seaton was trapped with him, he wouldn't have to rush to mark off his hit list. Seaton's fate could be decided later. Breaking out was now his top priority. It was only a matter of time before Dr. Rowburg would try to force him to stick his dick into someone.

He thought about the exchange between her and Seaton and shook his head. As far as he was concerned, there was nothing worse than losing the people you loved. Still, having an evil, sadistic bitch of a mother like her was pretty damn close.

KATHERINE CAME TO see Coy the next day, and not just to deliver his meal. She pushed a cart carrying trays of food and seemed genuinely surprised when she saw Seaton lying on the floor.

He had not moved since yesterday, and Coy had not bothered to check on him. The cell didn't stink, so he probably wasn't dead. Not that he would have cared if he were.

"He seems familiar," Katherine said. "I feel like I've seen him before."

"You probably have," Coy replied. "He used to be one of you."

She stared down at him with a confused expression, and he knew he had to elaborate further. Pretty girl, but she wasn't very bright.

"He used to be an officer. Turns out he's a shifter. Augustus Seaton."

"*That's* Seaton." She stared down at where the man lay, her gray eyes widening in disbelief. "He looks different with his hair down. He's pretty."

"Good thing I'm not the jealous type," Coy said with a smirk.

"Not what I typically go for though," she said. "I like my men a little manlier."

"I'm a man now, am I? Have I upgraded?"

She blushed, not looking Coy in the eyes. "I can't believe he was a shifter the whole time."

"Forget about him. I thought you were here to see me. Or, maybe I should just shove him under my bed so he won't distract you any longer. That is, if they didn't have cameras around watching our every move."

"Cameras? What cameras?"

"The ones in our cell."

"There are no cameras in your cell."

Well, that was interesting.

"Of course there are," Coy said.

"No, really. There aren't. We've been trying to get them installed, but the ambassador won't convince the sovereign to sign off on them. It makes sense, you know? We have the collars. They're effective. Cameras aren't really necessary. Though, we do have a few officers pushing to get them installed."

Coy didn't need her to tell him which officers those happened to be. He knew one of them had to be Fate. Still, considering all the horrible stuff the other officers got away with, it was no wonder the place didn't have cameras. No cameras—no proof.

She had a strange expression on her face, like she had just realized she'd shared a secret with Coy she shouldn't have.

He changed the subject. "That pretty wrist of yours wouldn't happen to have a watch on it, would it?"

She rolled her eyes. "It's six. You always ask me for the time. I bring you your dinner at six o'clock, every day."

"I told you, it's hard to keep track of time in this place."

"Maybe I should sneak you in a watch," she joked.

"Maybe you should." Coy grinned. He was serious. "Or, at least a few sheets of paper and a pen, so I can spend the rest of my days in here writing you love letters."

"We're not supposed to give anything to shifters."

"Who would know? It's not like they have cameras."

"I knew I shouldn't have told you that," she muttered and dropped her face into her hands.

"It's fine. I'm not going anywhere. I still have this, remember?" He tapped at the collar, snug around his neck. "Besides, there are a few things I want to say to you. Things that I can't say while others can eavesdrop."

"What things?" she asked.

Coy made a point of looking her up and down. His gaze roamed over her body, taking in the curve of her hips and the swell of her breasts. "Many things."

He heard footsteps.

"I have to go," she whispered before adding a quick, "I'll see what I can do."

MORE THAN ANYTHING, August was disappointed when he woke up. In the back of his mind, he had hoped Conlin would have just killed him in his sleep. At least then he wouldn't have had to deal with his present reality.

He sat up, and his back protested the movement. Conlin was lying on his bed, watching him with curious, mismatched eyes.

"So, you're not dead," Conlin remarked.

"Sorry to disappoint."

"Don't be. I can change that anytime I want."

August stood up, grunting and wincing at the pain that shot throughout his body. If he'd known that one day he would have ended up wearing a shifter collar, he would have designed it to apply a lot less force.

"What time is it?"

"What's it matter? You're in prison. Time doesn't mean shit here."

"It would be helpful if you answered the question."

"Since when have I ever given you any impression that I'd be willing to help you?"

"Forget it."

"It's forgotten."

August looked around the cell and spotted two empty food trays. Turning back toward Conlin, he understood the smirk on his face. He had eaten both August's dinner and his own.

Without speaking, he walked over to his new bed. Conlin had claimed the bottom bunk from the start, so it looked like August was going to have to sleep on the top. His body ached too much to climb up to it, but anything beat lying on the hard floor.

He could feel Conlin's eyes on him as he struggled to pull himself onto the top bunk.

"Make sure your feet don't touch my bed," Conlin warned.

August ignored him. His toes touched the metal frame beneath Conlin's mattress, but not the mattress itself. As luck—or lack of it, really—would have it, he lost his footing and had to brace against the edge of Conlin's mattress.

The top bunk seemed to ascend, rising into the air before he could reach it. Conlin had clipped him, his foot smacking August's shin so that he lost his grip on the bed frame and fell. His knees hit the frame with a loud crack before he landed, his back smashing against the floor.

He panted, body pulsing with pain as he stared up at the ceiling. Without moving his head, he shifted his gaze to Conlin, who stared down at him with a bored expression.

"I told you not to touch my bed."

"It was not on purpose," August replied. It hurt to speak.

"Not my problem."

He grunted when he sat up, moving slowly so the room wouldn't spin. It took effort to stand. His knees weren't broken, at least. He knew he wouldn't be able to make a second attempt at climbing onto his bed, so he grabbed the thin mattress off of it instead and laid it on the floor as far away from Conlin as possible—which wasn't far at all, given the cell's size.

His entire body hurt as he crawled onto the mat. He may as well have been sleeping on the floor. It was hard and uncomfortable, like lying on a bed made out of sand. At least he'd be close enough to the door to get his food once they delivered it again.

"How the mighty have fallen," Conlin mocked. "Literally." He snickered at his own joke.

After sleeping for what felt like an entire day, August really wasn't all that tired, but there was nothing else to do. He could only ponder how much the other officers must despise him and how his cellmate wanted him dead.

He'd been conditioned for this, he thought. He'd been alone all his life. Even so, he'd always held on to the hope that one day, someone, somewhere, would accept him for who he was. Now it was as if someone had hammered the final nail in his coffin. The Kingdom of Asuda was made up of two groups: humans and shifters.

August was hated by both.

He wouldn't be able to sleep, but he could try to figure out what to do next. Was he destined to spend the rest of his life in prison because of something he could not control? He didn't want to be here. He didn't *deserve* to be here. And yet, this was exactly where he belonged. He had put so many shifters in this place, had snatched them from their families and thrown them in prison because of what they were. They were shifters, yes, but they were also people. *He* was a person. How could he have been so foolish?

Somehow, someway, August had to fix this. Not just for himself, but for every other shifter caged behind clear walls like animals, like science experiments. No one deserved to feel like this. He had to take responsibility for it. He had to make things right.

The problem was, he had no idea of how to do that, or even where to start.

He glanced over at Conlin, who was still watching him, his well-toned arm folded across his chest. He winked at August with that fascinating, violet eye of his. Up until then, August had never felt threatened by a wink before. Conlin had more of a reason to hate him than anyone else in the world. If August was going to start righting his wrongs, he was going to have to start with him.

Chapter Twelve

YET AGAIN, COY'S new cellmate slept for most of the day—not that day and night had much bearing here. He was awake now, sitting on his mattress and staring up at the ceiling as if it would speak to him. He looked stupid, and just the sight of him annoyed Coy, but he decided not to dwell on Seaton for the moment. He wasn't important. What was important was that Katherine had come to see him.

She had a small stack of paper and an ink pen in her hand, but she was hesitant to give them to him now that he had a cellmate.

"Ignore him. He's not going to say anything. Are you?"

"Say anything about what?" Seaton asked from his spot on the floor.

"See."

She looked around, making sure no one was coming down either end of the hall, before she slid the pen and paper through the lunch slot, followed by their trays of food.

"Keep those hidden," she warned.

"I'll guard them with my life."

"And write me letters." She grinned.

Coy ignored the smears of lipstick on her teeth and grinned back.

"As many letters as you can read."

The grin was still on her face when she left. He could hear her humming as she walked away. He hid the items beneath his mattress. While his back was turned, he heard Seaton dart to the door, probably to grab one of the trays. Coy smirked to himself before walking back to grab his own food.

A few minutes into their meal, two guards walked down the hall, both of them stopping to look into Coy's cell as if he were a circus attraction. Something he was used to, given his former job.

"Enjoying the company, August?" one of the guards teased while the other laughed. They both smacked the cell door before continuing on their way.

"Are you going to eat that?" Coy asked.

Seaton glanced down at his partially eaten dinner. "Eat what?"

"That."

"What part of this is 'that'?"

"All of it."

"All of it," Seaton repeated. "Are you asking me if you can have my entire dinner?"

"Yes."

"No."

"No, you're not going to eat it, or no, I can't have it?"

"I'm not giving you my food."

"Tch. Selfish."

Coy watched him, unblinking, following each plastic forkful of food that Seaton shoved into his mouth. It must have made Seaton uncomfortable. After a few seconds, he turned his back to him and ate his food while facing the wall.

Coy smirked and stared at the back of Seaton's head. Yesterday, he had not realized just how long his hair was—but that could have been because he was thinking more about killing him than anything else. He was *still* thinking about killing him. Regardless, Seaton's beauty annoyed him. Even in the ugly, white uniform they had all been ordered to wear, there was a sense of unbelievable gorgeousness to him. Like he belonged on a balcony, addressing thousands of admirers below him.

"August."

Seaton turned around, his mouth stuffed full of bread.

"That's what that one officer called you."

Seaton was silent until he finished chewing his food. "That's what most people call me," he said.

"Rowburg called you Augustus."

Seaton snorted. "She's called me much worse."

"I can do better."

"I am sure you can."

Coy frowned, considering the best angle of attack. He needed more information from Seaton—both about his family and the prison. Just two short days ago, he had been an officer, strolling along the halls. Coy was certain he knew of the quickest, easiest way out of the prison, but he did not trust Seaton to just willingly tell him what it was. Not if he was Rowburg's spy, anyway.

His mind drifted into more turbulent waters. It was difficult not to think about his family when one of the last two people to see them alive was sitting right across from him.

"Did she suffer?" he found himself asking. He had not planned to, but the words had just burst from his lips like lava, hot and dangerous. They tore the scabs from his slowly healing wounds.

Seaton turned around again. He had finished eating. Coy tried to guess how old he was. He looked young. Maybe twenty-three, or twenty-four. Not much younger than himself. There was a look of sadness in his eyes, like he did not want to relive that day again. He would. Coy would make him. He needed to know.

"It was over for her quickly."

"Where is she now?" Coy asked. "Just rotting away on the kitchen floor?"

Seaton shook his head. "I followed protocol and called in her death to the Registry. She should be—" He looked away from Coy. "She should be buried on your land. I do not know if that's what she would have wanted, but—"

Coy put up a hand to silence him. "Enough. And Ari? Where is he?"

"I am not sure. A man took him away. Someone Fate called. So, Fate would know, I believe."

"I still don't believe you or any of this story. You know that, right?"

"That is fair," Seaton said.

"That is fair," Coy repeated mockingly.

He stood and advanced on Seaton, taking intense pleasure in the true terror in his eyes. Seaton pushed himself back against the wall, shoving the empty food tray out of his lap. When Seaton tried to dive to the left, Coy grabbed him, hoisted him to his feet, and then lifted him off the ground as though he weighed nothing.

"I am telling you the truth."

Seaton's feet only just scraped against his mattress, Coy's own only inches away, denting the thin material.

"Stop struggling." He lowered Seaton to his feet, fingers digging into his shoulders, feeling the muscles tighten and tense beneath golden-brown skin. "Did you kill her?"

"No, I told you. It was *Fate*."

"All right, fine. Let's say you didn't kill her. Let's say it was Fate. You didn't stop him, did you?"

"I…"

"Did you?" Coy repeated, a dark growl coming from his throat.

Seaton turned his head to the side. "I wanted to, but it all happened so fast, and I—"

"Didn't," Coy finished for him.

"No."

"Then that makes you just as guilty. Which means that you're going to help me."

"Help you do what?"

"You have information that I need to get the hell out of here."

"Get out?" Seaton released a dry laugh. "You cannot get out of here. The sovereign ordered for all shifters to be imprisoned indefinitely."

"I don't plan on waiting for the sovereign to change his mind. I'm breaking out."

"Breaking out," Seaton repeated. "Impossible. Someone would grab your controller and zap you within an inch of death."

"Your job isn't to worry about how I'll get out of here. Your job is to tell me everything you know about this place and how it operates. You can do it willingly, or I can beat it out of you. Either way works just fine for me. Are we clear?"

Seaton nodded. His dubious expressed cleared and became considering, almost—to Coy's confusion—eager.

"Good." He released Seaton's shoulders and moved back to sit on his own bed. "Now, start talking."

COY HAD WRITTEN down everything Seaton told him that seemed useful. Of course, this only pertained to the three levels Seaton had patrolled. It didn't matter. Some information was better than none. They all probably operated in the same way. At least Seaton's visits to the lab ensured that he knew how to get to the lower levels. Being on the fourth floor himself, Coy had never seen it, but Seaton had assured him that all guards used an elevator to transport shifters to and from the lab. There was, however, an emergency stairwell at the side of the building, only a fast sprint down the hallway from their cell. It was digitally locked from the inside, but if they could grab one of the officer's ID cards…

Beyond that, they would have to fly down three flights of stairs and then run like hell. When Seaton had described the grounds, Coy had already started to come up with tactics for scaling the prison's wall or sneaking past the gate, but Seaton had admitted, albeit embarrassingly, that the Registry had not even begun construction on one. Coy still found it hard to believe, but the Registry had always been elitist—it was no wonder that they hadn't bothered to update the security of what had apparently been an office building. They were so confident in their technology that they did not believe old-fashioned gates and electric fences would be necessary.

Their hubris would be their downfall.

Moreover, the prisoners were not as heavily guarded as he had previously thought. Three officers per three floors per shift. It was a cocky move and an ignorant one. The Registry had based the entire operation on the effectiveness of the collars. If the collars happened to malfunction, or if one of the shifters learned how to take it off—or, in Seaton's case, *knew*—the whole organization would crumble. Well, maybe it wouldn't crumble, but they would still have some shit to deal with depending on the shifter's animal type.

Especially if that animal happened to be a dragon.

Coy would have to make his move the next time they took him out of his cell to drag him to the lab or to the showers. The latter would be best. If they were taking him to the lab, and his attempt at escape was unsuccessful, he did not want to think about the type of torture Dr. Rowburg would bestow upon him. Perhaps he could tempt Katherine into swapping roles with one of the other officers, take him to the showers instead of bringing him his meals.

He used one sheet of paper to jot down a love letter full of false affection. He did not care about Katherine, but she was a cute girl, and so far, she had proven herself useful to him. There was no point in burning any bridges just yet, especially if a trip to the showers was plausible. Plus, he could use whatever information she was willing to give him to fill in some of the blanks that Seaton had left.

Coy surfaced from the well of his thoughts and blinked when he noticed that said ex-officer still hadn't returned. Hickman had rapped at their cell, his puffed-out face sporting a grin when he told Seaton it was time for his shower. As far as Coy could tell, Hickman made the two of them shower at separate times because he was too much of a lazy slob to monitor two shifters at once. Seaton had looked like a lost child walking next to a giant beast, Hickman's large hand gripping his shoulder and guiding him down the hallway. Coy hoped for Seaton's sake that the Registry had taught him how to defend himself from not only shifters, but from humans, too.

He was sure as hell going to need it.

AUGUST TRIED TO pretend that Hickman wasn't there, but he felt his gaze boring into him, staring at his exposed skin. The water ran slowly, more of a drizzle than a spray. The temperature was not nearly as hot as he would have liked it to be. He washed with a bar of soap that had probably been used by several other shifters that day. He had to use that same soap to wash his hair, as the prison didn't provide them with shampoo. He supposed that he was lucky they even provided soap.

"Had us all fooled, didn't you?" Hickman remarked.

August did not answer him. He was learning quickly that it was better to just be quiet than to engage in any sort of conversation with the officers.

"Oh, I guess you got water in your ears, huh?"

He heard Hickman's footsteps behind him, his boots squeaking against the wet tile.

"I asked you a question."

"I don't know what you're talking about," August said.

"Oh, but I think you do." He pushed August forward, forcing him to brace his hand against the wall to keep from falling against it. "You're lucky I don't kick your ass for what you did. No one would blame me."

"Keep your hands off of me," August spat. He shoved Hickman's hand away, which still lingered near him. It was a bold, but dumb, move. Hickman whipped him around and pitched him to the floor, laughing when August fell face-first against the hard tile.

"Who do you think you are, huh?" Hickman growled.

August attempted to push himself up, but a wet boot appearing at his back held him down. Using the strength from his anger and humiliation, he flipped to his side and gripped Hickman's ankle, trying to wrench it off of him.

All that did was make the officer angrier.

The second Hickman lifted his foot, August tried to scramble away, but Hickman caught him, grabbed him by his wet hair, and tried to slam his face against the floor. Quick thinking and quicker reflexes spurred August to flatten his hands against the floor so that they cushioned the blow. He kicked aimlessly, not caring what part of Hickman's body he came in contact with, just as long as he hit something. A pained cry tore from Hickman's mouth when August's foot finally made contact. Jackpot. He had just enough time to glance back for a perfectly aimed kick to the officer's face.

Again, he tried to get away, but Hickman tackled him. He managed to bite the inside of August's thigh hard enough to break the skin, and August screamed from the pain even as his fingers clawed frantically at Hickman's face. He must have scratched the officer's eye because Hickman cursed and covered it with his hand. August staggered to his feet and prepared to make a dash for the door, but Hickman's fingers wrapped around his ankle and began to pull.

"Let go of me!" August shouted, eyes locked on Hickman's hand as he tried desperately to shake it off.

"What in hell is going on in here?"

August looked up, his face dripping with dirty shower water, and saw Richards standing in front of him. He pleaded with his eyes, begging the director to save him. Yes, he had lied. He had fooled the Registry. He had made them all look like idiots for not recognizing that one of their own was a shifter. Still, he didn't deserve this, didn't deserve to be beaten by a sociopathic monster like Hickman.

"That's enough, Hickman," Richards ordered. "Take Seaton back to his cell."

August was afraid to speak. Richards had saved him, but he worried he might change his mind. He wiped both water—and quite possibly tears—from his eyes and dressed in the clean uniform that Hickman had given him when they first arrived at the showers.

Hickman was not pleased.

On the way back to the cell, he proved this to August by gripping him by the hair and smashing his face into the wall. Blood poured from August's nose. He could not tell if it was broken, but it ached more than all the other aches in his body combined. He had to use his uniform shirt to mop up the blood, staining it.

He'd have to wear it for the next three days.

"You may have gotten lucky this time, you little shit," Hickman muttered, "but Richards won't always be around to save you. Next time, I won't be so nice.

He leaned in, his lips pressed against August's ear.

"You know, I've wanted to stick my dick in you ever since the first day you enlisted. I backed off since Fate seemed to have laid claim to you. I got a lot of respect for that man. But now..." He grinned. "It's only a matter of time."

He grabbed August's face before he could pull away and forced a rough kiss on him, biting at his bottom lip until it bled. August jerked back, afraid to push Hickman off him lest he use the shock collar. He was still damp from his shower. Holding his breath, August kept his eyes averted, suddenly feeling numb. Not really feeling anything at all.

After a tense moment, Hickman scoffed. "Move," he ordered and shoved August down the hall with a sharp elbow smashed into the center of his back.

COY WAS MOMENTARILY distracted by Hickman pushing a bloody Seaton into their cell. Dr. Rowburg obviously noticed it too, but she did not acknowledge Seaton.

"As I was saying, Mr. Conlin. You can expect a visit from us soon. We will not be bringing you into the lab. We will bring the girl to you. Perhaps being in the comfort of your own cell with make things easier for you."

"I already told you, I'm not participating in your fucking breeding program."

"Yes, you have told me that, and as I told you, you do not have a choice. Either you will impregnate the female willingly, or you will be forced. I'm prepared for either scenario."

Dr. Rowburg left without another word to Coy—or her son, for that matter. Hickman followed her.

"What the fuck happened to you?" Coy asked.

Seaton didn't look at him. "I slipped."

He picked up his mattress with shaky hands and tossed it back onto the top bunk. Carefully, he climbed onto his bed, seemingly trying his best not to touch Coy's mattress.

He had. Coy had seen his toes brushing along the edge, but he let it slide. He looked like he had been through enough for one day. Everyone knew what type of sick fuck Hickman was, so he could only imagine what happened to Seaton while in the shower.

After a few moments of silence, Seaton spoke, his voice tired and weak. "What was that about?"

"Your fucked-up mom is trying to force me into a breeding program," Coy answered.

"A breeding program? Why?" Coy couldn't see Seaton, but he heard the shock in his voice.

Coy snorted. "How the hell should I know? She's *your* mom."

"This doesn't make sense. Why would she be trying to breed shifters? This is all wrong."

Coy rolled his eyes and let his head gently fall back against the wall behind their bed. "You're just *now* realizing how wrong all of this is? Why don't you start with why the Registry even exists in the first place."

August didn't reply, but that wasn't surprising. Coy hadn't expected him to.

AUGUST LAY ON his bed and prayed for sleep. When sleep did not come, he prayed for death. That was just as unsuccessful. Every time he closed his eyes, he saw Hickman's large body looming over him, clawing at him, trying to force his way inside of him. Richards had saved him this time, but Hickman was right. The director wouldn't always be around.

August had spent months training. He had learned how to protect himself in countless situations. Now, he was in a situation where all of that training was useless. He could not protect himself—not because he did not know how, but because he had no rights. He understood now why those shifters had given up. What was the point of fighting when the outcome would always be the same?

Below him, he could hear Conlin's deep, steady breaths, like gentle waves crashing against the shore. He knew his mother was a horrible person, but trying to force Coy to breed with other shifters was a new low, even for her. It was a different kind of rape from what Hickman or even Fate were capable of, but it was rape all the same.

He stared up at the ceiling, wondering why any of this had to happen. Maybe he deserved some of what had happened, but Conlin and the others were innocent. They did not deserve to be here.

He thought about Niami dressed in her blue dress with those pretty flowers in her hair. She had looked so happy then. Asuda's youngest person to ever successfully control her shifting. She had been a celebrity among her kind.

And now, she was locked away in a prison cell.

He saw something move in the corner of his eye. He glanced at the cell door and caught sight of a blue, little frog. It hopped awkwardly, almost as though it was patrolling the hallway. It made its way through the food slot and then fell to the floor without so much as a sound. He would have given anything to be that frog. To just hop right through that slot and then out the exit door to freedom.

He wondered how a frog even managed to get inside of the building.

August closed his eyes—and then snapped them open again.

A frog?

Looking over the side of the bed, he stared with wide eyes as the amphibian morphed gracefully into a little girl.

"Officer Seaton?"

August scrambled off the bed, careful not to wake Conlin as he landed on the floor with a soft thud.

"Niami, what the hell are you doing in here?" He snatched a blanket—thin enough to be a sheet—off the bed and wrapped it around her. "How are you... How did you..."

She wasn't wearing her collar.

He remembered how loose it had been the first time he had seen her in her cell. They had not made collars small enough for children because no child around Niami's age could shift, as shifting emerged during puberty. She still had a few years to go.

"I want my mommy," she whispered.

"I know you do." He lowered himself onto his aching knees and hugged her close. "But, right now you have to go back to your cell. Do it the exact same way you came in here, okay? You must make sure you get that collar back on. Do you understand? Get the collar back on and—"

"And what?"

"Niami, how many times have you shifted since you've been here?"

She held up four little fingers.

"Listen, there's something I need you to do for me. It might be scary. But..." August almost told her that it would help her see her mommy sooner, but he couldn't. He couldn't tell her that, not when he couldn't know if the plan would work. He couldn't lie to her. No more lies. Not when she was so scared and lonely.

"But it could help my friend. Could free us. Can you do that?" Friend. He almost laughed. That was the last word he'd use to describe his relationship with Conlin.

She nodded.

She was sweet and innocent and pure. What he was about to ask her to do could put her in danger. Yet, if everything worked out, he could get her back to her mother.

And Conlin would be a free dragon.

THEY HAD GONE over the plan three times. Niami was a smart girl, but she was also young. He wasn't sure how much of it she would remember, or if she would even want to do it when the time came. Even so, it was all they had.

Once she had shifted back and left his cell, August nudged Conlin's shoulder.

"Wake up," he whispered.

Conlin grabbed his wrist quicker than August's eyes could follow. He jerked him downward, pulling him closer until their faces were inches apart.

"What the hell do you think you're doing?"

"Nothing, I…"

"You what?" Conlin growled, sleepiness clinging to his words.

"We need to talk."

"About what?" He gritted out each word as if it pained him to speak. Conlin's grip was so tight that August's fingers were beginning to grow numb.

"I have a plan. One to get you out of here."

Conlin stared at him for a moment and then released August's wrist. He yawned, rubbing at one eye, while the other—the unnerving purple one—continued to stare at August.

"Let's hear it."

Chapter Thirteen

EVEN COVERED IN bloodstained clothing, Seaton looked poised and elegant. He ate his breakfast with the all the grace of a nobleman, his slender fingers gripping a peach and then bringing it up to his lips. He took a bite, and juice dribbled gently down his lips.

He wanted to punch him.

"Is there some reason why you are staring at me?" Seaton asked.

"I'm staring at you because I don't like you," Coy answered.

"All the more reason to look elsewhere."

Coy had been working on a plan that was almost crazy enough to work. He had figured out the basics and it all came down to Katherine. He had to convince her to swap job roles, had written so many love letters begging her to try. If he could persuade her to be the one to take him to the showers, escaping would become that much easier. Katherine was the key. Now he just needed to find the right lock, and he wasn't sure if that Seaton's little frog shifter girl was it. He doubted she would be able to distract Katherine long enough for them to knock her out and grab her ID card, but it was worth a shot.

"How'd you get away with it?"

"Away with what?"

Seaton looked annoyed, eyes narrowed and jaw clenched, each time Coy spoke to him. Coy was certain it had something to do with the fact that he had eaten most of August's breakfast, leaving him with only a couple pieces of fruit.

"With tricking the Registry into believing you were human. Didn't they do blood tests or something?"

"Of course they did," August said, "but my mother runs the lab."

"Then, shouldn't she have gotten in trouble for lying?"

"I told them that she was not aware of my being a shifter."

"Why in the hell would you do something like that?"

"Why does it interest you?" Seaton asked, snapping.

"It doesn't.

"Then stop asking me questions."

"I'll do whatever I want."

Seaton rolled his eyes and went back to eating his peach. He was not the best company, but harassing him beat sitting around doing nothing all day. Seaton did not speak much, but when he did, he was usually sarcastic.

"How old are you?" Coy asked.

"Why?"

"Because I want to know."

"My age is of no importance to you."

"Eighteen?"

"No."

"Twenty?"

"No."

"Twenty-one?"

"Do you have nothing else to do with your time?" Seaton snapped.

Coy grinned. It was too easy to annoy his cellmate. In the short time they had been forced into each other's lives, he'd learned many of the things that irritated Seaton and tried to do at least some of them every day. For instance, Seaton did not like being asked too many questions. He was rather private. Judging by how little he talked, he also did not like a lot of noise. Coy had taken to beating on the walls, the bed frame, or the toilet whenever he was bored.

"Know the first thing I'm going to do when I get out of here?" Coy asked languidly.

"Kill Fate?"

"Well, yeah." That had not been what he was going to say, but that was most definitely the first thing he was going to do. "I mean, provided it was him that killed my grandma, and not you."

Seaton said nothing.

"Know the second thing I'm going to do?"

"No," Seaton said, "but I am sure you will share it with me regardless of whether or not I care."

"I'm gonna find someone to fuck. Been in a bit of a forced dry spell, you know? Had to take care of myself these past few months."

"Yes," Seaton replied. A few seconds of silence stretched between them before he continued. "I heard."

"Did you now?" Coy snickered.

Leaning against the wall, he watched the slight blush spread along Seaton's cheeks. Seaton may have had a smart-mouthed comment for everything Coy said, but he could not hide his body's natural reaction to things that embarrassed him.

Coy decided to log that information into the back of his mind—for later.

COY HADN'T HEARD them slip in.

A hand was on him, inside his pants, stroking him. For a moment, he imagined himself dreaming of the touch of a past lover, teasing and caressing, waking him up in one of the most pleasurable ways. But then, he opened his eyes and saw Dr. Rowburg above him, her brown hand stuffed down his pants.

He jerked beneath her and smacked her hand away from him with a curse. She was not alone. There were others inside his tiny cell. The same female shifter from before, Hickman—who held the woman tight against his body—and a single lab assistant who looked like he did not want to be involved.

Above him, Seaton still slept. His long hair had fallen through the space between the wall and their beds. Lengthy locks of dark hair dangled a few inches away from Coy's arm.

"I told you what to expect, Mr. Conlin." Dr. Rowburg reached for him again. "I gave you the supplement while you slept. You should be feeling the effects soon."

He was *already* feeling the effects. He had never been a modest person, but sitting fully aroused around a bunch of people he hated wasn't something he could exactly be proud about.

"Bring the girl," she ordered. "Remove her clothing."

The woman tried to scream, but her mouth was taped shut. If the bulge in Hickman's pants was any indication, he was enjoying the struggle.

Coy had been too optimistic. Of course, things had not gone the way he had planned. When did they ever? Still, he could not allow this to happen. Not to him, and not to this woman. It was now or never. They had to try even at the risk of failing. Coy reached up, grabbed a handful of Seaton's hair, and yanked down on it. Seaton shouted, cursing and flailing on the bed above him.

"Seaton!" Coy shouted.

"W-What?" Seaton mumbled, his voice thick with sleep.

"A little help here," Coy replied, voice rising in panic.

"What are you talking—" Seaton began to ask before he cut himself off. Suddenly, he cried out, "Now! They're here! The bad people are here! Do it now!" His voice was loud enough to carry past their open cell door and down the hall.

"Be quiet, boy," Dr. Rowburg snapped. "This does not concern you."

Hickman dragged the woman closer to Coy and forced her onto the bed. Sweat rolled down Coy's face and neck, and he panted below her. She had a perfect body from head to toe. He could sink inside of her and stay there for days.

He shook his head, trying to shake those thoughts away.

"Stop!" Coy shouted. "I won't do this. Don't make me do this."

"*Ribbit.*"

Six heads all turned in the direction of the open cell door. Niami stood there, naked and giggling.

"That's what a frog says. Ribbit! Ribbit!"

"What the fuck!" Hickman cursed. "What the hell are you doing in here, kid?"

She did not answer. Instead, she lowered herself onto her hands and hopped backward. The first time, she hopped as a human child. The second, as a brilliant blue frog, speckled with spots of black.

"It's the frog shifter!" Dr. Rowburg screamed. "Get her!"

Hickman and the assistant bolted for the door, chasing after the girl, scrambling and diving along the hall in attempts to catch her.

"Stay back," Dr. Rowburg ordered, pointing at the remaining shifters. She made to rush out of the cell. Coy tackled her. He managed to get an arm around her neck, putting her in a headlock. She scratched at his arms, trying to break free. She was no match for Coy. Eventually, the flailing grew weaker and then stopped altogether.

When he released her, Dr. Rowburg lay on the ground, motionless.

"Is she...?" Seaton asked.

"No," Coy answered. "Do you want to change that?"

Seaton stared down at his mother and shook his head. "You should go. You'll need her employee ID." Seaton crouched down next to her and unclipped a laminated card hanging from her lab coat. After tossing it Coy's way, he pointed at the open cell door. "I need to stay and help Niami. And the other shifters. Go."

Coy started toward the door, but he paused to turn around and stare at Seaton, wasting precious seconds trying to make up his mind.

"Hurry up," Seaton urged. "You will only have a few minutes. If they sound the alarm—" He was interrupted by a blaring bell and flashing lights. "Go!"

Coy cursed and then grabbed ahold of Seaton's wrist, yanking him upright.

"You're coming with me. You can't help anyone from in here." He had made his decision. "And you?" he asked the female shifter as she scrambled to get her clothing back on.

"I have to go back for her," she said.

Coy frowned, uncomprehending. "We don't have time for that. We have to go *now*. Don't you hear the alarms?"

"I will not leave without her." She glared at Coy, and he knew trying to convince her was useless.

"Fine. Do whatever you want. Let's go." He yanked at Seaton's wrist and began to move out of the cell.

"I can't." Seaton tried to pull his hand free, but Coy's grip was relentless. "Let go."

Coy raced out of the room, pausing only once to grab their collars' controllers off of the hook next to their cell door. He rushed down the hall toward the emergency exit stairwell, dragging Seaton with him, whose protests fell on deaf ears. He knew the route. He had studied the map in the lab so much that he could have drawn it from memory alone. The floor was hard and unforgiving against his bare feet. He did not care. He ran faster.

Seaton struggled to pull away from him once more. Coy tightened his grip. He practically slammed against the door to the stairwell, lifting Dr. Rowburg's ID to the scanner. After the red light shone green, they burst through the door and down the stairs, running and panting the entire way down. He could hear voices coming from above them, feet slamming against metal steps. Some of the officers must have spotted them.

"Come on," Coy urged.

He moved quicker than he had ever moved before. The drug was in full effect, and it was painful and awkward to move. But he fought through it. He could see the exit sign just at the bottom of the stairs. They were almost there.

A shot rang out above his head. He ducked. Seaton had enough sense to do the same. Two more shots rang out, and they just barely managed to avoid the bullets as they ricocheted against the metal railings.

The exit door gave way with a push, and they were plunged into the welcoming murkiness of nightfall. He could see the forest just beyond the parking lot, could taste freedom. Coy felt only momentary guilt for the shifters left behind—there was no doubt that the Registry would update the security of the premises after their little prison break. In an afterthought, he dropped Dr. Rowburg's ID, knowing they wouldn't need it anymore.

Coy continued to run, gripping Seaton's wrist like a vice. He ignored the voice inside of his head telling him to go back and find Fate. As much as he wanted to get his revenge, he needed to find Ari first. Not to mention that he had dragged Seaton with him, and now he—annoyingly—felt obligated to be responsible for him. If he went looking for Fate, he wouldn't just be endangering himself. He'd be endangering Seaton, too.

They ran through the parking lot and into the dense forest that surrounded the prison. He heard more shots. The sound of bullets blared into the night in time with their rushing footsteps and the guards' demanding shouts. He kept running, even when it felt like his heart would explode, until finally both the shouting and shooting grew distant...and then silent.

They had moved so far into the dark forest that it would have taken more than a few officers to find them.

Coy stopped to rest, his heart beating like mad. He leaned against a tree to catch his breath, wanting to let go of Seaton's wrist but not trusting him to stay put if he did.

"I have to go back," Seaton said between ragged breaths. "Niami... I have to make sure she's okay. She was supposed to escape with us," he added distractedly, looking back the way from which they came.

"You're staying with me," Coy said, ignoring the guilt.

"She is just a child. I have to protect her."

"Ari was just a kid, and you didn't protect him. You owe me."

"I...I cannot..."

"Just until I find out the truth, once and for all. If it turns out that Fate really did kill Dinina, then I'll let you go back."

Seaton sighed. "What are we supposed to do?"

They may have escaped prison, but they had not escaped danger. They were still in Weren, which was filled with Registry employees. If they were not careful, they would be found in no time.

"We need to travel south," Coy said.

"South? Why?"

"We're going to Sago."

"Sago? Are you mad? It will take us over a week to get there on foot, and that's only if we run the entire time. What's in Sago?"

"Well, for starters," Coy said, "someone I can trust."

Chapter Fourteen

THE FOREST WAS a maze of trees, which at night became a gauntlet. They had stopped running. If someone was chasing them, they would have to do so on foot. It was impossible to drive a vehicle through the dense forest—too many hanging branches and uneven roots. Neither of them knew where they were going, save that they headed vaguely south. All they knew for certain was that they could not stop. They could slow down, and they could rest for a moment. Flat-out stopping was out of the question.

Conlin had more energy than August. More speed and stamina. Even when he was affected by the drug Dr. Rowburg had given him, he moved through the brambles with the stealth of a predator. August dragged himself along the tall grass and fallen leaves like an injured animal. He wanted to stop and think, to figure out their next move. He was dirty, sweaty, and exhausted, and he did not have a plan for getting them to Sago. At this point, adrenaline was the only thing that kept him moving.

As they moved deeper and deeper into the forest, the trees became larger. They towered over them like giants, the dangling branches their arms and the thousands of leaves their fingers, rustling when the wind blew.

Not knowing what they were doing—or quite where they were going—worried him just as much as the thought of any officers following them.

August stopped running.

"Keep moving," Conlin panted.

His face was covered in sweat. Even in the dark, August could see it dripping from his skin. He needed to rest, too.

"We need to stop for now."

"We can't."

"Conlin—"

"I said, keep fucking moving."

"And what?!" August snapped. "You expect us to walk to Sago in a *night*? Are you insane? Look at you? Look at your..."

He wouldn't say it. He couldn't say it. It had to have been painful, running with it like that, hard and straining against his pants.

"My what?"

"Nothing," August replied. "We need a plan."

"I already told you the plan."

"Yes, but your plan is terrible."

"You gotta better one?"

"No, but that's why we're stopping, so I can figure one out."

"Even if you were able to come up with something, what makes you think it would work?"

"My plan got us out of there, didn't it?" August huffed, swatting a bug away from his face. "Well, it got *you* out. I was forced out here against my will."

"You should be thanking me," Conlin said. "If you were still in there, Hickman would be paying you a visit."

August glared at him. For a glorious moment, he pictured punching Conlin in his smug face. One could dream.

"Fine. You've got ten minutes to come up with a plan. After that, we're moving again."

Conlin paced back and forth, waiting for August to come up with his plan. August could tell that he was growing more impatient by the second. He looked like he was ready to start running again.

"We need to know where we are."

"You'd know that better than me. I was knocked out when you fuckers brought me here."

"We are in Weren," August said. "And, what I mean is that we need to know where the forest will lead us, since we cannot go back to town—not if we want to avoid getting arrested. If we are indeed moving south and stay the course, we should hit the outskirts of Nenzo, Olra, and then Fiasu. But, I do not know those areas well enough to know what to expect."

"Did you study a map or something before they locked you up?"

"I believe what you are referring to is school. I took my education seriously. Though, I'm certain the same cannot be said for you."

"I had more important things to focus on. Like how hard I should punch someone who thought they could get away with insulting my intelligence."

They grew silent, glaring at one another. Their staring match only broke when a white hare interrupted it, sprinting past them like a fallen cloud rolling along the forest floor. They couldn't help but startle, although both pretended that they hadn't.

"Anyway, if the forest is gonna take us all the way to Fiasu, what's the problem? We get there, and it won't take us long to get to Sago. Fiasu's a small town. Smaller than Hamet."

"Well, first of all, the forest will only lead us to Nenzo, and after that we'll have to deal with the Olraian plains. Only then will we reach Fiasu. The *problem* is that Sago is on the other side. As in, the fastest way to Sago would be to go *through* Fiasu. I don't know anything about Fiasu."

"Fiasu's filled with peddlers and people trying to make money. No big deal."

"No big deal," August repeated. "It's an enormous deal. If the Registry alerts the rest of Asuda of our escape and offers a reward for our heads, there will be a mob after us."

Conlin shrugged as if having a group of money-hungry people after him would not have been a first for him. "Then, we'll just wear disguises."

"Disguises." August threw up his hands in exasperation. "A fantastic idea. Which costumes do you think would work best for someone with two different color eyes?"

"Oh, yeah..."

August sighed again. Their conversation was getting them nowhere. It would only be a few hours before daylight. Soon, they would need to find someplace to sleep.

"Anyway," Conlin said. "While you're thinking up a plan, we need to get these damn collars off."

August nodded. "Do you still have the controllers?"

"Yeah. This one's mine." He handed the controller to August.

"Hold still." August stood on his toes behind Conlin and sighed. "Could you bend down a little?"

Conlin crouched down lower than was necessary. August was sure he did it as a taunt. He was shorter than Conlin, but he wasn't *that* short. Carefully, he slid the back of the controller off, revealing a metal pin hidden inside. It was the width of a sewing needle. It felt like he was holding nothing between his fingers.

There was just enough light coming from the moon, allowing him to see what he was doing. Still, if he were to jab Conlin in the side of his neck with the pin...well, that would have hardly been his fault.

"Do not move."

He moved the pin along the slit where the two ends of the collar joined together. Holding his breath, he dragged the pin along the slit until the collar split, cracking like an oyster shell.

"You did it," Conlin said excitedly.

August held back a grin at the tone of his voice.

Conlin stood up so suddenly that he knocked August off-balance. He fell backward, pin flying out of his hand, ass smashing against a bed of grass and twigs. August was too tired to glare at him.

"Give me the other controller."

"Actually, I think I'll hold on to this for a while," Conlin answered, grinning.

The words hit him like a fist. He had just removed Conlin's collar, had given him back his ability to shift. He had freed the beast. A beast which probably still believed that August was responsible for killing his grandmother.

WAVES SPLASHED AGAINST rocks and rolled onto the shore. Coy had heard the creek ten minutes before he saw it. Seaton had protested the change in their route, but grew quiet once he saw the water, cool and glistening beneath the night sky.

They drank. The water burned at first—not because it was hot, but because their mouths were dry as deserts. Coy stripped down afterward, walking into the water, feeling its coolness lap against his skin.

He had torn the hem off of his prison uniform shirt and made it into a makeshift sling into which he'd tucked the controller to Seaton's collar. He saw the resentment in Seaton's face as it swung from side to side against Coy's chest like a pendulum. From the water, he watched Seaton undress and shake off dirt and leaves from his clothing before laying it flat on the grass. He kept his distance, something Coy found amusing. He didn't have anything Coy had not already seen.

Seaton tested the temperature of the water like a cat. Toes dipping inside, before sinking in altogether. He did not rush inside like Coy, eager to be cool and clean. He took his time, letting the water welcome him like the cautious hands of a first-time lover.

Coy did not like him, but the picture of him wet and dripping—his long hair clinging to his back and floating along the water—was a pretty one.

"Are you going to stare at me all night?" Seaton remarked bitingly.

"Why? Does me staring at you make you uncomfortable?"

"I happen to find it more annoying than uncomfortable."

"What's the difference? Either way, deal with it. Or, maybe I could just spend the next couple of hours pressing this button to give myself something else to do." He looked down at the controller hanging from his neck. If Seaton had something that he wanted to say, he kept it to himself. "We'll rest here for the night. The trees aren't as dense by the river, so we'll see anyone trying to sneak up on us. And I'll smell them."

"Can you not just fly us to Sago?"

Coy gave Seaton an incredulous look, wondering whether he was joking. "It's just as you said. If the Registry has alerted Asuda of our escape, people will be watching the skies for a dragon to fly by."

"There are other dragons in Asuda. How would they know it's you?"

"For one, I am not a small dragon. Two, all the others are back at the prison."

"You can't be that big."

"I am *very* big." He made sure to emphasize so that the statement had a double meaning.

Seaton rolled his eyes and began to make his way back to shore.

"How long do you think it will take to get us out of Weren on foot?" Coy asked Seaton's retreating back.

"I want to first wait until sunrise to make certain we're traveling south, but if we keep up our pace and only stop a few times a day, we should cross over to Nenzo in a couple of days," Seaton answered. "Nenzo is a moderately wealthy town, but if I remember correctly, the east side is mostly swampland. It may be hard to cross."

"Hard for you, maybe. I can fly," Coy remarked, deliberately contradicting himself.

Seaton didn't bother with a retort. He bent down to retrieve his clothing and then began to dress. Sweat must have dried into the clothing. It mixed with the bloodstains already there, creating an awful, unique smell that Coy easily picked up on even from a distance.

"You know," Coy observed, "it'd be easy to mistake you for a woman from behind."

"Do you ever consider keeping your mouth shut?"

"I consider a lot of things."

"Is not speaking one of them?"

"What was it like having Rowburg for a mom?"

The question must have caught Seaton off guard. He leaned against a tree, stiff as a broomstick. His wet hair saturated his shirt on both sides, his skin bleeding through.

"Was it as awful as I think it was?"

Seaton shook his head. "It was worse."

"Look, if it comes down to it. If they're closing in on us, and she's with them. I'll kill them. All of them, including her."

Seaton had pushed himself away from the tree as Coy spoke. His fingers were in his hair, fighting with the wet strands as he attempted to twist them into one large braid down his back.

"I will not hold it against you."

"You wouldn't care if I killed your mother? I know she's a bitch and all, but, really? You really wouldn't care?"

Seaton shrugged.

IF FELT LIKE they'd been walking forever.

If the Registry had alerted Asuda of their escape, they had heard nothing about it. Of course, they were still wandering through the forest, so they had no way of knowing. The news could have been all over Asuda by now.

And yet, August wasn't so sure about that. The Registry prided themselves, as an organization, on being adept. If two prisoners had escaped their walls, those who did not support the Registry would have even more of a reason to oppose it. If they were going to announce a shifter's escape, they would only tell their allies, who resided, naturally, in only the wealthy parts of Asuda. Since they were going south, the chances of them running into rich Registry supporters decreased, whereas the chances of them running into poor independents willing to do anything for money increased. They would have to take their chances with the latter.

"They're still coming," Conlin muttered. "They're far behind, but they're coming. I can smell them."

The news was frustrating. They had gotten so far ahead. How did the Registry even know what direction they were going? There was no way they could be using bloodhounds—most dogs avoided August. He couldn't imagine what they'd do if they caught a whiff of Conlin's dragon scent. Did the officers have some special device that...

August stopped walking.

"Oh, no."

The chip.

"What?" Conlin said. "Can't you walk and talk at the same time? We gotta keep moving. Didn't you just hear me say that they were coming?"

"They are going to find us."

"They won't if we keep moving." Conlin spared him a look and then walked back with a sigh when he saw that August hadn't budged.

"The *chip*."

"What? What the hell are you talking about?"

Dread consumed August and swallowed him whole, drowning him in an ocean of despair. Despite everything, they had gotten out, but no matter how much they increased their distance from the Registry, they would be found. Conlin was still chipped.

"The chip," August repeated, frustration spilling over into his words. "The one in your thigh. We can travel all day, but we will not get rid of them. They are tracking us. They are tracking *you*."

"Fuck."

August slumped against a tree. He felt defeated. Among the chaos of their escape, he had never thought to even consider Conlin's chip.

Conlin pulled down his pants. August got whiplash from turning away. "Come here. I need your help."

"My help with what?"

"Stop asking questions and just get your ass over here."

August shook his head slowly, looking up at the canopy above them and not at anything below Conlin's waist.

Out of the corner of his eye, August saw Coy gesture downward as he said, "Feel it for me."

"Are you *insane*?" August exclaimed, stunned. He was depressed by the news, too, but not enough to do anything sexual with Conlin before they were hauled back to prison.

"No, stupid. The chip. Find it. I'm going to need you to hold it in place while I cut it out."

Yes, Conlin was definitely insane.

"You can't be serious."

"Get over here," Conlin growled.

August moved toward Conlin until he stood in front of him. He lowered himself down to his knees and dragged his fingers along Conlin's thigh. His cheeks burned at their compromising position. Conlin's skin was warm beneath his touch, his dark hair smooth. Finally, he felt a lump beneath the skin the size of pill capsule, and he pressed down gently on it to make sure it was the chip.

"Found it."

"Good. Don't move."

Talons broke the skin and pierced through flesh. Conlin cursed and gritted his teeth. "Push it up."

August did as he was told, his fingers wet with blood. The chip popped out of Conlin's thigh. He removed his hand, and Conlin tore a strip of fabric from his already tattered shirt and used it to stop the bleeding. The wound was superficial. The chip had only been under the skin and so would not cause any significant problems other than a bit of soreness. It was unfortunate that they did not have any antiseptic, so August made a mental note to keep an eye out for infection.

"There," Conlin said. "Now we have nothing to worry about."

August was silent for a moment. "Right." They still had plenty of things to worry about. He wiped his hands off on his own bloodstained shirt. He was starting to look like abstract art. "Are you okay to keep moving?"

"Of course. It takes much more than that to bring me to my knees," Conlin said with a leer.

August didn't bother to hide his eye roll. "Spare me the details. We should stop for the night soon."

Conlin nodded. "Let's head back to the water, so I can get rid of this thing once and for all."

"That is a good idea," August replied. "Perhaps you can wash the wound, too."

They began to walk back in the direction of the water. Conlin glanced down at the makeshift bandage wrapped around his thigh. "Thanks, by the way."

August responded with a slight shrug. "Don't mention it."

THEY MADE CAMP near a massive tree. If it could be called that, as camp consisted of only the two of them, surrounded by the woods.

August worried about food. Conlin had disappeared into the darkness, presumably to remedy this, but August doubted they had many options. Now that they had gotten rid of the tracker, August was a little less worried about the Registry finding them. They deserved a few hours of rest before they started moving again. Regardless, they needed to be careful, as the Registry would have the advantage in numbers. Then again, Conlin could shift if they were in any real trouble. Still, who knew what weapons the Registry had built in preparation for dealing with him? Ironically, August probably would have known had he stayed in the lab. Not that he would have been in this situation had he done so.

The Registry had once claimed that protecting humans and shifters were their number one priority, but August had come to understand this as a facade. Even if the sovereign's daughter had not been attacked, something like this still would have happened. The Registry did not exist to protect. It existed to punish. To torture. To break a shifter down until there was nothing left except an empty husk of a human form.

Conlin returned, holding his shirt like a sack. He stopped in front of August and opened it. Fish fell from the wet fabric like they had been cut from a net. He bent down to grab one of them, smirked at August, and then opened his mouth. Suddenly, his breath was fire. It blew from his mouth. Beneath the flames, fish crackled and cooked. When he was finished, he used his fingers to split the fish open. Talons. Much like his grandmother's, except longer. *Sharper.*

His entire hand had been encased in flames, yet it was unscathed.

"Useful," August noted.

Conlin winked at him and bit into the fish like an animal, tearing into bones and scales. August cringed.

"What's your animal, anyway?" Conlin asked, still chewing even as he began to roast another fish.

"It is of no real importance."

"Useless, huh?" Conlin tossed a well-cooked fish over at August. "Something weak? Like a rabbit or squirrel?" He chewed with his mouth open.

August curled his lips back in disgust. "No."

"Weaker? Like what, a hummingbird? You're a hummingbird, aren't you?"

"I am *not* a hummingbird."

"That's it, isn't it?" Conlin laughed. "You're a fucking hummingbird."

"You are a moron."

Conlin had been considerate enough to split his fish open, too. August picked at it, grabbing out bits of meat with his fingers.

"No, I'm a *dragon*. And *you* are a fucking *hummingbird*." He laughed again.

They ate in silence after that. All things considered, Conlin was a decent cook. August could only imagine the things he ate as a dragon. He had bit through that fish like a grizzly bear chomping salmon.

After dinner, Conlin offered to keep watch while August slept. August was wary of the offering but too tired to come up with potential scenarios of how Conlin could murder him while he slept.

"Wake me up when you are ready to switch shifts." He lay on his back, his head resting against his interlaced hands.

Conlin said, "'Night, hummingbird."

MOST OF THE time, Coy didn't like complaining. It never solved anything and only made the situation worse. He kept this thought in mind even when he was tempted to grouse about how tired he was of walking. They'd been at it for most of the day.

"It's freezing," Seaton whined, rubbing at his arms. "I wish I had something warmer to wear."

And Seaton had been griping about the weather for just as long.

"Well, crying about it isn't going to make things better for you, is it?" Coy replied.

Seaton huffed and tried to arrange his hair so that it completely covered his arms. "I'm not crying."

"Might as well be," Coy retorted.

Based on the calculations Seaton had given him earlier, they were several hours away from crossing the border between Weren to Nenzo when the storm started. Neither of them had expected it, and Coy had only smelled it seconds before it started.

They sprinted past trees, slipping on mud as they searched for shelter. The river followed them, playing a splashing melody of heavy raindrops. Their thin, drenched clothing stuck to their skin. They had to shout over the falling rain slamming against the ground to hear each other.

"Keep going!" Coy urged. "We'll seek shelter under the biggest tree we can find. It's going to be impossible to keep going in this weather. We'll have to…" Coy squinted, trying to make out the odd shape in the distance.

"Have to what?!" Seaton shouted back. He wiped the rain from his wet face with an even wetter hand.

"Look." Coy pointed straight ahead.

It was a house. Well, a shack—but to them, it was a five-star resort. It would shield them from the rain, which was all Coy cared about.

They rushed forward, kicking up mud as their toes dug into the earth. They reached it and then bolted inside. They did not even bother to check if it was inhabited by someone else.

There was not much within. A mat that looked like an animal had either died or given birth on it. A broken chair that sat in the corner of the room like a disfigured, abandoned doll.

No food. No water. No clothing.

Still, it would keep them dry.

"Do you think it's okay for us to be here?" Seaton asked. "What if the owner comes back?"

"You think someone owns this beat-up shack? If anything, random people use this thing when hunting. Or to fuck. Or escape the weather. Same thing we're using it for. We must be getting closer to Nenzo."

"I guess." Seaton didn't sound too confident. Coy didn't have the patience to convince him.

"We're out of the rain, aren't we? Stop being so paranoid about everything."

"We are fugitives," Seaton remarked wryly.

"We're innocent," Coy disagreed. "Well, *I'm* innocent. I still don't know about you." He stripped, peeling off his clothes as if they were a second skin. He laid them in a corner of the room, standing tall and obscenely nude in the small shelter. "You better do the same, or you'll be walking around in damp clothes all day tomorrow."

"You are rather domestic for a dragon," Seaton said after a pause. Coy expected to turn and find himself being ogled, but the ex-officer was watching the storm, expression thoughtful.

"Nina wanted to make sure I could be independent, so I wouldn't die if anything happened to her. I guess she was thinking ahead of time," Coy admitted, words soft, lost in a fond memory of her trying to teach him how to properly fold laundry.

"Why do you refer to her by name like that? She was your grandmother, was she not?"

"Yeah, so?"

"So, why do you not call her grandmother?"

Coy snickered. "She thought being called grandmother made her seem old."

"She did not look very old."

"She was, but dragons age slower than everyone else. How quickly do hummingbirds age?"

"I told you, I am not a hummingbird."

"Sure you're not."

Coy walked over to the mat and flipped it over. It was less dirty on the other side. No stains. Just dirt and dust. He lay down, unbothered by his nudity. He had grown used to being nearly naked in front of people. Being completely naked wasn't much different.

Besides, it wasn't like he had anything to be shy about.

"I will keep watch if you want to sleep," Seaton offered.

"I suppose I could catch a bit of sleep while we wait out the storm."

"Sleep well."

"Thanks," Coy said. "By the way, if you try to steal your controller off me while I'm sleeping, I'll burn that pretty face of yours."

Seaton huffed.

THEY WOKE UP early, still worried about the Registry finding them and eager to get moving. Seaton had not taken Coy's advice about taking off his clothes to dry. He walked like a crab, widening his thighs to keep his pants from sticking to him. He tried to be discreet about it. Coy smirked at him to let him know he was doing a terrible job of it.

As they walked, the trees began to thin and gave way to swampland. Seaton excitedly pointed out that they must be nearing, if not already in, the territory of Nenzo. Eventually, they discovered a path of solid ground and followed it. It seemed to stretch on for hours, but it beat trying to trudge through murky water.

For someone who had never experienced life outside of Hamet or Sago—disregarding the several weeks he spent at the prison in Weren—Coy adjusted to the change in their surroundings with ease.

Seaton was less willing to adapt.

He swatted at flies and mosquitoes—both of which seemed attracted to him. "We're going to be in trouble if we're still on this path at nightfall," Seaton warned. "Can't make a camp when half the land is covered in swamp."

"We're bound to run into a shelter or two along the way."

They continued south, feet squishing and squelching against the ground beneath them.

"Where are you from, anyway, hummingbird?"

"Osin."

Seaton had obviously given up on trying to stop Coy from calling him by his new nickname. Coy smirked to himself, looking away.

"What's it like?"

"Beautiful. And clean. No swamps."

Coy snickered. "You're not used to any of this, are you?"

"I've never broken out of a prison before."

"I haven't either, smartass. I mean *this*. Nature. The wilderness. You can't handle it."

Seaton frowned. "I had a pretty sheltered life."

"Yeah, no fucking kidding. With a mom like Rowburg, I think anyone—" He paused. "Someone's coming."

He grabbed Seaton by the arm, went off the path, and crouched down, hiding behind the tall, thick reeds surrounding them. Coy pulled Seaton close, making them a smaller target. Seaton's back pressed heavily against his chest as they waited in silence, both watching to see who would come down the path.

He had learned to ignore the weird smell that emanated from Seaton's body. Now that he was so close, whenever Coy inhaled, the scent assailed him. It frustrated him because he *knew* that smell, only he did not know why or how. He wanted to pull Seaton back and breathe him in just as much as he wanted to shove him and tell him to get away.

It was infuriating.

After what felt like hours of waiting, a man walked down the trail. He stuffed his hands into his pockets and shook his head. His pants were unbuttoned, as if he'd left somewhere in a rush. An unlit cigarette hung from his lips.

"Where is…? If she finds out, I'm dead," the man muttered to himself. "Will she…will she smell her on me? I should have showered. I shouldn't have…" He looked down at his wristwatch. "I need to hurry."

They stayed put until they could no longer see him and then carefully stood up.

"I wonder what that was about," Seaton commented.

"Looks like he cheated on his wife."

"How did you get that from those rambles? He smelled like a brewery."

"He smelled like sex." Coy stared in the direction from which the man had come, spotting a large, white house in the distance, at least a mile or so away.

Seaton scoffed. Wordlessly, they continued down the path.

"Tell me more about Osin."

"What do you want to know?" Seaton asked after a moment, chewing on his lip.

"Doesn't matter. What's your home like?"

Seaton smiled, perhaps lost in thought. It was the first time Coy had ever seen him smile, as far as he could remember. It made him look sweet and innocent, like he could do no wrong. Coy almost snorted. He knew that wasn't true.

"It is surrounded by roses. There's a garden out back that—"

"A garden?"

"It's a hobby. A therapeutic one."

Coy thought about his grandmother and Ari. "You lived alone?"

"I think you know the answer to that question."

"How'd they catch you, anyway? If you'd gone so long without anyone knowing. What happened? What'd you do wrong?"

"It was Fate," Seaton admitted. "I don't know if he had gotten suspicious, or if he just wanted to check on me after I left work so abruptly. He must have seen me, either when I shifted, or when I shifted back. He hit me in the head with his gun, and that was it."

"Why'd you shift?"

"I told you, I cannot control it. I do not know when it'll happen. I just *feel* it. Once I learn the science behind it, then I can—"

"Science." Coy snorted. "There's no science behind it. Shifting is based on emotions. If you can't control your shifting, it means you can't control your emotions. If you can't shift, it's because you're fucked up, emotionally," he reiterated helpfully.

"Thank you," Seaton said, sarcasm dripping from his words like snake venom. "I had no idea I would be receiving therapy from someone who thinks it's normal to bite into the entirety of a fish."

Coy grinned. "You're just mad because you can't shift. One, because you don't know how. And two, because I have this." He pointed down at the controller resting against his chest.

"You are a child." Seaton rolled his eyes and then seemingly caught sight of what Coy thought was a wad of trash lying on the trail. "No way." He rushed forward, pulling ahead of Coy, and then bent down and snatched the trash from the ground. "Look."

Coy jogged to catch up with him and saw the crumpled money in his hand.

"That must have been what that drunk was going on about. And look over there." He pointed over at the house he'd noticed a few minutes ago. "Maybe we can pay someone for something to eat."

Seaton frowned, and Coy saw the hesitation on his face.

"I don't know. Nenzo may not be very welcoming to escaped shifters."

Coy shrugged. "If not, we'll do what we have to do."

"I hope it won't have to come to that," Seaton muttered.

Chapter Fifteen

IT DIDN'T HAVE to come to that. The doorman barely spared them a glance before letting them in despite their harried state, strange attire, and August's questionable collar. August wondered if it had anything to do with the fact that the house was a brothel.

The ladies of this Nenzo brothel welcomed anyone as long as they had money. Fortunately, that bumbling drunk had paid for August and Conlin to each enjoy a night of luxury.

Despite the relatively early hour, women were scattered about the room like sparkling ornaments. All shapes and sizes and varying shades. A buffet in Conlin's eyes—a complicated puzzle in August's.

"Have you gentlemen decided?"

The woman who spoke was the lady of the house. Her brown hair, peppered with gray around the hairline, was pulled into a loose bun on top of her head.

"I'll take those two," Conlin said.

"Those two" were full-figured, large-breasted women who were nestled on the couch together, touching each other and giggling. August was certain it was for show. He bet they did this anytime a client walked through the door. If Conlin noticed, he did not care.

"And for you, sir?"

"Just the room, please," August replied.

From the look on her face, his answer had not been one she was expecting, but she was prepared for it. "If you prefer men, we also—"

"The room is fine," August assured.

"As you wish. I'll have Laura show you to your room. If you happen to change your mind, you'll see she's well-equipped to handle any of your needs."

August didn't know what that meant and did not care.

Conlin was tugged away by the two women, both clinging to either of his arms and guiding him down the hallway and up the stairs. August rolled his eyes.

Laura, a young woman with reddish-blonde hair, led him up the same stairs and stopped before an open door. "If there's anything else I can do for you, please let me know. You're paying as much for this room as you would for one of us. Wouldn't you like to get your money's worth?"

"It's a lovely room, thanks." He stepped inside and shut the door before she could breeze past.

It had not been an exaggeration. The room was lovely. A large bed was pushed against the wall adjacent to him. A couch decorated in a pattern of flowers rested below a pair of casement windows. The floor was hardwood, creaking like old stairs when August walked across it.

August sighed happily when he saw the bathroom. The bathtub-shower, sink, and toilet called to him like old friends, welcoming him after a long time apart. He decided to take a bath, turning the tap to let the water run. They had been traveling for days, living off nothing except berries and fish. He was covered in sweat and grime and couldn't wait to relax in a hot bath and then eat anything that wasn't a fish or didn't grow from trees.

He watched with a mixture of disgust and fascination as the tub of translucent water became a cauldron of muddy broth. He was covered in bug bites, and the particularly nasty one on his upper thigh—courtesy of Hickman—had scarred and wasn't looking to disappear anytime soon.

After scrubbing away the worst of it, he took a shower to rinse off the remainder of the dirt that clung to his skin. Tiny bottles of shampoo and conditioner sat on a shelf built into the wall. He helped himself to them.

Once out of the shower, he felt better than he had in days. Maybe Conlin would stop complaining about his smell now—not like he had room to talk. He smelled more than August.

A blue satin robe hung on the bathroom door. August slid it on and shivered. It seemed like ages since he had worn something that wasn't covered in dirt, sweat, or blood.

The bed looked inviting, covered in fluffy pillows and cotton sheets. He grinned and fell face-first on top of it, letting his body sink into the mattress. The sheets smelled clean, flowery and sweet. Even if they hadn't been, he would not have cared. He had slept outside on the ground beneath trees. Sleeping on sex-stained sheets was top-class compared to that.

The bath—and shower—combined with the relaxing fragrance of jasmine and vanilla proved too much for him. Sleep claimed him in seconds.

However, it did not claim him long.

He woke up to chorus of shouting. For a brief few seconds, he thought the Registry had found them. That was until he realized that the shouts were actually moans coming from the room next to his.

He did not need to guess whom those moans were coming from.

"Damn it," he muttered.

He used two pillows to cover his ears, pressing them hard against his face to drown out the cries of passion leaking through the unfortunately thin walls. He just wanted to sleep, but the women were so loud, shouting and squealing like gutted pigs. A show to build up the confidence of their customers. Was it necessary for them to be so loud? Conlin was already cocky enough without their help.

It took nearly an hour for the noises to stop. August pulled the pillows away from his head and settled onto his back. Finally, he could get some much-needed rest.

COY LAY ON his back, hands tucked behind his head. His guests for the afternoon, Lynn and Justina, splayed out next to him. Justina was asleep, her head resting on top of his chest, hair tickling his skin. Lynn was still awake, her blue eyes staring up at Coy in admiration.

"How soon will you be leaving?" she asked, her voice sounding faraway. Probably because he was drifting to sleep.

"Tomorrow morning."

She nuzzled her head against Coy's chin like a cat. "You can't stay longer?"

"Got things to do."

"What's this for?"

"Mm?"

He closed his eyes, but the sudden yell coming from the next room over made him open them again. Sounded like Seaton was finally learning to enjoy himself.

"You hear that?" he asked with a sleepy smile on his face. "I didn't think he had it in him." Glancing to the side, he saw Lynn leaning over the nightstand, her fingers pressing the button on the controller he had left there for safekeeping.

"Shit. Don't do that." He snatched the controller from her manicured hand. "Sorry!" he shouted, hoping Seaton could hear him on the other side of the wall. When he did not get a response, he climbed out of the bed, ignoring Lynn's protest, and stepped out into the hall.

Seaton's door was unlocked, so he peeked inside.

Seaton lay on top of the bed, panting and gripping the collar around his neck. He did not move when Coy stepped into the room, but his eyes darted Coy's way, acknowledging him.

"Uh...hey. Sorry about that. I was dosing off, and one of the girls got curious."

Seaton mustered up enough energy to throw one of the pillows at him. It fell a foot away from the bed, several feet away from Coy.

"*Asshole.*"

"You okay?"

"Get out."

"Really. I swear it wasn't on purpose." Coy scratched sheepishly at the back of his neck. He really did feel bad for Seaton. Getting shocked by the collars hurt more than anything he had ever experienced. "Do you want me to—"

"Go away?" Seaton snapped "Yes, I would like that very much."

"Uh, okay. I guess I'll, um, see you tonight? We'll talk more about the plan. Figure out where to go from here?"

Seaton's only answer was a glare.

AUGUST COULDN'T SLEEP. The series of shocks from the collar had woken up both his mind and his body.

It was his first time in a brothel. The funny thing about brothels was that, if you weren't fucking, there was nothing else to do. No television to watch, and no books to read. Just a bed—for fucking—and a bathroom to wash away the evidence.

What was so great about sex, anyway? He wondered if maybe he should call Laura and see what the fuss was all about. He wasn't exactly sure if he was attracted to her, or any woman for that matter, though the lady of the house did say they had men available, too...

He decided against it.

Instead, he thought about his own version of "the plan," as Conlin had called it. Conlin's plan only consisted of getting his revenge on Fate and finding Ari. If and when he managed to do that, the Registry would still be after him. They would have even more reason to recapture him if he killed one of their own, especially someone as respected as Fate. Conlin would have to spend the rest of his life running from the Registry. If that's what he wanted to do, that was his business.

August had no desire to spend the rest of his life fleeing from anyone. Though the mere thought made him panic, he acknowledged that he had to learn more about the attack on Noralani. He had no real way of knowing, but he was certain Fate knew more about it than he had shared in the lab. If he and Conlin got their hands on Fate, August could force it out of him. Then he could decide where to go from there.

The sovereign had not always hated shifters. It was even rumored that his wife had been a shifter. One or both of his daughters might grow up to become one. None of it added up.

He wished his thoughts had not been so diluted by all the things Fate had told him. He would have done anything Fate had told him just to receive his praise.

August had spent his entire life trying to please people. The first time he went off to do his own thing, to follow a path that he wanted to take, it ended up backfiring on him. Regardless, he couldn't let one mishap, no matter how huge it was, be the deciding factor in how he lived his life.

Somehow, someway, he would convince the sovereign to free the shifters. He could not let them rot away in cells they didn't belong in. They deserved to be in their own homes with their families and friends, people who loved them. They didn't deserve to feel lost and lonely and useless.

Like him.

He would help Conlin, and he would save the shifters. Once he had done that, he would leave Asuda. He would find some faraway land to explore. He would start over, start fresh. Somewhere no one knew him. He wouldn't take just what was thrown at him—he would live the way he had always wanted to. He would have friends, maybe even a lover.

For the first time in his existence, he would truly experience *life*.

August fell asleep with a smile on his face.

THE SKY WAS dark when Coy woke up. The ladies were gone, probably attending to other customers. Maybe sleeping in their own beds. Coy neither knew nor cared.

He climbed out of bed, clutching his robe closed, and slipped out into the corridor. The next-door room was still unlocked, which meant that he had not changed his mind. It was a shame. Getting laid would have probably relaxed him. It always worked for Coy.

He opened the door. "Hummingb—" No. He was certain that he was still pissed at him for the little accident with the collar. It was probably best to call him by his first name for the sake of damage control. "August?"

It was too bad though. Coy did not see the harm in the nickname. It was cute. Hummingbirds were cute. Useless—but cute.

Just like August.

Carefully, Coy sat down on the edge of the bed. August slept on his back. He reminded Coy of a doll with long eyelashes and even longer hair. His lips were that natural kind of pink that made him look like he was wearing lipstick. His thighs were parted just enough to show off smooth skin, except for the mark on his thigh in the shape of teeth. It looked too old to have come from any of the ladies. Everything above that was well-hidden beneath the robe he had fallen asleep in.

He was as beautiful as he was when they first met—maybe more so now because he was covered in neither the black Registry uniform nor the white one. Coy leaned down to get a better look at his face.

His lips looked soft.

"Can I help you?" August muttered, grogginess lingering in his tone.

Coy sat up and cleared his throat. "Wanted to talk about the plan, but you were sleeping."

"So, you felt it necessary to sit on my bed and wait for me to wake up?"

"I thought maybe you had died. You know, from earlier."

August shoved Coy away from him.

"Come on," Coy complained, catching himself before he could tip over. "I said I was sorry. I was falling asleep. Otherwise, I would never have let her do it."

"And you expect me to believe that?"

"I'm serious."

"Spare me."

"Okay, look. You want to make things even? Fine. Here." He turned so that his cheek was facing August. "Punch me."

"What?"

"Come on. Punch me as hard as you can. I won't even try to stop—"

He had not been prepared. More importantly, he had not expected August to have such a powerful right hook. He'd been in the middle of speaking when he felt the force of it, August's knuckles smashing into his face so violently that he bit down on his own tongue, hard enough to draw blood.

The room fell silent.

He held his cheek in his hand, cradling it like a child. His tongue was a puddle of blood, wet and throbbing in his mouth. August stared at him, his brown eyes narrowed in satisfaction. Coy opened his mouth and blood dribbled down his lips and onto his chin. He swallowed, cringing at the taste.

August's eyes widened with realization.

Coy caught him just before he tried to lunge off the bed. He was strong—stronger than he looked—but not stronger than Coy. It took effort to get a hold of both of his wrists and pin them down against the mattress, yet he managed it.

"I'm sorry," August pleaded. Without the use of his arms, he flailed his legs, but Coy slid between them, widening his knees so that even if August did try to kick, he would only manage to kick at the air. "I didn't mean to."

"Funny," Coy growled. "That sounds awfully similar to what I told you."

"You told me to hit you."

"You didn't let me finish what I was saying."

"We're even now." He writhed beneath Coy, jerking like a fish snatched from the ocean.

"Stop fucking squirming."

"Get off."

Coy smirked down at August's struggle. He got a sick sort of satisfaction out of watching August trying to break free of his hold. Probably something in his dragon blood that made him enjoy seeing something beneath him. Coy liked power. He liked being in control. He liked staring down at August, strong but helpless.

And so pretty.

"You know," Coy began, leaning down so his lips were near August's cheek, "I wouldn't even need to shift to kill you right now." His words were hot against August's ear. "I could just bite through a vein in your neck. Right here—right now. It'd happen so quickly that you'd be dead before you could scream."

"I said I was sorry." August whimpered.

"You were a smart kid in school, right, hummingbird? Do you know what dragons used to eat before they evolved? Come on. Take a wild guess."

August did not speak.

"They ate *people*." Coy dragged his lips along August's cheek and then down to his neck. That scent was still there, stronger than ever. Coy hated it—and *craved* it. "I wonder how you taste." His tongue was a snake, slithering against August's neck until it reached his ear, just beneath his earlobe.

It was supposed to be a joke to punish August for hitting him so fucking hard. He just wanted to scare him, to teach him his place, but then...

"What's that?" Coy asked. Something hard had jabbed his thigh.

"N-Nothing," August answered. He froze, blinking rapidly.

It was *definitely* something.

"*Nothing*," Coy repeated. He rubbed his thigh against it. "Is this what *nothing* feels like?"

"Please," August breathed out. Coy noticed the reddening of his cheeks as he closed his eyes.

"If so, then I gotta say, hummingbird—" Coy continued to move his thigh, making August gasp beneath him. "—nothing feels a lot like *something*."

He looked down at August, who had seemingly grown brave enough to open his eyes and stare back up at him. Coy knew that look. It was a look that asked, *Will there be more?* He had been on the receiving end of it multiple times.

"You like that, hummingbird?" Coy pressed down firmly. His body reacted to the strangled cry that fell from August's mouth.

"Was that a yes?"

There was a brief knock before a voice called, "I brought you dinner," as the door to August's room suddenly began to open. "I figured you could use something to eat, and after that, maybe we could—" Laura's sentence stopped short, and her eyes widened at seeing the two of them together.

Coy released his hold on August's wrists and sat upright, turning so that his body faced the wall opposite of the door. August sat up as well, his cheeks flushed, snatched a pillow, and used it to cover his lap.

"T-Thank you."

"I'll just sit it here." Laura placed a dinner tray on top of the dresser next to the door and left as quickly as she'd come.

"I guess," Coy began, haltingly, "we can go over the plan later."

August nodded. "R-Right."

"Well, uh, goodnight."

Coy hurried out of the room—leaving August alone on the bed—to think about what had just happened. When he reached his own room, he shut the door with a quiet curse and then fell face-first onto the bed. What the hell had he been thinking? His mind was a cloud of confused thoughts and feelings. He was frustrated with himself, with August, and with the woman who had interrupted the two of them. How far would they have gone if she had not barged in? Would August have let him keep going? And if so, why? More importantly, why did Coy care?

He thought about August lying beneath him on the bed, eyes half-lidded and lips parted. How could someone so annoying be so beautiful? He had wanted more. They had *both* wanted more. He thought about the needy expression on August's face, and the pleading tone of his voice. His own body reacted to the memory, his cock stirring at the thought.

"Go away," he muttered against the mattress.

There was no way he was thinking about any of this right now. Thoughts like that belonged at the very back of his mind. He refused to let them to the forefront.

August ate his breakfast in silence and alone. He thought about his home and wondered whether his house had been ransacked by the Registry once he had been thrown in prison. He tried his best not to think about Conlin, or what had almost happened between them.

Conlin's room was quiet. It had been quiet since Conlin had woken him the night before. As annoying as it had been to listen to women screaming, he would have preferred it to the silence—at least it would have helped him think that whatever had happened last night was not that big of a deal.

And really, it hadn't been.

Conlin had just been teasing him. That was the type of person he was. It wasn't his fault August's body had a natural reaction to it. It would have happened with Laura, or any of the other ladies in the house. No big deal. Nothing to waste time thinking about.

So, why couldn't he stop thinking about it?

They were leaving today. He had mixed feelings about it. On one hand, he wanted to continue their journey. On the other, one night of sleeping on an actual bed made him loath to leave it again, even though Laura had tried once more to convince him to use her services. This time, instead of food, she had come to him wearing nothing but a silk robe and a strap-on dildo. Its solid, purple surface protruded from her body, large and obscene. August had quickly declined the offer.

He couldn't bring himself to eat the banana that came with his breakfast.

Conlin came to get him not long after he had finished eating.

"You ready?"

August nodded. "I'm going to miss this place," he said. "Well, the bed. Not too sure about the company."

Conlin chuckled. "You should learn to loosen up every now and then."

They descended the stairs. Paintings of the girls followed them, lining the hall in wooden frames.

August's lip quirked up involuntarily as he remembered the punch he had landed. Conlin's expression alone had been worth it. "Was I loose enough for you last night?" he teased unthinkingly.

"No," Conlin said, "but if we had kept going, you would have been. You and your—" The corners of his mouth tugged upward into a smirk. "—*nothing*."

August's eyes grew wide as he realized the mistake he had made in his wording. He turned away from Conlin and stared at the wall.

"Moron," he muttered.

They said their goodbyes to the ladies. Conlin's goodbye consisted of slobbering kisses and unsightly gropes. August exhibited more courtesy, thanking the lady of the house for her hospitality. He avoided eye contact with Laura.

"You gentlemen do come visit us again." She held the door open for them, her pale fingers adorned with rings that sparkled under the sun's rays.

Conlin was the first to step outside. Upon following him, August had only a moment to admire his quick reflexes before Conlin grabbed him and ran.

The Registry officer gave chase.

Chapter Sixteen

THEY RACED DOWN the path, Coy gripping August's wrist tightly. The officer was behind them, screaming for the two of them to stop running.

Between gasps, August said, "That's Julius Hale. He enlisted the same time I did."

"Do you think one of the girls gave us up?" Coy panted.

The longer they ran, the denser the area grew with civilization. Vehicles sat parked alongside the road like grazing cows. They needed to guide Hale farther away, or they risked someone spotting them—or worse, someone getting hurt.

"Not likely," August breathed out. "Maybe he was here for the same reason you were."

Coy conceded the point—had anyone tipped off the Registry, the brothel would have been swarmed by officers within minutes.

They changed course, heading back to the swamp, its reeds swaying in the distance. Concrete slowly gave way to mud. Finally, a single tree rose before them, marking the point between solid ground and where the land eventually gave way to the dampness of swampland. The two of them crouched behind the tree, its wide trunk shielding both of their bodies from Hale.

"No sense in hiding," Hale called. He had the same drawl as the ladies back at the brothel did—slow and deep, like he was seconds from falling asleep. "What's the matter, Seaton? Fucking Fate wasn't enough for you? You had to go and fuck the dragon, too?"

Coy turned to look at him, wide-eyed, mouth agape.

"Best thing for you to do is come back with me. You and your dragon boyfriend. Can't be held accountable for what I'll do if you don't come willingly."

"Did you really fuck Fate?" Coy demanded, not caring that they could be seconds from death.

"Are you serious?" August moved to stand, but Coy gripped the front of his shirt.

"Did you?"

August smacked his hand away and stood up. "I need you to distract him. I'll handle everything else."

August dove away from their tree, narrowly avoiding a bullet, and dashed into the reeds. Coy wasn't sure if Hale was using tranquilizers or real bullets, but he had no desire to find out.

"You had no business working for the Registry in the first place," Hale mocked. "Pretty thing like you ain't worth nothing more than a whore."

"*Hey.*" Coy stepped out from his place behind the tree, trying to distract Hale from closing in on August. "So, this is who they sent to drag me back? A Nenzoian hick?"

"Fuck you, dragon." Hale fired off a round of shots that Coy dodged by jumping back behind the tree. "Go ahead and shift, dragon," Hale taunted. "The whole world will see it when you do. Registry's gonna chop you up into little, bite-size dragon nuggets. Just like they did to that old bitch grandma of yours."

Incensed, Coy pulled away from the tree. "What the fuck did you say?"

August had told him that his grandmother was buried on their land. Had the Registry really dissected her? He wouldn't have put it past Dr. Rowburg to slice up his grandmother all in the name of her sadistic experiments.

Had August lied to him?

"You got balls, dragon. I'll give you that. But, you ain't a very bright one." Hale laughed and aimed his gun at him.

Coy did not have enough time to jump back behind the tree.

Hale fired, but the bullet went up unto the air rather than straight ahead. The gun fell from Hale's hand and landed in the muddy grass below. His neck had been split open, the skin sliced apart, reminding Coy of the fish they'd been catching and gutting. Blood poured from the wound like a crimson fountain and stained Hale's fingers when he tried to hold it closed.

He fell forward, and August stood behind him, his fingers wet and red. He held a knife, standard-issue. He must have grabbed it off of Hale before attacking him.

Coy looked from August to Hale. He felt relief at seeing the officer dead, couldn't muster up any guilt. More importantly, he had questions for August, ones that he doubted August would be willing to answer. And, even if he did, who was to say that he wouldn't lie?

"I didn't... I can't believe..." August put his hand over his mouth, eyes wide with horror.

"We gotta get rid of the body," Coy said.

THIRTY MINUTES OF walking—and dragging a lifeless Hale behind them—led them to a swampy river. They stuffed Hale's pockets full of rocks and then dumped his body into the water, where it sank. Feeling uneasy, August had tucked Hale's knife back in its sheath. If he'd noticed, Conlin chose not to mention it.

August remained silent, staring at the body disappearing into the depths.

"Well," Conlin said. His arms were folded across his chest. He stood in front of August, an unmovable object.

"Well, what?" August replied.

Conlin narrowed his eyes at him. "Did you?"

"Did I *what?*"

"Don't give me that shit," Conlin growled. "Did you fuck Fate?"

"What difference does it make?"

"It makes a lot of fucking difference as to whether I can trust you."

August inhaled. His anger from before had gone nowhere. It was still there, still festering inside of him. He had just killed someone for Conlin's sake. What would it take for him to *believe* that August was on his side?

"I do not have time for this." August tried to walk around him.

Conlin grabbed his shoulder, his calloused fingers digging into August's skin. "I'm not done talking to you."

"No!" August shouted, jerking away from Conlin's grip. "No, I did *not* fuck Fate. Since you have to know so badly, I have never *fucked* anyone."

Conlin frowned and tilted his head warily. "He said your mother cut up Nina."

August shook his head. The weight of what he had done was finally settling on him.

"You believe everything anyone else tells you. I just killed someone for you, Conlin. I have done *everything* you have asked of me." He felt like he was being broken apart from the inside, like everything that held him together was crumbling away. "I'm out here suffering because I wanted to prove to you that I didn't kill your family. That I'm trying to *help* you."

"August—"

"You believe what someone told you, someone who was trying to *kill* you. But you won't believe *me*."

He wiped at his eyes, smearing tears against his cheeks. Hale was a bastard, but he probably had a family. Parents. A wife. Maybe even children. He had taken him away from all of that, and for what? For the person he had protected to accuse him of lying.

He felt sick. Not like he was going to shift. Just sick.

"Look, I believe you, okay?" Conlin reached out a hand for August's shoulder, seemingly trying to calm him. August smacked it away.

"Don't touch me. Just—" He pushed past Conlin and gave up trying to wipe away the tears. They seemed intent on flowing, so he let them.

"August..."

"Don't," he said. "Just, don't."

CONLIN HAD GIVEN him space.

They had not spoken since they dumped Hale's body into the river. As they followed the path downstream, the water was a constant reminder of what August had done for such an ungrateful creature as Conlin.

He thought about the brothel—about Conlin on top of him, rubbing against him—and felt disgust for how his body had reacted. He had actually *liked* it. He was stupid. He was always so *stupid*.

They had been walking for hours. The sky was a sea of stars. Little by little, the swamp gave way to plains of grass and the occasional tree.

"Let's stop for tonight," Conlin suggested. "I doubt that guy had the chance to call in any backup. Even if he did, it'll be awhile before they even come close to finding us."

August did not want to stop for the night. He wanted to keep moving. The farther they got, the closer he would be to being free of Conlin, but the weight of the day's events had worn him down. He was tired and hungry.

It was the same routine as usual. Conlin caught fish and built a fire, unconcerned about the smoke trail it'd create. August was less impressed by his fire this time around. In fact, if he had not known Conlin was fireproof, he may have been inclined to push him into it. He was still considering it.

"So you're still mad at me, huh, hummingbird?" Conlin asked.

August plucked meat out of his fish, scooping up the bits of white flesh with his fingertips, and put them into his mouth. He glanced up at Conlin for a second and then went back to his food.

"Guess that's a yes. Here."

August looked up just in time to catch something flying at his face. It was the controller to his collar.

"I suppose you think this will make me think better of you?" He sat the fish on his lap and, after wiping his hands on his pants, cracked the controller open like a walnut. The pin was there, smooth and sleek.

"You can't really blame me."

"I can do whatever I want."

Conlin sighed. "I said I was sorry." He hadn't.

"Yes," August said. "I agree with you. You are. The sorriest excuse for a person I have ever met."

"Fuck you." Conlin threw a fish head at him. It sailed through the air before hitting August's thigh.

August plucked the pin out of the controller and then reached behind his head. He breathed a sigh of relief when the collar popped off his neck, turning his head from side to side to stretch out the tense muscles. He rubbed at the skin, which was smooth and sensitive under his touch. With another sigh, he tossed the collar into the fire and the fish head back at Conlin.

"Fuck *you*. Imbecile," August retaliated.

"Pretty boy."

"Brute."

"Asshole."

"*Dragon*."

Conlin smirked. "*Hummingbird*."

August rolled his eyes. Being rid of the collar had lifted his mood. "We should be in Olra in a couple of days."

It was something he wasn't looking forward to. He had enjoyed visiting Olra in his childhood, but Olra was Niami's hometown. Knowing that he would be traveling through it left a sour taste in his mouth. He told himself that he was doing this for her, that he would fix the problems that he had caused for her and the other shifters. It would not be easy. Still, he would do it. He would not be able to live with himself otherwise.

"You want me to take first watch?" Conlin asked.

"It does not matter. If you are tired, you can sleep."

"No, you go ahead. I have some things I need to think about anyway." August said, "Okay."

"Sleep well, hummingbird."

"Don't do anything stupid while I sleep, *dragon*."

THE RIVER SEEMED to go on forever. They followed the water, kicking rocks and pointing at scurrying animals. August thought about Hale's lifeless body sitting at the bottom of the river several miles back and sighed.

"Check it out."

August looked over at Conlin to see him pointing toward a tree. There was a blanket there, stretched out, its corners held down by two pairs of shoes. In the center of the blanket was a wicker basket. Next to the basket were two bottles of wine.

"Con—" August hesitated. Conlin had taken to calling him by his first name, and August wanted to do the same. "Coy..." He prepared himself for the look of displeasure on Conlin's face, but it never emerged.

"Shh." He waved his hand, silencing August. "I'll be right back."

August half smiled. There was something he liked about being on a first-name basis with Coy. It made him feel less like escaped fugitives and more like friends. Well, maybe not friends, but at least associates.

He shook his head while Coy made his way over to the blanket. He snatched up the entire thing, using it like a sack to carry the basket and bottles. He came back with a grin on his face.

"Was that really necessary?" August asked.

"What? I got you a blanket, didn't I?"

"Let's continue. If we do not get out of Nenzo soon, I will go crazy."

"You mean, you haven't already?"

August ignored him.

He watched as Coy opened one of the bottles of wine and guzzled it. "Pretty good stuff. Wanna try?"

"No, thanks."

"Can't handle your alcohol, or not old enough to drink?" Coy questioned.

August rolled his eyes. "I'm twenty-two."

"So it's the first one then?"

"Imbecile."

They were still a few hours away from crossing over to Olra when August decided to stop and rest. Coy had finished the first bottle—entirely on his own—and was moving on to the next one. He was also becoming louder and clumsier by the second.

"I can keep going," Coy protested.

"Just lie down and be quiet."

"Come on. Let's go." Coy grabbed him by the wrist, trying to tug him back to his feet. "We're almost there."

"Coy, please." August yanked back his arm. Coy's tight grip and his drunken, awkward footing caused him to fall on top of August.

"Get off me, you simpleton."

He tried to push Coy off of him, who was already heavy—and heavier still now that he was inebriated. Coy stared down at him with a smirk.

"How's your *nothing* doing, hummingbird?" When August didn't respond, Coy taunted him further. "What? That sharp tongue of yours all outta ammo?"

"Release me."

Judging by the widening smirk on Coy's face, the demand had amused him. "May want to reconsider your choice of words. But..." He looked August up and down, his mismatched eyes locking on August's exposed shoulder. "I could release you, if that's what you want."

"P-Pervert."

August held stock-still. He knew what would happen if he struggled, and Laura would not be there to interrupt them this time. Coy was warm and heavy against him and smelled distinctly of the forest. Despite having little opportunity to bathe, it was not an unpleasant smell. Coy's thighs were like hot lead pressed against him, forcing his own thighs open to the point where his legs trembled from the weight.

"Your eyes are closed. You scared to look at me?"

"I'm protecting them from the droplets of spit you can't seem to hold in your mouth."

"Ah," Coy said. "There's that sharp tongue again. I was starting to miss it." Coy lowered himself even further, nuzzling his face against August's neck.

"You are very drunk."

"And you," Coy said, "are very *pretty*."

The compliment was enough to make August blush. He swallowed thickly and gasped, his nerves getting the best of him when he felt Coy's hand trailing down his side.

"D-Don't," August stammered. He had already made so many mistakes in his life. He did not want losing his virginity to be one of them, especially not to Coy, and definitely not while he was drunk.

"I won't," Coy said, and he didn't.

A second later, he was asleep, his warm breath blowing steadily against August's neck.

STARS PEPPERED THE sky, shining brightly against a vast blanket of darkness. Alongside the moon, they reflected off of the river, gentle ripples of water warping the scene above. Yet somehow, the image was just as beautiful.

For a few moments, August quietly watched Coy, his bare, broad shoulders resting heavily against a tree. He seemed to be in his own little world, digging absentmindedly into his teeth with a thin piece of tree bark. He was also, surprisingly, completely sober. He must have burned through the alcohol quickly—which August secretly thought was a blessing. He didn't think he could handle a hungover dragon.

"Your mom ever teach you it's rude to stare?" Coy asked, holding the piece of bark between his index and middle fingers like a slim cigar.

August did not startle—he *didn't*. "You flatter yourself. I have better things to do than stare at you."

"Guess she never taught you that it's rude to lie, too."

"Do you honestly think that *anyone* would want to sicken himself by watching you stab blindly at your teeth like that? It is *repulsive*. Who knows how many animals have marked that tree over the years. I am nauseous just thinking about it."

Coy tossed the strip of bark away and rolled his shoulders. "I thought you liked trees. You know, the nectar."

"What are you talking about?" August asked, exasperated.

"The nectar. You drink it."

"Nectar is found in flowers. You're thinking about sap."

"Nectar. Sap. It's all the same. The point is, you put that little beak of yours all over the plants and trees that animals have pissed and shit on, and you're grossed out by a little bit of bark."

"For the last time," August snapped, "I am not a *fucking* hummingbird."

"Oh." Coy grinned. He pushed himself to his feet, his hands brushing at the dirt clinging to the back of his thighs. "You're using the dangerous, big-boy words." He approached August, a taunting smirk tugging at the corners of his mouth. "How'd that taste on your tongue?"

"Be quiet."

"What's up with your eyes?"

His eyes? August blinked several times, wondering what Coy meant. It was a strange question, considering the person who has asked it had two different color ones.

"My eyes? What do you mean?"

Coy leaned down, his own mismatched eyes narrowing as he stared into August's.

"I don't know. They look different. Lighter. Have they always been this color?"

Barely keeping his shock in check, August quickly turned away. He yanked nervously at his hair before he began to comb through it with his fingers, using the long, dark locks to shield as much of his face as possible. This could not be happening. Not now of all times. He hadn't even experienced any other telltale signs that would have normally alerted him.

"I do not know what you are talking about. Maybe there was something in that tree you were eating that has caused you to hallucinate. Either that, or you are still drunk."

"I was cleaning my teeth."

"Yes, well, you did a tragically mediocre job at that."

"August."

"What?"

"Let me see your eyes again."

"No. They are just eyes, Coy. The same as they have always been. Let's rest for tonight."

"Yeah, I guess you're right," Coy said.

COY HAD WOKEN up over an hour ago, and August was still missing. He was starting to regret letting him take the collar off.

He had spent thirty minutes or so looking for him, wandering aimlessly through a field of tall grass. He'd thought about calling out to him. If August had gotten lost and was heading in the wrong direction, it had the potential to set them back after hours of traveling. However, he also worried about someone hearing him and coming to investigate, only to find an escaped shifter wandering around.

It was better to stay quiet, go back to camp, and hope that August would turn up soon.

Coy was tired, but he could not sit down. He ran the risk of August coming back and not seeing him. The longer he waited, the more worried he became. Had August run off, or had someone captured him?

He wasn't sure which one of those possibilities bothered him the most.

Another hour passed. Coy felt like he was back at the prison. He had to avoid doing anything that could have informed August of his location. No fire blowing—no shifting. He just had to sit there and wait. After spending a few weeks in prison, waiting was the last thing he wanted to do.

After what felt like an eternity, August finally showed up. He stumbled through the field, his bloody shirt popping up from the grass like a wildflower.

"Where the fuck have you been?" Coy growled. "We lost two hours because of you."

"Sorry," August said. He spoke softly, his words barely above a whisper. It was as if his body was there, but his mind was someplace else. "I didn't feel well."

"You couldn't have told me that before you ran off?"

"Sorry."

"Whatever. Let's go."

Coy stomped forward, and August followed after him. He was a ghost, drifting through the fields, his hair blowing around him. Coy was worried about him, but he was too angry to ask if he was okay. His eyes were back to their normal brown color. They had been amber yesterday. Coy was certain of it.

August could barely keep up. Annoyed with his August's slow pace, Coy slowed down his own.

"What's going on with you?" he asked. "You're acting weird."

"I shifted."

"Is that why you were gone so long?"

August nodded. "I was afraid I would never shift back."

"That's because you don't know what the fuck you're doing."

"Thanks for stating the obvious."

Coy slowed until he stopped walking. Wind rustled around them, blowing his hair about his face.

"Look, I already told you. Shifting is influenced by your emotions. You'll never learn how to do it successfully if you don't get those under control. You know what happens when you shift without being in control of your emotions?"

August shook his head.

"People die, August. You kill people."

They continued walking.

Coy watched as August opened his mouth several times as if to speak.

"If you have something to say, then say it," Coy ordered.

"Is that—" Coy heard the hesitation in his voice before he continued. "—what happened to your grandfather?"

"Yep," Coy answered without a hitch. He was not ashamed, nervous, or upset that August had asked him, or even that he knew.

"Why did you do it?"

"Because it was my first time shifting, and I didn't know what the hell I was doing—it was ruled as self-defense. Also, because he was evil, abusive, and a fucking tiger."

"What's wrong with tigers?"

Coy said, "*Everything.*"

THE OLRA REGION was mainly comprised of plains, a steady source of produce for the surrounding regions. Its only city, of the same name, was a quiet, walled community. Unfortunately, officers guarded its sole entrance. They had no choice but to avoid the city, but its outskirts stretched out promisingly before them.

August wanted to leave the moment they arrived. The ground was covered in periwinkles, the same type that Niami wore in her hair before the Registry—before *he*—plucked her out of Olra and threw her in prison.

A barn sat in the middle of the plains, its chipped paint rusting beneath the sun. Off to the left of the farm, cows snatched grass from the earth with their teeth. Off to the right, horses.

"Are you seeing what I'm seeing?" Coy asked.

"A farm?"

"Do you see the horses?"

They were standing next to each other looking at the exact same thing. Of course August saw the horses. He was finding that, with Coy, it was simpler just to give him whatever ridiculously obvious answer he was looking for.

"Of course I see them," August answered.

"If we grabbed a couple of them, we'd hit Fiasu in no time."

"We are not stealing horses, Coy."

Coy ignored him and made a beeline to the gate where the horses stood, tall and majestic, eating hay and swatting away flies with their tails.

"Coy," August whispered. There had to be people nearby, and he did not want to risk being heard. "Get back here, you idiot."

Coy opened the gate. They were going to steal a horse, August acknowledged wearily. Coy tried to lure one of the horses away from the others with an apple he'd snatched off a tree. Still, none of them seemed particularly interested. It was too much of a risk to jump inside, so he tossed August the apple and rounded the gate, probably hoping to sweet-talk one of the horses away from the others.

The moment August caught the apple, one of the horses trotted over to him, its teeth square and large. August took a step back. If it came any closer, running would be his next move. The horse continued to slowly advance on him, its teeth sticking out from its mouth, trying to reach for the apple. It left the gate, tail swishing, large, muscular body following August with each backward step he took.

"Keep going," Coy said, his words hushed. "Get as far away from the farm as you can. I'll catch up to you."

August shot a glare at him, at a loss at what else he could do. Giant, brown eyeballs watched him with curiosity. August had never been this close to a horse in his life. Sweat rolled down his neck. He clung to the apple with dampened palms as if it were keeping him alive—he chanced a glance down at the horse's hooves and let out a weak groan, praying that it would.

He had expected to learn a few things on this journey, but finding out that he was scared of horses was not one of them.

He moved backward until his shoulders pressed up against a tree. The horse was still moving toward him, those big teeth nipping at the air. August closed his eyes and waited for his inevitable death.

Unwillingly, he opened them when the horse took the apple in its mouth with the gentleness of a mother cat carrying her kitten. August melted against the tree and watched as those teeth chomped down on the fruit with ease. When it was finished, the horse moved closer to August.

"That's it. I don't have any more," August whispered panickily.

The horse moved even closer, nuzzling its long face against August's cheek. August brought up a hesitant hand and rubbed the horse's head, its coarse fur gliding between his fingers.

"New girlfriend?" Coy asked. He was on foot.

"I thought you were getting another horse."

"Yeah, well. That plan didn't work. I don't think they liked me all that much."

Coy took a step closer. The horse turned around and made a shrieking noise at him, nostrils flailing.

"*Fuck.*"

Apparently, this horse didn't like him either. They had a dilemma.

Coy knew how to ride horses. August did not. The horse liked August. It hated Coy.

"You'll have to get on first to keep it calm. I'll ride behind you."

"I don't want to," August whined. "I can't."

"Stop being a baby."

"What about a saddle?"

"It'd be nice," Coy said, "but we already stole one of their horses. Doubt whoever owns that farm would be willing to just hand over one of their saddles."

"So, we have to do it, what? Bareback? I've never ridden, let alone bareback"

Coy scratched at his eyebrow, giving August a funny look. "Yeah, well, that's pretty obvious," he muttered. "Just get on the horse, August."

THEY CONTINUED THROUGH Olra. August felt like a puppet, listening to the instructions that Coy gave him from his spot on the back of the horse.

The day was sweltering.

The horse, whom August had affectionately named Rose once they discovered she was a girl, moved slowly. They would need to reserve her strength and energy for when they got closer to Fiasu. August had gotten used to the slight rock of his hips whenever Rose took a step, but he was still adjusting to Coy rubbing against him from behind. Each movement she made caused him to brush against August in a way that would have been inappropriate if they had not been on horseback.

"So, this is Olra," Coy remarked. August could feel the heat of his body against him—something that he may have taken guilty pleasure in if it were not so unpleasantly hot.

"A small part of it, yes. Olra is actually a—"

"What happened to your dad?"

"What?" August was brought up short by the offhand question. Wary, he turned his face slightly, looking at Coy from the corner of his eye.

"I know Rowburg's your mom. But your dad. What happened to him?"

"He died."

"Did she kill him?"

"No," August said. He remained quiet for a couple of seconds before adding, "At least, I don't think she did."

"So, what happened to him?"

"He was sick. I'm not sure with what. I was pretty young when he died." *Had* his mother killed him? "What about you?" August asked, deciding to ponder this later. He had enough to deal with. Trying to figure out whether his mother had murdered his father was far too much to take on.

"What about me, what?"

"Your parents? What happened to them?"

"Dead."

August thought about Coy's file. He had not looked for any information about Coy's parents. Had he killed them, too? Just like he'd done to his grandfather?

"I didn't kill them," Coy said, as if reading August's thoughts. "My dad made a lot of bad decisions. Cost him and my mom their lives. Nina raised me since I was six. She was more like a mom to me than a grandmother."

"I truly am sorry about what happened to your family, Coy," August admitted. "I wish—"

"Nothing we can do about that now. When people die, they stay dead. While the living stay dead inside."

"That's a rather morose thing to say."

August cried out when he felt Coy's hand gripping his hair, pulling his head back. He squeezed his heels against Rose, the action signaling for her to stop.

"It worked," Coy said, grinning.

"What worked?"

"I can use your hair as reins."

August smacked his hand away. "How are you an adult?"

"Doesn't your neck get hot with all this hair?" Coy grabbed August's hair again, lifted it up, and piled it on top of his head.

"Let go of my hair," August said.

"Or you'll do what?" He tugged on August's hair again, tilting his head so that August was forced to look at him from upside down.

August looked at Coy's lips. They looked soft, pink. Like flower petals. He wondered if Coy was a good kisser. He was probably a good kisser. Even if he wasn't, August had never kissed anyone, so he would not have known the difference. August licked his lips. Coy mimicked him and then leaned down until his face was just a few inches away from August's. When he was so close that August could almost *feel* him, he chuckled awkwardly and sat up.

Coy released his hold on his hair, smiling at August's undoubtedly confused expression.

"Want to speed things up for a just a bit?" he asked. "See what your horse girlfriend can do?

"I guess," August answered, unsure.

Coy grinned. "Then hang on, pretty boy."

Chapter Seventeen

THEY RODE FOR hours but slowed down considerably so they wouldn't burn Rose out. They had already stopped a few times to rest and relieve themselves. August's inner thighs ached, and his legs felt like noodles. If Coy was having the same issues, he did not act like it.

Once they'd reached Olra, they had strayed from the river that had supplied them, but it became apparent that they needed to head southeast until they hit it again. Rose would need to drink soon, and the wine bottles they had filled with water would need to be replenished. Besides, they needed food. August was sick of fish, but at least they wouldn't starve to death. Coy did not seem to care one way or another.

Thanks to Coy's sense of smell, they found it. This part of the river was unlike anything August had ever seen before. Sparkling water splashed against rocks. It cascaded down from a cliff and dived into the waiting pool below. A massive rock sat in the center of the river, misshapen and angled like a giant, broken fishtail.

They dismounted Rose and let her drink. As much as August wanted to rush into the water, he had to tend to Rose. She still had not fully warmed up to Coy.

Coy, on the other hand, acted like a toddler. He raced forward, stripping off his clothing, his skin darkened even more from spending days wandering outside beneath the sun. August watched him, his eyes roaming over Coy's body, lingering at his ass for a few seconds before he blushed and ran his fingers through Rose's mane to distract himself.

"He is a moron," August whispered to Rose.

"Heard that," Coy shouted. He was already waist-deep in the water, his skin wet and glistening.

After tending to Rose and making sure she would not get the urge to run off and go exploring, August picked up Coy's scattered clothing and folded it in a neat pile on the grass. After undressing, he did the same with his own. He pretended to ignore the gaze he felt on him. He knew Coy was looking. Coy always looked. He was never discreet about it.

August joined Coy in the water but did not swim to him. Instead, he moved toward the waterfall, eyes widening in amazement when he noticed there was actually space behind it. Holding his breath, he went beneath the water and swam to the other side. When he came back up, he watched the rushing water splash in front of his face. He held a hand out, letting it fall on his fingers, cool and refreshing. He could see why Olraians loved their land so much. If he lived there, he couldn't imagine leaving.

He thought about Niami.

"Hey."

August cried out and slammed back against the solid rock behind him. Coy's eye—the violet one—was open and staring at him. The other was closed, blocking out the water spray.

"What the hell is wrong with you?" August snapped.

Coy laughed. "What? I just wanted to see what you were doing. This place is pretty nice, isn't it?"

August glared at him and moved to the side when Coy pushed through the waterfall to stand next to him.

"It's beautiful."

"You know what else is beautiful?" Coy asked.

August rolled his eyes. He knew what was coming next.

"Me."

"Would it kill you to learn what privacy is?"

"Privacy," Coy repeated. "What are you trying to keep private?"

Coy ducked beneath the water before August could answer. August huffed and looked at the surface of the water, trying to figure out where he had gone. A few seconds later, he found out when a hand gripped his ankle. He tried kicking Coy's hand away, cursing just seconds before Coy pulled him under.

August came up sputtering. His hair was in his face, blinding him. Coy pulled him back down.

He came up a few seconds later, swinging at the air.

"Stop, you fucking asshole." Even with water in his ears, he could hear Coy laughing. He swung again. Another miss. "Would you please grow up!"

"Or what?" Coy said from directly in front of him. His wet hand gripped August by the wrist and pulled him so that his back met the slick rock behind them once again. He leaned in, his hard chest flush against August's own. "What exactly will you do, hummingbird?"

"I know what you are doing," August said. "And you can forget about it because it will not work."

"What won't work?" Coy asked. His breath was warm. It smelled of the apples they had eaten earlier.

"Your—" August searched for a word. "—*ways* won't work on me."

"My ways?"

He felt his eyes on him, even though his face was almost entirely covered by his hair. Coy's hand grazed his face, pulling the strands back so that he could see his eyes.

"And what ways would those be?"

"Disgusting."

"Disgusting," Coy repeated, emphasizing his Hametian drawl. He made a noise that sounded like a tick of a clock. "Still so tight."

"Excuse me?"

"You gotta loosen up, hummingbird. You wouldn't even have a drink with me back in Nenzo."

"I told you I don't drink."

"You don't drink. You don't fuck. What do you do?"

"Participate in intelligent conversation."

"Yeah, you and the horse seemed to have lots of scholarly topics to discuss."

"I'm surprised you know what that word means," August rebuked.

"And I'm surprised you're okay with letting whatever that creature is crawl all over you."

"What creature?" August looked down and saw a bug clinging to his hair. He flailed about, swatting it off. It landed in the water and floated away. *"Coy."*

Coy laughed and swam away. After a moment of glaring, August swam after him.

AFTER THEIR MUCH-needed break at the river, they traveled a few more hours before stopping for the night. The stolen blanket had been destroyed, ripped apart to make makeshift reins for Rose. What was left of it was so thin that they may as well have been sleeping on the ground. Coy lay on his back. August lay on his side, facing away from him. There was space between them, but not much. Coy could have reached over and touched August if he wanted to. Still, he had messed with him enough for one day. August really did need to loosen up.

"What are you going to do when this is all over, hummingbird?"

"What do you mean?" August asked, voice muffled in his arm.

"I mean, once you've helped me get my revenge against Fate. What will you do?"

"I'm going to find a way to free the shifters," August said, as if it was the most obvious answer one could have to such a question.

"That's stupid," Coy said. "Not to mention impossible."

August fidgeted, not looking back at him. "I'll figure out a way."

"You'll get yourself killed is what you'll do."

"Why do you care?" August asked. "It's not your problem."

"You're right, it's not."

"Then, why did you ask?" August questioned. He flipped over onto his back, glaring.

Coy shrugged. "Just curious."

"Whatever."

August was only four years younger than Coy, but he seemed much younger. Too sheltered. Too naive. Killing one officer was one thing. Taking on the entire Registry was a whole different beast. Going against the Registry meant going against the sovereign's orders. Even Coy wasn't willing to take things that far. August had guts—the guts of a kid who had yet to understand how the world really operated.

"If you weren't so selfish, you could help," August offered.

"Like you said, it's not my problem."

"You're a shifter, aren't you? Don't you care about what happens to the rest of us?"

"Yes, but I'm a shifter who doesn't make a habit of getting involved with stuff that doesn't affect me directly."

"But, it does affect you. It affects all of us."

"Says the person who was parading around like a human just a few weeks ago."

"Forget it," August muttered. "You don't understand."

"Oh, no, August. I understand a lot more than you think," Coy growled. "You think being a martyr is going to stop you from your guilt? You think just because you want to save them means it's going to happen? That if you try hard enough, you can just fix all the bad shit that's happened to them? You want to fix things? You want to make things better? Start by bringing back my fucking family."

August fell silent.

"There are some things you won't ever be able to make right, August. Even if you somehow did manage to have them freed, all the shit they've been through doesn't just disappear. Take your own advice. Grow up."

August didn't reply.

BREAKFAST WAS FISH. Coy ate as much as he could without exploding. August ate just enough to sustain him for another day. He did not seem to have much of an appetite.

They mounted Rose and rode in silence. Occasionally, August would lean down and praise Rose for her hard work. When the silence became too loud, Coy would make a snide remark. August would reply with something short and curt—his normal response to most of Coy's sarcasm—but it wasn't the same. His heart wasn't in it.

It should not have bothered Coy. He meant everything he had said last night. Maybe he could have said it a little less harshly, but August needed to know the truth. You could fix broken things—not broken *people.* Not a single shifter who had ever seen the inside of one of those cells would ever be the same, including himself. There were just some things you couldn't repair no matter how much you wanted to. Growing up as he had, he had learned that the hard way.

August hardly spoke to him. It annoyed him that August thought he could stop communicating with him just because he did not want to face the truth. He had called Coy childish, but August was the childish one. And so what if he didn't want to talk? Coy didn't care. He didn't need to talk to August. All he needed to do was find Fate, kill him, and avenge Dinina. First, he needed to go to Sago.

He had to find Amira. Then, everything would start to fall into place.

From the back, August was all hair. While they rode, Coy had gotten used to playing with it when he was bored, winding it around his fingers and twisting it together in a poor attempt to braid it. August had let him do it. Probably to keep him from getting bored, and thus intolerable to be around. Coy hated being bored. He missed whittling.

He reached down, lifting a few locks of August's hair off his back, wanting to occupy himself.

August said, "Could you let go of my hair, please?"

It was a logical request. It was August's hair, after all. And yet, it set a fire in Coy that was ten times hotter than the one swirling in his throat.

"Oh, so I can't touch your hair now?"

"Well, it is *my* hair."

"Fine." Coy pushed August forward, creating a space between their bodies. "I didn't want to touch your stupid hair anyway."

August said nothing. He simply pulled his hair forward so it rested on his chest.

Coy knew he was being ridiculous and petty—he *knew* it—but he didn't want to apologize. He only apologized when he was sorry, and he wasn't sorry. August was just a dumb, stubborn kid who refused to accept reality.

They continued traveling in silence. It was starting to drive Coy crazy. It had only been a few hours, and although he did not want to admit it, he missed their banter. August was a spoiled brat, but he was fun to talk to.

"How long are you going to stay mad at me?" Coy asked.

"I am not mad at you," August replied, his fingers gently combing through Rose's mane.

"How many times are you going to lie to me?"

"I am not lying to you."

Coy snorted. "Well, that's two so far."

August shrugged. "I assumed you didn't want to hear anything I had to say."

"That's what you get for assuming."

August took to braiding a few strands of Rose's mane. "It seems to be the only thing I'm good at."

Coy sighed heavily, his breath blowing against August's hair.

"Could you please stop breathing on me?"

Coy sighed again, blowing his breath in the same spot as before.

Apparently fed up, August jerked back his arm in an attempt to blindly hit Coy in his face. Coy caught his arm with ease and yanked it back until it was folded over like a pretzel, the sharp angle causing August to cry out in pain. He pulled August backward like he'd done once before, so far back that he had to arch his torso and look at Coy from upside down. Rose stopped moving, possibly sensing something wasn't quite right with her riders.

"Did you forget how much stronger than you I am?" Coy asked.

"As if you would ever let me."

Coy smirked.

"Well?" August said. He stared up at Coy, almost looking expectant.

"Well, what?" Coy repeated. "Oh, you want me to let you go, huh?"

"No." August said, "I want you to kiss me."

The confession was a shocking one. Certainly one Coy had not been expecting to hear August admit. He was not sure if he should smirk or pout. It had almost been too easy. He supposed he just had that effect on people.

"So, you want a kiss, huh?" Coy licked his lips.

"Yes." August did the same.

"I guess I can do that."

Coy leaned down, eyes closed. He had to give it to August though. He'd held out longer than anyone else Coy had ever met.

The kiss was a jolt to the ribs. Mainly, because August had not kissed him at all. He had waited until Coy was close enough to jam his elbow into Coy's upper abdomen. Coy jerked back, wheezing, and August sat up, swinging his hair back behind his shoulders.

"You can play with it if you really want to," August said. "It actually feels kind of nice."

Chapter Eighteen

A MURKY SKY and fields of dying grass. Naked trees and litter that blanketed the ground. It had been beautiful once. It wasn't anymore. It was dark, dirty, and depressing, but they had reached it: Fiasu.

They probably should have celebrated, but the land was so dreary that it felt inappropriate.

"This is Fiasu?" August asked.

He and Fate had only been assigned one shifter from Fiasu, and he had ended up dead thanks to Fate. They had not gone deep into the town, just far enough to find the fish market, which was where the shifter had worked.

"This is Fiasu," Coy confirmed. "Hamet's not looking so bad right now, huh?"

"I never thought Hamet looked bad," August said. It was a lie. A flat-out lie. Hamet was terrible. Hot and dusty and filled with people who were so lowbrow it made him uncomfortable even being there.

"Bullshit," Coy said. "I know what uppity pretty boys like you think about where I'm from."

August considered mentioning that Fate was also technically from Hamet, but he decided that it would only put Coy in a foul mood. "So, I've upgraded from pretty boy to uppity pretty boy? Is there a difference between the two?"

"Yeah. One of them is afraid to suck cock with the light on. Wanna guess which one that is?"

August rolled his eyes, sidestepping a bedraggled Fiasian who gave him a funny look. "Can you go three seconds without thinking about sex?"

"Can't help it. It's in my blood."

"Thinking about sex is in no one's blood."

"Not true. Dragons mate at least five to ten times a day. That's why our lives are longer than other shifters."

"Is that true?" He had never read anything on the topic. Though, the mating rituals of dragons were not something he had ever considered before.

Coy snickered. "No."

"Idiot."

They walked along the dusty road. Beyond Fiasu's dingy dwellings, precarious, rocky hills loomed in the distance, separating Fiasu from Sago. Traversing them would be the fastest route to their destination, but it was arguably safer to travel through Fiasu and take the direct road to Sago. As long as they were careful, they would reach it in no time.

Rose was at August's side, trotting along quietly. They were going to have to get rid of her soon, as the cliff-like terrain would not be safe for her. August did not want to, but their plan had not involved him caring for a horse. Hopefully, there would be someone—a good person—who would be willing to take her off their hands. Someone who would take care of her, or at least make sure she got back to Olra.

The town grew even drearier when they reached the town center. Most people paid them no mind. Occasionally, someone would stare at them and then go back to whatever they had been doing.

His clothing was filthy, covered in blood, and nearly see-through. And yet, August still felt overdressed. Women sauntered by in skimpy dresses that hid nothing. They smiled at Coy, offering him a good time for a fair price. Coy responded charmingly, flirting with each of them, but ultimately declined their invitations.

"You still have money," August pointed out. "I'm surprised you didn't take them up on their offer."

"Not everything made with sugar tastes sweet," Coy said.

"What's that supposed to mean?"

Coy ruffled August's hair. "I'll tell you when you're older."

August smacked his hand away and sighed. The farther they moved down the road, the more populated it became. Vendors lined both sides of the street. People came and went, shopping, bartering, and arguing. Fiasu was an extremely small town—smaller than Hamet—but it was so heavily inhabited by people desperate for money, it was like trying to walk to the back of an overcrowded bus.

"Someone's coming," Coy cautioned. "Try not to make eye contact."

A man approached them, so filthy that his skin looked gray. Bits of food clung to his matted, salt-and-pepper beard. It reminded August of bugs caught in a spider's web. When he opened his mouth, three teeth hung down from his upper gums. The bottom had two fewer than that. One blue eyeball stared at Coy. The other, covered with a milky white film, stared elsewhere with the gaze of a dead fish.

August looked at the ground uncomfortably. He would not have a problem avoiding eye contact.

"How much you want for the horse?" the man asked, each word was long and hissed out. If a snake could speak, it would have spoken exactly like this man.

"It's not for sale," August said.

"Everything's for sale here," the man shot back "For the right price, even you."

"Get lost, buddy," Coy warned.

The old man stared Coy up and down. He pursed his lips and rubbed his chin, observing Coy like he was a purebred in a dog show. It was rude, but August grudgingly understood the gesture. Coy was unlike most people. Strong and intimidating, he towered over the old man. His chest was broad and peppered with dark hair, while his curls dangled from his scalp and framed his face. In short, Coy had a physical appearance that mastered the art of rugged masculinity, but still held a sense of boyish softness to it.

August wondered if it had something to do with him being a dragon.

"Not as much money for you," the man eventually concluded. "You aren't as pretty as the other one."

"Let's go," Coy said. He pushed past the old man, pulling August along with him. Rose trotted next to August, brushing her face against his side.

"You'll be back," the man called. "When you need the money, you'll be back. They always come back."

"That was terrifying," August muttered.

"That," Coy replied, "was years of drug use. Let's hurry up and get the hell out of this town."

They continued down the path, passing by fish markets, meat shops, and fabric stands. The food smelled delicious, and they still had money left. August had never tried food from Fiasu, and Coy would not let him change this fact.

"Nothing is as simple as paying for a meal and eating it in Fiasu," Coy said. "You'll wake up in a ditch a few hours later, naked and bleeding."

"Why would you assume something like that?"

"I told you, my dad made a lot of bad decisions before he died."

August had questions, but he didn't pry.

Farther down was more of the same. More vendors. More filthy people covered in rags trying to buy Rose, buy one of them, or both. It was not until they reached a small stand with a woman nursing a newborn that August felt hope that Rose would go to a home that could provide for her. She stood out like a tulip surrounded by weeds. She was clean, well-dressed, but not overly so. Her skin was the color of pecans. Not gray.

"We're not actually from Fiasu," the woman admitted after they approached her with a greeting and a few exchanged remarks. "We're from Olra. My husband is a doctor. We come here a few times a month to help the sick and elderly. The doctors here are...not very reliable."

"We found this horse in Olra," August said. It was not a complete lie.

"Oh," said the woman, likely surprised by the offhand comment. "Then, why didn't you bring it back to its owner?"

Coy elbowed August in his chest. "We were in a rush and didn't have time to turn back. She took a liking to my friend here. We figured we would try to make sure she found a good home if we couldn't get her back to Olra."

"Oh, well. In that case—" She smiled. "I'll do my best to make sure she gets back."

They lied about the circumstances of how they'd acquired her, but not about the farm they passed. She nodded in understanding, concluding that the horse must have escaped from the farm. August winced to himself, feeling a little guilty. She would probably find out the truth when she brought her back. That didn't matter. Rose would make it home.

"Goodbye, Rose," August said. He rubbed her back gently, nuzzling his face against the side of her long neck.

They thanked the woman and offered to pay her for her troubles. She declined and wished them well on their way.

"Missing your girlfriend?" Coy teased.

"You're just jealous that there was one lady who liked me more than she liked you."

Coy laughed. "Gotta admit. It's not something that I'm used to."

ALTHOUGH FILTHY AND generally uncomfortable, the streets of Fiasu were easy to traverse despite the crowd, offering little danger. Unwittingly, they let their guard down. That is when, of course, everything fell apart.

Trouble came in the form of a poster displaying their faces. There was a single photograph of Coy. His mismatched eyes stared straight ahead, and his cocky grin showed a mouthful of clean, white teeth. It was the same photo from his file, only blown-up.

However, there were two photographs of August—one from the day he'd graduated from the Registry's boot camp, dressed in the all-black uniform of a Registry officer. The other, taken a few minutes after he had woken up strapped to a table in the lab, hair down and eyes wide and afraid.

Stunned by the images, August almost missed the face turning toward them. A kid stood next to the poster, tattered shirt hanging off his bony shoulder, rolling a bread roll back and forth in his palm. If it had not been for Coy's commanding presence, the kid probably wouldn't have noticed them.

He stared at Coy first, then at August, then at the poster, and finally, at the part of the poster that listed the monetary value of their whereabouts.

"It's them!" the boy shouted. He jumped up and down, his bare feet pattering against the hard pavement. "It's them!" He repeated it over and over again like a chant as he pointed at August and Coy, his small, stubby finger wiggling with excitement.

This drew the attention of others, who made the connection quicker than either of them expected.

They ran.

It had been easy to escape the officers in the forest of Weren. There had been more places to hide or branches to use as weapons if someone got too close. In Fiasu, there was nothing. Only rundown buildings and masses of people pouring into the streets. The only saving grace was that many of them were sick, weak, or old. They moved slowly, but not slowly enough where the two of them did not have to run as fast as their legs could carry them.

They raced through the streets, the excited, gray mob behind them. Coy held his hand. Not his wrist or his arm. His hand. It was a ridiculous thing to think about given their situation, but the fact would not leave August.

They turned a corner, kicking up rocks and broken glass, and spotted an open doorway. They slipped inside the dilapidated building and slammed the flimsy door closed behind them. After letting go of his hand, Coy picked up a rotting plank of wood and propped it up against the doorknob. It would not hold for long. August looked around. An old, stained mattress lay in a corner of the building, two used syringes next to it.

"Inside!" they heard a voice call. "I heard them go inside."

"Fucking bitch," Coy growled.

They ran up a staircase of metal and down a hall. They found a window, already broken, edged with shards of glass like a shark's teeth. Coy kicked out the remaining glass and was the first to climb out, his broad shoulders getting scratched on the tiny pieces he had missed in the process. He perched on the sill, motioning for August to join him. August was more dexterous, exiting the window without a single cut.

The distance from the window to the ground wasn't too high. Coy jumped first, as casual as if it were something he did on an everyday basis. August followed suit, and Coy caught him a few inches before he hit the ground.

August thought about how he had fallen back in their cell, when Coy had tripped him. He still remembered the sound his knees had made when they cracked against the bed frame.

"Come on," Coy urged, taking his hand again as he guided them forward.

The moved quietly, holding their breaths as they skittered down an alley. August wanted to get out of it as quickly as possible. Nothing good ever happened in an alley.

They had to jump a fence, its warped wood buckling and splintering under their weight. They maneuvered their way through Fiasu's backstreets, hiding behind anything large enough to shield them from view.

Coy had been right. Fiasu was a small town. Eventually, its dreariness gave way to the rocky hills. August doubted they were still being chased. Even if they were, eventually the Fiasians would give up. The only people who seemed crazy enough to constantly keep running were him and Coy.

THEY TRAVELED THROUGH the cliff-like hills, sweaty and exhausted. The rolling land stretched far, seeming almost never-ending. It took a lot to wear Coy down, but moving through the uneven terrain was starting to get to him. Maybe it was because he knew they were so close to Sago. It felt like every step they took equated to two steps back. He knew that wasn't the case. He had been on the run for so long—he just wanted it to all be over. He needed a boost of adrenaline, something to keep him going. Something to remind him that they were getting close to their destination.

Next to him, August seemed even more tired. He didn't complain though. He kept trekking along, eyes set straight ahead, determination plastered on his pretty face. Coy felt a sense of pride for how far he'd come. He could imagine how many people in August's place would have given up, and still, August pressed on. Whether he felt a sense of obligation, or just wanted to prove himself, Coy appreciated his commitment to seeing things through.

"How much longer?" August asked.

"We're close," Coy answered, trying to be optimistic. "It's in the air. Can't you smell it?"

"If by *it* you mean grass and sweat, then yes. I can definitely smell it."

Coy snickered. "Hang in there, August. We're almost there."

August turned toward him, one eyebrow quirked high on his face. "Are you feeling okay?"

"No worse than usual," Coy replied. "Why?"

"It's just that..." He flipped a lock of hair over his shoulder. "Nothing, never mind," he said before turning away.

Coy had not missed the beginning of a smile on his face before he did so.

THEY STOPPED WALKING, but it was only to take in the sight before them. It didn't seem real. Coy almost felt like pinching himself, but he was afraid if he did, he'd wake up from a dream and find himself right back at the Registry prison. It was real. It had to be. He could see it. He could *smell* it. About two hundred feet ahead of them—so familiar, vivid, and breathtaking—stood *Sago*.

He was covered in dirt, sweat, and mosquito bites. Still, Coy grinned. He glanced at August and saw that his mouth was also pulled into a bright smile.

Their bodies were the wind. They whipped through the stretch of land that remained, cheering as they did so. It wasn't Hamet, but it was close. They were almost there. One more town to cross, just one more.

Coy did not doubt for a second that they could do it.

His feet touched Sagoian soil first. August was right behind him. There were not done yet. Sago was filled with twists and turns. Dangerous cliffs awaited them along with ankle-breaking ditches hidden by grass. Sago's landscape was as beautiful as it was treacherous. To outsiders, it was a risk walking on anything but the clearly marked paths.

To Coy, it was a second home.

Chapter Nineteen

COY HAD NOT stopped grinning since they had crossed the border into Sago. He walked the dangerous land with ease, hand gripping August's own, guiding him past deep holes and slithering snakes. He pointed out parts of the landscape: the thorny bush he had tripped over while drunkenly stumbling around late one night, the tree he'd lost his virginity under...

"You lost your virginity under a tree?" August repeated dubiously.

"I was seventeen—she was nineteen. It was the greatest night of my life."

"What was her name?"

Coy shrugged. "Don't remember."

"You are a pig."

Coy smirked.

They chatted and laughed as they made their way down from the hills, Sagoian dwellings steadily popping up around them. Night had fallen upon them. By Coy's estimations, they still had about an hour to go until they reached Amira's pub.

Coy thought back to the determined expression on August's face when they had been crossing over from Fiasu. He glanced over at August, noting how he looked more relaxed now, but still steadfast.

"I gotta admit, hummingbird. I'm impressed."

"Impressed about what?" August asked, scratching at his arm.

"You don't look like it, but you can hold your own. When I first saw you, I thought you were a spoiled pretty boy who wouldn't last a day as a Registry officer." He snickered. "I guess I was still right to some extent of that. But you're not as bad as I thought you'd be."

"Thanks," August said. "Unfortunately, I cannot say that the feeling is mutual."

Coy laughed. "Yes, you can. You just won't." He pinched August's side and moved his hand away before August could hit him.

"Once we find your friend, what will we do next? You have yet to share that part of the plan with me."

"First thing," Coy said, "we'll ask her to take us to Hamet. There's something in my room that I need to get. Something important. Then, we'll hide out in Sago while you fill me in on everything you know about Fate. Amira can drive, so she can transport us. That'll help keep our faces out of sight."

"You're betting a lot of things on this friend of yours. What if she does not want the responsibility of all of this?"

"She won't," Coy admitted. "But, she's my closest friend, and she loves me. Besides, who can say no to a face like this?" He grinned.

August snorted. "It's much easier than you think."

THEY HAD NOT reached Amira's pub. That is to say, they *could not* reach Amira's pub. The route they needed to take was blocked by both police officers and Registry guards. They did not seem to be looking for anyone. Rather, they were just waiting, staring at the road in front of a building that had music blaring out into the streets.

"What is that place?" August asked.

"A hotel. I'm not sure why there's so much activity tonight."

They hid in a grove, watching as cars pulled up and then slowed down. Windows were opened, and drivers leaned out to chat with the officers. Sometimes, they were turned away. Other times, they parked and went inside the hotel. The officers continued to stand in the road.

"Do you know any of them? Is one of them Fate?" Coy asked, anger rising. That would have put the icing on their cake. If he could have killed Fate without having to track him down, it would have made his life ten times easier.

August bent forward to get a better look. "I can't tell from here. We need to get closer."

They moved from their spot behind a tree, rushing forward and ducking behind others as they advanced. Eventually, they got as close to the hotel as they could without being spotted. Coy hid behind one tree, one broad shoulder peeking out, while August chose another a few feet away. His slimmer figure was completely out of sight.

"I don't think any of them are Fate. Though one of them does look familiar."

Coy heard the strain in August's voice. Quickly, he glanced back at the hotel. The familiar-looking officer was Hickman.

"Let's just wait it out and try to figure out what the hell is going on," Coy said. "Nothing brash, okay? We'll take care of him when the time is right," he offered kindly.

August nodded.

MORE VEHICLES ARRIVED—cars, vans, and some carriages that were usually only seen in the richer, more traditional parts of Asuda. Coy tried to identify some of the people going inside the hotel, only to discover that he had never seen any of them in his life. If Amira had been here, she would have known at least half of them. Possibly even all of them.

Amira was a font of information and could help Coy get the answers he needed. She had always been capable of that, even when they were kids. If he was going to succeed with his plans, he needed her help just as much as he needed August's.

Regardless, he wouldn't be able to risk trying to pass the guards. There were too many of them. They would see him for sure. And if he shifted, one of them could notify the Registry and he would end up back in prison, lying helplessly on Dr. Rowburg's experimenting table. Coy hated waiting, but it was his only option for now.

He wondered if Fate was inside, but he knew he could not just waltz in to find out. At least, not as they were now—Fate knew both of their faces all too well. Hell, their faces were probably plastered all over Asuda by now.

More people entered the hotel. They wore fancy clothes and high-heeled shoes. Beautiful women clung to the arms of old men. Handsome men escorted aging women up the small steps and through the door.

Was it some kind of party?

Coy leaned against the tree and looked for a sign, something that would give away what was going on inside. He wished he had made more of an effort to befriend someone other than Amira. Sure, he had associates in Sago, but none he actually trusted. As far as he was concerned, most Sagoians were like Fiasians. They would give up their own mother for a quick payday.

He watched as a woman climbed out of a car. Her long legs glistened beneath the light of a lamp post. Another woman climbed out next to her, petite in comparison to the first woman.

"Listen, honey. I'd love to drop everything and work on that. But, I have a party to run. Handle it on your own, okay? You can do it. I have faith in you," the tall woman said, sounding both encouraging and stern, warning that there would be hell to pay if the shorter woman screwed up.

Coy knew that voice.

Amira.

Confusion set in. Why would Amira be surrounding herself with Registry officers? Had August been right? Had she turned her back on him the moment he had been arrested? She had eaten dinner with him and his family, both as Raul and as the woman she had grown into. Had she just given up on him? Despondent, he watched her enter the hotel.

He thought about long nights spent at her pub, about how he had helped her drag out drunks and clean up vomit. There was no way Amira would turn her back on him. It had to be something else.

And then, he thought about the flyer.

The blue paper had been taped to the bar. Coy had commented about her advertising it so early. It had been for a party, another shindig filled with people from all over Asuda. They were to come from far and wide to engage in risky, obscenely sexual activities. A sex party. No, not a sex party.

She had called it an "extravaganza."

Amira had not forsaken him. The one constant in his life that wasn't dead hadn't turned her back on him. Well, at least he hoped she hadn't. It was too early to tell, but he had faith in Amira. She had never let him down before. There had to be a good reason for the presence of Registry officers.

He glanced at August, who'd been quiet the whole time, and wondered what was going through his head. They were too far away to talk to each other—August had moved even closer to the hotel after seeing Hickman. Coy had great hearing, but he was not a mind reader, and August couldn't read lips. Still, he needed to let August know where they were and what was happening. He tried to get August's attention without having to speak, but August was too busy glaring at Hickman.

"August," Coy whispered. August didn't appear to hear him.

August's fingers were digging into the bark of a tree. His shoulders tensed as he leaned forward. He looked like he was about to charge. Coy cursed inwardly and knelt to pick up a fallen acorn. He threw it, relieved when it bounced off August's shoulder. August whipped his head around, falling back on his heels.

"What?" August whispered.

"I know what this is," Coy mouthed back.

August furrowed his brows, frowning. "What?"

"I know what this is."

"I can't understand you."

As if a greater power had taken pity on their pathetic attempt to converse, the guards moved out of the street, back to the front of the building. They still ran the risk of being seen, but at least they could actually whisper without being heard.

"I said, I know what this is," Coy repeated.

"Then stop wasting words and tell me," August whispered back.

Coy glared at him. Why did he always have to be so sharp-tongued? There were so many other things Coy could do with that tongue. Like snatch it out of his mouth and beat him with it.

"It's a party."

August looked at him with overly exaggerated amazement. "I would not have guessed that on my own. Thank you, Coy."

He would make sure to take care of August and his smart—though amazingly beautiful—mouth later. However, right now was not the time for banter. Right now was the time for putting their plan into action. Amira was inside the hotel, which meant that they needed to be inside the hotel *with* her before the officers found them. They couldn't just waltz in there, either. They needed disguises. Good ones. Ones that wouldn't alert the Registry to the fact that two escaped shifters were walking among them. Coy had never needed a reason to wear a disguise in his life.

He did not have a clue of what to do.

THE NUMBER OF people walking inside the hotel seemed endless. Coy and August watched, each still hidden behind a tree. The rough brick exterior of the building did nothing to mask the sounds of music and laughter, which spilled through the entryway and into the grove.

A wagon pulled up, its paint covered in dirt and rust. Six people—four women and two men—spilled out of the vehicle. Their clothing, silk pants and skirts, hung low on their hips and dusted the ground as they walked. Their vests and brassieres were adorned with jewels in intricate patterns, shimmering in the artificial light. Each of them wore jewelry, some more than others. One of them, a heavy woman with skin the color of walnuts and a round belly that jiggled when she moved, led the others toward the entrance. Coy may not have known who they were, but he knew *what* they were the moment they stepped foot out of the wagon: dancers.

Seconds later, another vehicle arrived. The exterior was so clean that it shone in the moonlight. He watched as the driver climbed out and then rushed over to open the passenger door. The driver's large body blocked most of the passenger's, but Coy was able to make out a head of blonde hair. Something about that hair seemed familiar, only he couldn't picture the face it belonged to. Maybe they were one of the many guests that visited Simone's.

He needed to tell August about Amira, so he needed to get closer to him. With the amount of noise pouring out of the building, whispering would be less effective.

"Hey, hummingbird, I'm coming over to you."

"What? No. Are you crazy?" August replied, eyes wide and voice panicked.

Most of the Registry officers had gone inside, while the few remaining were distracted by the crowds. Who knew when the next opportunity would arise?

"Coy, you idiot. Stay where you are."

Coy, of course, did not listen. Narrowing his eyes, he watched and listened intently, waiting for the opportune moment to run across the bare space between the two trees they each hid behind. He perked up when an attendant came down the steps toward an elderly man and a startlingly beautiful young woman.

The man seemed to have trouble walking, and he needed both the assistance of the attendant and the young woman to help him up the three steps that led to the hotel. Coy saw his chance. With everyone focused on the elderly man, Coy rushed forward. In his haste, he did not notice the mass of twisted aerial roots in his path. He tripped, falling hard onto his knee, before he jumped back up and bolted forward until he came to rest behind August.

He felt August trembling in front of him, shoulders shaking, hands coming up to cup his mouth. For a second, he thought August was crying, that he'd been so afraid Coy's movement would get them both caught that he could no longer contain his emotions. It wasn't until he leaned in, shoulder resting against August's, that he realized August was laughing. He was trying to muffle the sound with his hands.

"Screw you," Coy muttered. "How the hell was I supposed to know there were roots there?"

"Well, we *are* in a grove," August said, his words breathless as he fought to hold back his laughter.

"Roots are supposed to be in the ground. Not on top of it."

"*We're* going to be in the ground if those officers catch us. Please tell me you have a plan."

August turned so that he was facing Coy. Clearing his throat, he took a small step backward, creating enough space between them so their bodies were not touching. Coy resisted the urge to pout at the slight distance August put between them.

August shook his head. "Actually, never mind. Your plans are terrible. Tell me where we are, and I'll come up with the plan."

"No need," Coy said. "I have a friend inside. She's hosting the party. All we gotta do is get to her. She'll help us figure things out from there."

"A friend," August repeated, dragging the word out in mocking disbelief. "That party is swarming with Registry officers. How can you be sure she's still your friend? How do you know you can trust her?"

Coy stared down at August. Even in the dark, he saw discomfort flash across his delicate features.

"I have more of a reason to trust her than you."

August opened his mouth to reply, but he closed it after a tense, silent moment.

The wind blustered around them, blowing a lock of August's long hair against his face. The end of it stuck to the corner of his mouth when he spoke.

"I hope you know what you're doing," August muttered.

"Of course I do," Coy said.

Without thinking, he reached down and brushed the hair away from August's face and then looked away when he realized what he had just done. "I always know what I'm doing."

Coy did not know what he was doing.

He knew he needed to somehow get Amira to come outside, but he had yet to figure out exactly how to do that. He couldn't just walk inside and ask for her. While he could change his hairstyle and clothing, there was nothing he could do about his height, his build, or his eyes. Coy spent just as much time in Sago as he did in Hamet, and someone was bound to recognize him, especially from his work at Simone's. He trusted Amira, but he doubted there was anyone else around who wouldn't give him up to the Registry for a shiny reward.

Still hidden behind the tree he now shared with August, he watched as more people poured into the hotel. The men wore classy suits in bold colors like cobalt, maroon, and juniper. The woman wore short skirts and dresses that hugged every swoop and curve of their bodies. He thought about the dancers. The leader had stepped through the entryway with confidence, her long, dark hair swaying behind her.

Her hair...

That was it.

Reaching up, Coy snatched the makeshift hair tie August had made from a scrap of the blanket they had stolen. No longer pinned up, his hair tumbled down his back in thick waves, the ends coming to rest just a few short inches above his waist.

"What the hell are you doing?" August asked, reaching back to grab at his hair, and then turned around to face Coy.

"It has to be you."

"Do you ever say anything that even remotely makes sense?"

"A disguise," Coy clarified. "We'll dress you up, and you'll go to the door and ask for Amira."

"Did you forget that there are *Registry officers* in there?"

"Too many people in Sago know who I am, so I can't do it."

"I'm a former *officer*, Coy. There is a chance that I actually *know* some of the officers in there."

"Yes, but there's also a chance that you *don't*. Plus, it'll be easier to dress you up."

"And what exactly would I be dressing up as?"

Another vehicle pulled up in front of the hotel. This one looked expensive, like it had cost more than every other vehicle parked along the curb. A single woman climbed out of it, clothed solely in red. Her back was bare, save for the several strings that hung from both shoulders and connected in the middle at the small of her back. They formed an upside-down arch, swaying with each step she took toward the entryway. Her shoes, the same red color of her dress, clicked against the pavement. She practically smelled of money. Perhaps a resident of Skiana. Maybe even Askia.

"Well..."

In his periphery, Coy saw August follow his gaze to the woman. They stared at her retreating back until she disappeared into the hotel lobby.

"Oh, no," August said. "Absolutely not."

"You have to," Coy urged. "It's the only way we're going to be able to get in contact with Amira."

"I am *not* dressing up like a *woman*, Coy. It is out of the question."

"August—"

"I said no."

"It'll just be—"

"I'm not doing—"

"You *owe* me."

"—it." August let out a defeated sigh. "I want it to go on record that this is a terrible idea which will not work. You are an idiot, and we are going to get ourselves killed."

Coy was satisfied when August failed to argue against owing him. "Noted."

"Fine," he gritted out, folding his arms across his chest. "And what am I supposed to wear?"

Coy smirked. "I know just the thing."

"JUST THE THING" was the gaudy drapery Coy had spotted hanging on a clothing line outside some poor victim's house on their way to the hotel. August almost felt bad for stealing, but his humiliation served as fitting penance, he thought. He watched as Coy used his talon to make quick work of the fabric, the sharp claw cutting through the material like a surgeon's knife through skin.

"This works pretty great for tailoring, huh?" Coy said without looking up.

August folded his arms and waited as Coy continued to gussy up the drapes. When he was finished, he handed the torn pieces of thick, emerald polyester fabric to August.

"One's a skirt. The other's a…" He made a crude motion that August assumed was the universal gesture for "breast" in Hamet. "You tie it around them."

"I don't have *breasts*, Coy."

"Yeah, but you need to make people *think* that you do. Even flat ones."

"Fine."

August did not have the strength to argue. Coy's plan was terrible, but it was the only one they had.

August undressed, pulling off his shirt and shoving down his pants. Although his back was facing Coy, he still felt Coy's eyes on him. At least it was night and thus shady enough that Coy wouldn't notice his blush.

He needed Coy's help to tie the upper portion of the World's Most Hideous Outfit around his chest. Afterward, they strategically rested his hair on his shoulders, covering up the parts of his chest where his breasts would be if he had he been a woman.

"We need makeup," Coy announced.

"I'm sure we'll find plenty lying around in the forest," August remarked.

The sarcasm was lost on Coy.

"You're right. Wait here."

Excluding the quest for the gaudy fabric, they had been hiding behind the same tree for almost an hour. Where the hell else was August going to go?

Coy came back a few minutes later. His hands were cupped together, and he took careful steps—probably looking out for more aerial roots— as he crossed the forest floor back to their hiding spot. August glanced over at the hotel to make sure none of the officers were nearby.

"Look what I found." He opened his hand, revealing a handful of small red and blue berries.

August stared down at Coy's hand in confusion. "What are we supposed to do with those?" Maybe he could put them in his hair or something, but he didn't really see the point of it.

"We grind them up," Coy said. "They're your makeup. It's what Nina used to do when she wanted to be all glamorous. Here. Close your eyes."

August did as he was told. He cringed when he felt a slippery wetness spreading across his eyelids. It was not a pleasant feeling, but at least it smelled nice. After Coy finished with his eyes, he went to work on his lips, smearing the juice from the berries against them, painting them with the tip of his finger.

"Let the juice dry before you open your eyes," Coy warned him. "Berry juice stings like a bitch."

"How would you know?" August questioned with a smirk.

Coy shrugged. "Sometimes I like being glamorous, too."

August chuckled. "Anything else I should know?"

"Yeah," Coy said. "I used to lick the juice off my lips as a kid." He snickered. "I still do."

August smiled.

"All right. There. You're done."

"How do I look?" August asked. He slowly cracked open one eye, wanting to be sure the juice was dry before he fully opened both of them.

Coy gazed down at him, his mismatched eyes roaming over August's body, making him feel both nervous and insecure.

"I'd fuck you," he finally said. "Flat chest and all." He grinned.

"Is there anyone you *wouldn't* fuck?"

"Hey, there's plenty of people I wouldn't fuck."

"Are any of those people actually alive?"

"Some of them," Coy answered with a wink. He then brought his berry-stained hands to his mouth and gave them a lick. "Mmm. These are pretty ripe. I may have to grab some more of these."

"Stop thinking with your stomach and focus on the plan," August scolded. "What am I supposed to do? Who do I ask for? What if something goes wrong?"

"It won't," Coy said. "Just go to the door—ask for Amira. When she comes, tell her you're a friend of mine and that I need her help."

"What if she doesn't believe me?"

"Don't worry. And, if things go wrong..." Coy trailed off. "They *won't* go wrong. It'll be fine. Now go."

"Coy—"

"August, trust me."

The situation was too dangerous, and it was bound to end in chaos. August had a million questions, and Coy had not convinced him that he was not about to walk to his death. It was not that he didn't trust Coy in particular—August just didn't think it was possible to trust anyone under these circumstances. Regardless, he was entirely out of options.

Chapter Twenty

THE HOTEL DOOR was closed. August assumed this meant that all the guests had arrived and the party had officially begun. His heart hammered in his chest as he approached the threshold. He thought about what he would say. More importantly, he thought about *how* he would say it. He had never attempted to sound like a woman before. What did women even sound like? The only woman he knew well was his mother, and she was aggressive and downright terrifying. He doubted that was the act he was supposed to put on when he asked for Amira.

August glanced back at the grove, seeing Coy's head peeking out from behind the tree. His curls had grown since the first time August had seen him. He looked like a child in the middle of a game of hide-and-seek. A giant, hairy forest child.

August knocked on the door.

It was answered a few seconds later by a short man with a receding hairline. He stared at August, one of his dark eyebrows raised high.

"Can I help you?"

August cleared his throat. "I am looking for Amira," he said in the highest pitch he could reach without causing severe trauma to the lining of his throat.

"I see," the balding man said. "And you are?"

"Au...lina. My name is Alina."

"What business do you have with Amira?" he asked skeptically.

"We are...friends."

"Friends, right..." The man looked August up and down and shook his head. "I'm sorry, but Amira is very busy at the moment. Please come back lat—"

"Okay, okay," August conceded, berating himself for what he was about to do. "I knew it was silly to try to trick someone as obviously intelligent and handsome as yourself. The truth is..." He bit his lip for a second and tasted berry juice on his tongue. It was sweet. He understood why Coy had licked it off. "I'm a performer."

"A performer?"

"Yes. A dancer. I was hoping I could convince Amira to allow me a chance to dance. I won't charge a thing. I'm hoping—" He lowered his voice. "I am hoping to find a rich man to take care of me." He leaned forward, his berry-stained lips close to the man's ear. "And I'll do whatever he wants me to in return."

"I...see." The man gave August another up-and-down look. August knew that look. It was not one he was unfamiliar with. Hickman had been particularly fond of it.

"One moment." He shut the door, and for a moment, August thought that the plan had not worked. But then, a few seconds later, the man opened it again. Amira was not with him.

"Right this way," he said with a grin, taking August's hand and leading him inside.

HE HAD EXPECTED more when he entered the hotel, but there was not much happening inside that he could see. Structurally, it was beautiful—large pillars covered in intricate designs rose to the ceiling and polished marble floors reflected the stunning painted murals—but it was fairly small. There was an aroma of food, but he didn't see any, nor did he see many guests. He supposed that was a good thing. Occasionally, one of the few people would glance at him. He could not tell if the expressions were ones of confusion or amusement, and he did not stay in one place long enough to find out.

The bald man—whose name, he said, was Alexander—led August down a long hall to the side of the antechamber. There were doors on each side, some closed and others opened to reveal comfortable-looking beds and rather interesting, intimidating furniture.

They arrived at one door, which was cracked open. August could hear a woman barking out orders as if she were commanding a ship. His heart was already racing, but it beat even faster when he felt Alexander's hand rest against his lower back.

"Amira can be a bit...unapproachable," Alexander warned. "Do your best. I'll be waiting for you."

"My best," August repeated, but Alexander gently shoved him inside the room and shut the door behind him.

The room was filled with people. From what August could tell, they were all waiting to perform for Amira. Apparently, she was going to handpick the entertainment for the night's festivities. Great. That was just great. He had never danced in his life.

"And you are?" Amira asked. When August didn't respond, she approached him, striding through the room like a queen inspecting her royal court. "I believe I asked you a question."

"O-Oh," August said, voice breaking. "Alina. A friend of mine suggested I come dance for you."

"Is that so?"

He nodded. "He is a dancer himself. He does this whole act with fire. You would love it." August had never seen Coy dance before, but his file listed his place of employment, as well as his occupation.

Amira's eyes widened, and a small gasp slipped from her lips.

"All of you out," she ordered. "Right now."

August was certain everyone in the room was just as confused as he was, but they dared not question Amira's demand. The entertainers began leaving the room, all walking in single file. He started to follow after them, but Amira stopped him.

"Not you," she said. "You stay."

HE HAD MADE a mistake. He had made a mistake, and it was going to get August killed. Coy wanted to go inside, but such reckless thinking would ruin everything. August was inside, but that did not mean he was in trouble. Coy was just going to need to play it by ear and see what happened. If he noticed any type of commotion, he would make a move. Until then, as difficult as it was, he would have to wait.

To pass the time, he ate the leftover berries in his hand and tried to come up with a plan of how to rescue August if things turned sour. His only option was to shift, something he still did not want to do. It had been so long since he'd shifted—he wasn't sure if he would be able to retain his senses. Besides, he didn't know who was attending the party. Some of them—mainly the Registry officers—probably deserved to die, but there were others who were innocent. Even just Amira's presence was enough of a deterrent. He would not be able to live with himself if he killed her by accident during one of his draconic rampages.

Although Coy hated to admit it to himself, he was going to have to trust August to get things done.

AMIRA TOWERED OVER him, her wide, brown eyes staring down at him in disbelief. "You can't expect me to believe that."

"It's true," August confessed "I know it sounds insane, but it's entirely true. You have to believe me."

"I don't *have* to do anything," Amira said. "And I certainly don't want to."

"I... *This*." August gestured at his face and clothing. "This was all his doing. He told me to ask for you and said that you could help us. He is outside hiding behind one of the trees. I have to get back out there and let him know I'm safe."

"You can't go out there. Not looking like that. You may have been able to convince Alexander, but that's because his eyes are shit and he thinks with his dick. If anyone else looks at you for longer than a few seconds, they'll get too curious for comfort. If you and Coy are going to hide out in here, we're going to have to come up with better disguises."

August left out a breath of relief. Even if she may not have believed him entirely, she was at least willing to give him the benefit of the doubt. More importantly, she was going to get him out of the horrible outfit and makeup Coy had convinced him to wear.

"So, what's the plan?" August asked. "Is there a window or something that the two of us can climb in and out of?"

Amira laughed. "Oh, no, honey. I have something much more elegant than that."

AMIRA'S DEFINITION OF "elegant" differed from his own.

August stared in horror at the outfit Amira held in front of him. It was a lot of things: leather, revealing, and provocative, but it most certainly was *not* elegant. Worst of all, it was made for a woman.

"I don't understand why I have to be a woman *again*," he complained. Now that he was inside, he could dress as a man and no one would notice him. Amira had to have *something* that he could put on that would still work as a disguise without forcing him to wear yet another skirt.

"You should be happy that you have the body and face to pull it off," she said, unimpressed. "Now, take that hideous thing off. We have a lot of work to do, and it's only a matter of time before someone comes looking for me. I'm supposed to be hosting this thing, you know."

"You want me to get undressed?" August looked around the room. "Right now? In front of you?"

She quirked an eyebrow at him. "You don't have anything I want," she said. "Trust me."

He was long since fed up with having people asking him to trust them.

He pulled off the ugly outfit made out of even uglier drapes and tried not to blush when Amira stared at him. She left him for a moment, moving into the attached bathroom. When she returned, she carried a bowl of water in her hands and a can of shaving cream.

"What are you going to do with that?" he asked.

"I'm going to shave your legs."

"What? Why?" August stepped backward until his heels hit the wall behind him.

"Because, if you're going to be a woman, you're going to be a convincing one."

"Not all women shave their legs."

"That's true," Amira acknowledged. "And I admire your feminist critique, but right now, we don't have time for that. I'm sure there are some men at this function that admire a woman in all of her natural, hairy beauty. But there are even more sexist, misogynistic pigs down there who think the only thing a woman should be is shaved. You don't have that much hair on you, but it's enough to get noticed. So, it's coming off."

Amira forced him into a chair, and August covered himself with his hands while she shaved his arms and legs. When she was done, she ushered him to the bathroom and made him take a ridiculously quick shower. He sighed and reached down. His legs felt like satin underneath his touch, smooth and hairless. When he stepped out, Amira was waiting for him with an assortment of perfumes and lotions.

August almost felt like taking his chances with the Registry.

The sensation he felt when he slid black latex over his body made his cheeks burn. The embarrassment only grew when Amira stood behind him, tightening the many laces at the black of the dress.

"I was planning to auction it off to the highest bidder. Coy owes me big for this."

"Why do I feel like..." August reached behind himself, feeling along the back of the dress. "Why do I feel like my ass is showing?"

His ass *was* showing. Upon first seeing the dress, he'd thought the laces would stop just around his mid-back. August traced them down to nearly the bottom edge of the dress.

His ass was most definitely showing.

"You can't expect me to actually wear this out there. This is insane."

"We need to keep the attention off of Coy. If that means people will be staring at that pretty ass of yours rather than him, then so be it."

"But my—"

"Stop complaining. It's a great ass." She smacked him on said ass to emphasize her point. "Now, turn around and look at me."

August turned around, red as a beet. "I feel ridiculous."

"Tonight, it doesn't matter how you feel. All that matters is how you look. Now, sit down. We still have to do your makeup."

IT TOOK TWENTY minutes to do his makeup and another twenty for his hair. He was certain that Coy thought he was dead by now.

Amira had a bag full of high-heeled shoes. And, although some of them could fit him, he may as well have been a newborn fawn walking in them. Amira decided to forgo the shoes altogether.

"With a dress like that, a woman doesn't need shoes," she observed.

After the entire ordeal, she led him back into the bathroom and to the mirror.

"I look—" He shook his head in disbelief. "—like I belong in some type of fetish sex dungeon."

Amira stood behind him and grinned. He could see her reflection in the mirror as she admired her handiwork. "Congratulations," she said and rested her hand on August's shoulders. "You look like a Sagoian."

"Now, there's just one thing left to do."

"And what's that?" August asked, terrified of the answer.

"Well, it's not enough to look the part," she said. "You have to be able to play the role."

"Role?" August asked. "What role?"

Amira did not reply. He had the sinking feeling that he was going to find out firsthand.

ALTHOUGH THE CONTENTS inside the bag he held were light, August felt like he was carrying a boulder. There was almost no one in the hall, and only a few people in the antechamber. He felt eyes on him, but given what he was wearing, these people did not seem very interested. He could not imagine what they must have been used to seeing. He did his best to ignore the soft chatter. His hair tickled the sections of his back that were exposed to anyone willing to look.

He exhaled when he finally stepped outside, relieved that no one had approached him, and stared at the tree that he knew Coy was hiding behind. Taking a deep breath, he walked toward it.

Chapter Twenty-One

SOMEONE WAS COMING.

Coy had seen her step out of the hotel. She stared in his direction, and he pressed closer to the tree, hoping she had not noticed him. He could smell her coming closer, her sweet perfume drifting through the air. He didn't know who she was, but if she recognized him, it would lead to disaster.

He thought about what to do. The trees were too spaced out for him to make a run for it. She had seen him. He knew she had. He did not want to hurt her. Maybe he could knock her out just for a little while. By the time someone came looking for her, he would already be lost to the darkness of the night. Only, that would mean abandoning August, which—he realized with an exceptional amount of surprise—was something he did not want to do.

"Coy."

She knew his name. *Oh, gods.* She knew his *name.* How did she know his name? Because his name was infamous throughout Asuda. That's how. His name and photograph were probably on a wanted poster inside the hotel. He had to knock her out. That was his only option.

"Coy," she repeated.

Coy poked his head around the side of the tree and saw her. It was hard not to notice her legs. They stretched long and high, her oiled thighs glistening beneath the moonlight. He let his gaze roam over her. She was certainly beautiful. Quite possibly, she was the most beautiful woman he'd seen in his life. It would have been a shame to injure her in any way.

"Stay back," Coy warned. "And don't scream. I don't want to hurt you."

"What?" she exclaimed. "It's me, you idiot. Amira's inside. I found her."

"*August?*"

"She came up with a plan to get both of us inside. You have to put these on." He tossed a bag his way. Distracted, Coy barely caught it in time.

"Why are you *dressed* like that?" Coy asked. "You look…"

"Coy, we do not have time. You need to take off your clothes."

"You probably shouldn't be saying things like that to me when you're dressed that way," Coy murmured.

"Coy—"

"I know, I know. I'm taking them off."

August turned around, allowing Coy a moment of privacy to get undressed. It was not a very wise move, considering the back of the dress.

"*Jesus*," Coy whispered and shook his head. What the hell had Amira done to August? Coy tried not to look at him, tried not to look at the way the dress was laced down the entirety of his back, at the way the undersides of his thighs looked so smooth and toned… Eventually, he forced himself to look away, hyperaware of his own nudity.

Coy cleared his throat. "Did you know the back of that dress is, uh…unfinished?"

Covering his ass with his hands, August whipped around. His mouth hung open, and Coy raised an eyebrow at his shocked expression.

"You act like you've never seen it before. Stop staring at it," Coy muttered.

August blushed and turned away again, this time keeping his hands down to shield his ass from Coy's gaze.

"You're one to talk," he muttered under his breath.

Coy opened the bag and stared at the contents inside. "What the hell is this?"

"We're supposed to match." He turned back around just as Coy began to slide himself into the black leather pants. They fit lengthwise, but not exactly in width. He could not fasten them. He was not exposing himself, but there was nothing he could do to hide the tuft of dark pubic hair.

"This mask is…" Coy trailed off. "What the hell are the people in there into?"

August shrugged. "Your guess is better than mine."

Coy knelt down and let August help him into the mask. It covered the entirety of his head and, like the pants, was made of black leather. There was a zipper down the back that allowed them to slip it on without too much of a struggle. There were also zippers in the front: one for each eye and one for his mouth. Coy played absently with the zipper over his mouth. Opening and closing it repeatedly. Coy bet that August wished he could zipper his mouth shut without the use of a mask.

"When we are inside, you can only open the left-eye zipper. I doubt people will pay as much attention to that eye. Though, it may be best if you kept them both closed when we first enter. You will be temporarily blind, so I will guide you."

"Yeah, got it," Coy said, still toying with the zipper. "So, what's the plan?"

"We go in. Amira brings us to an empty room on the first floor with a patio door facing east. If anything happens and we need a quick getaway, we can go through the door and straight into the trees."

"Told you she'd know what to do." Coy grinned.

"She shaved my legs."

Coy laughed. "How was that?"

"They're soft." He stuck out one leg, balancing himself on the other. "Want to feel?"

Coy laughed again. He reached down and ran his hand up and down August's leg just below the knee. "Yeah, they actually are pretty soft." He flicked August's knee before standing upright. "All right. You ready?"

August nodded.

"Then, let's do this."

August led the way.

Coy followed behind him, listening to his commands: *keep straight, slow down, watch your step...* It was unnecessary. As soon as August had turned, Coy had unzipped the left-eye zipper so he could stare at August's ass as they walked. He probably should have felt guilty, but he didn't. After everything he'd been through, he should have been able to look at all the asses he wanted, *especially* August's.

Coy zipped it shut once they reached the door. A moment later, he felt August grip him by the hem of the mask and pull him forward as they stepped inside the hotel. Door closing behind them, Coy could only hear a muffled din of conversation and music. Their steps echoed ominously as August led him through the room. He heard another door swing open. The noise hit them at full capacity.

"Dear gods," August whispered.

"What? What are you seeing?"

"QUIET. SOMEONE'S COMING," August muttered, regretting this plan twofold.

This room was far grander and much larger than the antechamber. There were people everywhere. Many were dressed similar to him. Others wandered around the room in elegant gowns or expensive suits. The air around him was thick with lust. One group of people was particularly difficult to miss. They talked, kissed, and touched each other in plain sight, as if they were the only people in the room.

He stayed silent when a couple walked past them, their eyes glinting in a way that made August feel like a fresh piece of meat in a wolf's den. The man's gaze lingered on him for just a few seconds longer than the woman's before they turned a corner.

Looking around the room, August spotted Amira speaking to one of her guests, a man wearing a black suit and a red, silk shirt. His greasy, black hair shone beneath the ceiling lights. For a second or two, August had been convinced it was Fate, but realized that both this man's body size and his height didn't match. He let out a breath of relief.

"I see Amira," he whispered. "I'm going to guide you over there. We have to walk past a lot of people. Keep your head down."

Coy gave a single nod.

August began to guide Coy across the room, bombarded by music and boisterous chatter. He still felt everyone's attention on them, each glance discomfiting. The high-class attire he'd seen when the guests were arriving now appeared sparingly. Most people had changed, some of them into outfits that were even more revealing than his own.

"Is that Katherine?" Coy whispered.

August first looked back at Coy—who had unzipped an eye slit—and then followed his line of sight. Spotting said woman, he realized he recognized her. She was the one Coy had sweet-talked into helping him back when they were imprisoned.

"Damn. Didn't expect her to be into this type of thing. Feeling like I kind of missed out. Glad to see she was able to go on without me."

August rolled his eyes.

Amira stood only a few brisk steps away. Opening his mouth to call to her, August's words died on his lips even as his steps did not stutter until he stopped beside her. From his previous angle, August had not been able to tell with whom she was speaking: Callas Fate, Asuda's ambassador...and Daniel Fate's kin.

Before August could turn and run, Callas's eyes found his.

"And who is this beauty?" Callas remarked, interrupting his own conversation with Amira. "I make an effort to know every single beauty that Asuda has to offer, and I have never seen you before."

August could feel his eyes widen to match Amira's. Coy stood close behind him—August tried to focus on the warmth of his body, grounding himself.

"Come on, now. Do not tell me that you are shy," Callas teased. "You cannot be. Not dressed like that."

"Ambassador, sir," Amira began. "Please allow me the pleasure of introducing you to Alina. Alina, this is Callas Fate, the Ambassador of Asuda." Now that he could see Callas up close, he noted the similarities of his features to Fate. They both had those same evil, green eyes and that ridiculously pale skin.

"Alina," Callas repeated. "What a lovely name. And who is that behind you?"

"Oh," Amira said. "That's... That's..."

"His name does not matter," August declared, trying not to panic. "He is my toy for tonight. It is a pleasure to meet you, Ambassador."

"Your toy," Callas said. "And what a fine toy he makes. May I?"

"If you wish." August held back a wince. "But he's in training. So, nothing above the neck, if you could be so kind." He felt Coy tense next to him and couldn't blame him. Knowing that Fate's relative was about to touch him had to be too much for him.

"Of course." Callas nodded. "I do so admire a woman who knows what she wants."

He stepped over to Coy and looked him up and down. "Very nice." He reached over and gently pressed his fingers against Coy's abdomen before dragging them downward. They slid along Coy's skin, caressing it, passed over his navel, and then stopped to tangle in the coarse pubic hair.

"Very nice, indeed." He lowered his hand farther still, grabbing Coy through his pants, and murmured appreciatively when he heard Coy grunt. "He's built like an ox."

"Why, thank you," August said with a seductive smirk. At least he hoped it looked seductive. On the inside, he felt like screaming.

"I don't suppose I could convince you and your toy to put on a private show for the Ambassador of Asuda?" he asked, his green eyes shimmering with hope.

"I'm sorry, Ambassador," August replied. "Tonight, my toy and I are just here to observe."

"I understand. But it did not hurt to ask, my beautiful, ah… What did you say your name was, again?"

"Alina," August answered.

"Alina, right. Where are you from, Alina?"

"Osin." He smiled and hoped Callas would hurry up and leave.

"Osin," Callas repeated. "Yes, of course. I've visited a couple of times. A quaint, little town."

"I hate to interrupt, Ambassador," Amira said, no remorse in her tone, "but there are still many people I need to introduce you to."

"Yes, yes, of course. Well, Alina, my dear. Perhaps, you will join me for a drink later when things get a little more...*interesting*."

"I'd like that," August lied.

With an apologetic look back, Amira guided Callas away. He hoped she could ditch the ambassador soon. She had not told him which room he and Coy would be staying in, and he wanted to get away from these people as quickly as possible.

"That was strange," August whispered.

Coy said something, but the mask made it difficult to understand. August stood on his toes and reached up to unzip the mouth opening.

"What?"

"I said, at least he didn't grab your dick."

SOMETHING WAS HAPPENING.

The lights had grown dim, and guests were moving through a door into another room. August did not want to follow, but he had no choice when the staff began to usher in the stragglers. Even worse, he had not seen Amira since their run-in with the ambassador. The longer they stayed around others, the more they risked being discovered.

They stepped inside, and August's eyes grew wide at the sight. The room was large and designed like an arena. Rows and rows of chairs surrounded the center stage, set at different levels so that guests had to climb stairs to reach them. August spotted at least four semiprivate compartments above the nosebleed seats. These sections contained no chairs at all, but rather a space covered by sheer drapery. August could just make out couches, food, and bottles of wine. If not for the unusual crowd, this might have been a regular outing to the theater—the drapery alone reminded August of velvet curtains.

"Right this way, mistress," an usher said and led him and Coy up the stairs. August said nothing as they walked up to one of the private spaces. "Madam Amira reserved this for you and your toy. I've placed a pillow on the floor for him. Please enjoy."

August waited until the young man was gone to speak. "What the hell is happening?"

Coy looked around, his hazel eye taking in the scenery around them. "You don't want to know."

"Have you been to one of these parties before?"

"A few years back when these things first started. I hadn't known what it was at first, but Amira had begged me to come dance for them. Apparently, they send the entertainment away once this part starts. But, because they liked me so much and because I was in good with Amira, they let me stay."

"So, what is this, then?" August asked. "What are they going to do?"

"It's pointless to explain. You're going to see it anyway. You might as well sit down and get comfortable. We're not going anywhere anytime soon."

August wanted to know more, but Coy seemed done with the topic. Resigned, August took a seat on the soft couch behind him. The velvet caressed his bare skin. Coy followed suit, kneeling on the pillow in front of him like an obedient pet. August almost commented, but thought better of it.

"I can't believe we've gone this far without anyone noticing us," August remarked.

"Don't jinx it." Coy stretched himself out on the floor and ran his hand up and down August's leg, chuckling. "They really *are* smooth."

"Cut it out." He pulled his legs away, holding them up in the air, and then lowered them onto Coy's back, digging into his shoulder blade.

Coy winced and fell flat onto the floor.

"Serves you right."

"It didn't hurt. It's like getting a massage. Do it again."

"I am not a masseuse."

"Come on. It's the least you can do," Coy urged. "It'll help me forget the fact that I got my dick grabbed by the ambassador, of all people. You know, Fate's relative? I wouldn't be surprised if he was in on all of this."

"I thought you enjoyed having your dick grabbed." August tapped Coy's back with his heels, pressing down hard enough to knead the tense muscles.

"He's not my type."

"*You* actually have a *type*?" August snickered.

"Of course I do. Pretty eyes. Soft lips." He smirked up at August. "Nice ass."

August jabbed his heel into Coy's shoulder and reveled in his grunt of agony.

"Guess the cut of that dress suits you more than I thought."

August rolled his eyes. "Idiot."

THE FIRST PERFORMANCE was hard to watch. August stared wide-eyed at the scene below. A man was strapped face-first to a giant piece of wood shaped like a cross. He was dressed a lot like Coy, clad in leather pants, back and feet bare. His outstretched arms were cuffed at both ends of the cross, accentuating his muscular frame.

Two people stood several feet behind him. One man and one woman. Unlike the man strapped to the cross, they were not wearing leather. The woman wore a gown, its shimmery, blue fabric glistening beneath the light of a crystal chandelier. The man wore the same fabric, except in the form of pants which swished along the floor when he walked.

They kissed. It was not a sweet and gentle kiss, which August would have expected of a couple. It was wild, hungry, and *rough*. The man gripped her by the shoulders, pressing her against him hard enough to raise her feet off the ground. August could just see where her nails bit into his skin, leaving angry, red lines and specks of blood in their wake.

And then, they brought out the whips.

The first crack was loud enough to make him jump in his seat. The man cuffed to the cross cried out, his knees buckling against the wood. The whip flew through the air with ferocity before it smacked against his back again. The strike was sharp and precise, though not quite strong enough to break the skin.

"Why are they doing that to him?" August asked.

Coy had sat up from his lounging position and now had both the left eye and mouth zippers open.

"Because he likes it," Coy explained.

Another crack of the whip.

"Who could possibly like being beaten like that?"

"More people than you'd think. Most of the people at this party came here for the stuff that's happening down there."

August winced at a cracking sound followed immediately by another. The man and woman had begun to take turns. The whips snapped through the air like snakes striking at prey.

"So, they're just going to spend the night beating him?"

"Not exactly."

The sound of the man's shouting echoed off the walls. No one deserved to be beaten like that...except maybe Fate. It seemed to last forever, but eventually, the whippings stopped. August watched as they slowly unshackled him. He did not know the man. Still, he pitied him.

They turned him around, his reddened back facing the cross but not actually touching it. The woman spoke to the man in the shimmery pants. He cursed their distance. He wanted to know what she had said. Not that it mattered. What happened next was enough to make August forget about her entirely.

August watched, dumbfounded when the blue-clothed man lowered himself to his knees. He unfastened the other man's pants with haste, exposing his shockingly hard cock to the room before wrapping his lips around it.

"Dear gods," August whispered and dropped his gaze to stare down at his lap. He could not look at people doing something so intimate—and obscene—in front of an audience. He put his hand against his forehead, as if he were shielding his eyes from the sun. Despite himself, he slowly looked up and then gasped as he saw the man on his knees shoving his face into the freshly beaten man's lap.

"It's just a blowjob. What? Is Osin filled with a bunch of shy virgins? Or is it just you?" Coy wondered out loud.

"Be quiet." August retorted.

"Are you?" Coy asked, staring up at him.

"Am I what?"

"A virgin?"

August crossed his arms and looked away. "That's none of your business. Stop asking so many personal questions."

Coy snickered. "I already know you are. You told me."

August used his knees to nudge Coy forward and away from him. "Then why are you asking me?"

"I just wanted to see you blush."

"I will not give you the satisfaction," he said, trying to prevent himself from blushing.

Up until he'd met Coy, he had never even seen another person *completely* naked. Coy had been the first to break that twenty-two-year-long streak. Now, not only was he seeing another person's cock, but he was also watching—while pretending otherwise—another man suck it.

"This is just the first act," Coy said.

August just stared at him. There was a cry from down below. August automatically turned and caught the whipped man jerk his hips forward, shudder, and slump before jerking upright again—undoubtedly due to the pain in his back. When the man in shimmery pants moved away, it was to show off the whipped man's wet, flaccid cock.

"It only gets better from here."

AUGUST AND COY definitely had different meanings of the word "better." After the spectacle with the whips, another couple took the stage. Thankfully, there were no more beatings, though there was certainly more sex.

The next pair were a man and a woman who rolled around on the floor, kissing and touching and tearing off each other's clothes. August spent most of his time looking anywhere but the display. Even Coy seemed to have more fun watching August than the entertainment.

After them were two women. They looked like royalty as they made their way to the center of the room. Diamond and gold jewelry twinkled beneath the lights, dark skin glistening and extravagant gowns flowing behind them as they moved.

They mesmerized the crowd. Each slowly wound their hips, moving about the floor. Occasionally, one would help the other remove a portion of her clothing. Gradually, they revealed more of their flesh.

August gazed down at Coy, who seemed to be enthralled with the scene below them. His reaction was only more evident when the women ended up completely naked, each of them touching and caressing the other's skin. An unmistakable groan slipped from Coy's lips when one of the women lay back on a couch, her legs spread wide, showing off her sex. This was followed by another groan as the second woman slid her face between the first woman's thighs.

"Ah, Alina. There you are."

The voice startled August. He glanced down at Coy, who had already closed both the eye and mouth zippers and lowered his head.

"How are you and your toy enjoying the festivities?" Callas asked.

"Well, *I'm* certainly enjoying them, Ambassador," August said, after a pause.

"It seems your toy is enjoying them as well." Callas motioned down to the obvious bulge in Coy's pants.

That idiot.

"Yes, well. I may have let him sneak a couple of peeks." Callas began to lean down, his hand reaching out toward Coy's cock. Moving his foot before Callas could get his hands on Coy again, he pressed his toes against the tent in Coy's pants, rubbing at the bulge with his toes. "Among a few other things."

"I see," Callas said. He watched August molest Coy, the sole of his foot sliding back and forth against his covered erection.

August heard Coy grunt, felt him lean into August's caress. "Was there anything I could do for you, Ambassador?"

"Not really," Callas admitted. "I just wanted to make sure the beautiful Alina from Osin was enjoying herself...and her toy."

"I assure you I am enjoying us both." He smiled.

"Do you mind if I finish the rest of this performance with you?" Callas asked.

"Of course not. Please have a seat."

August held back a sigh when Callas sat next to him. Callas began rambling on about another such party he had attended, comparing the extravagance between the two. August barely kept from scrunching his nose at the scent of stale wine. Worse, his leg was getting tired, but he knew he couldn't stop with Callas sitting next to him. It felt like an eternity before the two women below finished their performance. Whimpers and moans filled the room and then roars of excited cheering. Finally, a staffer announced a brief intermission, and Callas excused himself.

"Sorry," August said, pulling back his leg. "He was probably going to touch you again if I hadn't done that."

"It's nothing," Coy said. "Thanks."

It didn't look like it was nothing. August looked down at his foot. Did he have some type of special talent?

"Finally," Amira said. Startled, August and Coy both looked up. August smiled to himself, imagining the face Coy pulled when he realized the mask impeded his vision.

"Of course, I'll take your pet to the restroom. I'll make sure he stays on his best behavior," she said loudly enough for anyone nearby to hear her.

August nodded. Not sure what Amira was planning, he trusted her to do it without anything going wrong. Amira took Coy's wrist and helped him to his feet.

"Right this way."

She led Coy through the opening in the sheer curtains, her high heels clicking against the hard floor.

August leaned back against the couch and sighed. He was tired but far too apprehensive to try to sleep. Besides, he needed to be alert in case Callas came back. Maybe if he closed his eyes for a second, it would give his mind some time to relax. He gave it a try but had to sit up a second later when he heard someone coming.

"Mistress."

It was the usher who had guided him and Coy to their seats. He held two small flutes, champagne bubbling inside.

"Compliments of the ambassador. For you and your toy."

"Thank you." He accepted the drinks. "Send the ambassador my thanks."

"Of course, mistress." He retreated past the sheer curtains, leaving August alone.

August picked up one of the flutes and smelled it. He had never tasted champagne before—or any other type of alcohol. Bringing it to his lips, he took a curious sip, and his eyes widened at the taste. It was *delicious*. Unbelievably smooth and amazingly sweet on his tongue. He finished the glass in a matter of seconds and then looked over at Coy's.

Just one little sip of his drink wouldn't hurt.

Chapter Twenty-Two

COY WALKED WITH only one of the eye zippers open, letting Amira lead him to who knows where, keeping track of the route. Her palms were sweaty where she gripped his hand. It took everything for him not to grip her back. It had been so long since he'd seen her, since he'd talked to her. Coy knew a lot of people, but he could count the number of true friends he had on one hand, using exactly one finger.

She pulled him to the right.

"Almost there," she said.

He listened to her footsteps as they marched, letting the rhythm distract him from the unpleasant feeling of not being in control. She turned right again into a vacant room and then shut the door behind them. Seconds later, Amira threw herself against him into the first hug he'd had since losing his family.

"Oh, Coy," she exclaimed. Her long arms gripped him, holding him tight against her body. "I thought you were dead."

Coy had to wrench an arm free from Amira's hold to open up the mask's other zippers. "Dead? Gimme a little more credit than that."

"How did you do it?" Amira asked. "There're Registry officers looking for you all over Asuda. Some of them are here—with Callas."

"Yeah, I know. August and I saw them. He said you had a place for us to hide out?"

Amira nodded. She hesitantly released her hold on Coy, perhaps worried that he'd disappear if she let him go.

"The event lasts for three days. You two can stay in this bedroom for the duration. Afterward, I'll bring you both back to the pub. Registry officers come in from time to time, but they don't stay long. You and August can stay upstairs with me until we can figure out a plan. How did the two of you even meet?"

Coy scratched at his head, realized the mask prevented him from doing so properly, and dropped his hands down by his sides. "He's a shifter I escaped with. And, uh, a former Registry officer. He used to work with Daniel Fate…"

"He what?!" Amira yelled. "With *Fate*? How do you even know you can trust him?"

Coy rested his arms on her shoulders. "I know how it sounds. Trust me, I do. It's a little complicated."

"A *little*?" Amira shook her head, and Coy could tell she thought working with August was a bad idea. "See, this is why I didn't bring the two of you straight here in the first place. I knew it had to be something like this. Coy, you can't trust him if he worked—"

"Amira, please. If you can't trust him, trust me. I know what I'm doing. August is… He has my back, okay?"

The stern expression on her face relaxed. "It almost sounds like you have a soft spot for him."

He snickered, brushing off the comment. "Yeah, well. I wouldn't go that far."

"Well." She sighed. "As long as you're sure about this."

"I am."

"Okay." She nodded, as if trying to convince herself that if Coy could trust August, then she could, too. "Okay," she said again.

"You're the best, Amira."

"Tell me something I don't know." Unable to contain themselves, they hugged once more, laughs edged with a hint of desperation "I'm so glad you're okay, Coy." The smile fell from her face. "At least physically. I was sorry to hear about Dinina. Do you know where they took Ari?"

Coy shook his head. "Not yet, but I'm going to find out. I'll tell you about everything as soon as we're out of here. For now, we should probably go back for August. I can't tell if the ambassador is trying to fuck him or me."

"Probably both of you."

"I didn't know he was into this type of stuff." After a pause, he added, "Do you think he had anything to do with all the shifters being locked up?"

"It's possible," she answered. "You'd be surprised what that man is capable of. Come on. Let's get you back to your mistress." She grinned.

Coy zipped up his mask. "Lead the way."

COY CURSED. THEN, he cursed himself for leaving August alone.

They found August reclining against the couch, his brown eyes staring up at the ceiling. He had found a way to loosen up his dress so that the top part of it hung off his shoulders. It looked like he had attempted to get the dress up and over his hips but gave up because of how tightly it clung to his skin. The tip of his index finger rested against his lip, smearing the red lipstick that Amira had painstakingly painted on him to perfection. He did not seem to register their presence.

"August, what the hell," Coy whispered.

August looked at him. At least, Coy thought he was looking at him. There was a faraway glint in his eyes, like he was looking past Coy and staring into the abyss.

"There you are," August slurred. "I've been waiting for you." He leaned over and picked up an almost empty flute. The bit of liquid left inside splashed against the sides. "I only drink... My only drink..." He laughed and shook his head so hard that his hair whipped about his face. "I only drank a little bit of yours." He murmured something incoherent, and his body slumped over the side of the couch.

"*Fucking hell*," Coy muttered.

"Give me that." Amira snatched the flute out of August's hand and sniffed it. "Damn it."

"What? What is it?" Coy asked.

"Callas. He does this all the time. The drug itself is harmless, but he'll..." Amira trailed off while looking down at August. "He'll probably be a little difficult to handle for a while."

"What do you mean by that?" Coy asked, watching as August dropped his hands to his thighs, dragging them back and forth along the smooth skin, smearing lipstick between them.

"It's a drug. Popular in this type of setting. It's already potent as it is, and from the looks of things, he's had more than someone his size can handle."

"Fuck," Coy muttered.

"If that's what it takes," she replied. "Aren't the two of you...?"

"No, it's not like that," he snapped, telling himself that he didn't sound disappointed.

She shrugged. "Could have fooled me."

Coy let out a frustrated growl. He was not going to fuck August, and neither would anyone else, especially not Callas. He was just going to have to get him back to the room and have him sleep it off. Fortunately, the last performance would be starting soon. Maybe he could drag August away before anyone noticed that Alina was being led around by her toy, instead of vice versa.

"Amira!" a voice called. Coy could just make out the form of one of Amira's staff on the stairs below.

"Gotta go," Amira said, wincing. "Just..." She stared down at August and shook his head. "Just keep him quiet."

"Right," Coy said.

With a lingering look, Amira finally turned and left, waving to the man below.

Sighing, Coy lowered himself to the pillow in front of August's feet, pausing briefly to yank August's dress back up. "I can't leave you for a second."

"You were gone longer than a second. You were gone so long." August leaned down so far that his lips nearly brushed Coy's cheek. "I thought you were never coming back." He dragged out the last word, his mouth lingering so dangerously close to Coy's face.

"Sit back and shut up," Coy ordered. "Why the hell would you drink something knowing it was from Callas?"

"It tasted so *sweet*." He shifted in his seat and raised his leg, bringing it up to just below Coy's waist. Coy caught his foot before he could brush it against his cock like he had done earlier.

"You liked it before." August pouted.

"You need to get ahold of yourself."

"What if I want you to get ahold of me?"

Coy stared at August's painted lips as he spoke. The seduction in his words was unmistakable—but so was the slur. Again, August tried to caress him with his foot.

"Knock it off." He pushed August's leg away. This happened several more times before August finally gave up.

"I'll let you touch mine," August whispered. He reached down, grabbing the hem of the dress. He tugged at the fabric, trying in vain to get it above his waist, but it was too tight and would not go up any higher than it already was. Coy mentally scolded himself for being disappointed when the dress would not budge.

This was getting out of hand.

"August, please. I'm begging you. You're going to ruin everything if you don't stop this."

"Fine." August fell back against the couch with a sigh. "Be that way."

Coy had to remind himself that the person above him was not August. Well, it *was* him. Only, his sense of thinking had been altered. Coy would not be responsible for letting him do, or say anything, that August would regret. Coy would be the first to admit that he enjoyed teasing August mercilessly, but he would not let August suffer at anyone else's hands, least of all Callas's.

Watching August was a struggle. He moved and squirmed on the couch, whimpering and gasping as he attempted to touch himself. He was too out of it to figure out how to get the dress off, so he just slid from side to side on the couch. Eventually, he obviously figured out that if he opened his legs wide enough, he could slip his hand between them.

It was fine, Coy told himself. The last performance had started and many of the other attendees were doing the same thing as August. It wouldn't be a big deal if someone walked past and saw him fondling himself—just as long as they didn't see his cock. Luckily, Coy sat in the way, his body blocking August's lap. Besides, even if anyone saw, most probably would not have cared.

Coy watched August's inexperienced hands trying to extract pleasure. He had known August was a virgin the moment he'd seen him, but he did not realize the depth of that presumption. Dr. Rowburg was a monster. An evil woman who made sure he was hidden from the world and all of its experiences. Coy wondered if this was the first time August had touched himself. It probably wasn't, but it didn't look like he did this sort of thing very often. He almost felt sorry for the life August had been given. *Almost.*

August gasped, and the sound went straight to Coy's cock.

"Okay, that's enough," Coy growled. He grabbed August's hand, pulled it away, and pinned it down against the couch.

Below them, two men had taken the center of the floor. Like the two women before them, they danced around, enticing the crowd. Coy was not impressed. He could dance better than them any day of the week. He missed dancing, he thought sadly—and then bitterly. He missed his family and his freedom and his dignity, too.

August made a few attempts to free himself from Coy's hold before giving up. He tried with the other hand, but only ended up with it pinned down, too. Without the use of either of his hands, he opened and closed his knees, trying to use the friction from his thighs to stimulate his cock.

Coy was exhausted. He spent more time keeping August under control than actually watching the performance, not that it really mattered. Like every other performance, it would end in sex. He wondered how August would have responded to watching two men fuck had he not been drugged, compulsively humping the air.

Callas was despicable.

The performance ended, and the audience cheered. Coy stood up and helped August to his feet. He could barely walk, stumbling around like the ocean roiled beneath him. After a few clumsy steps forward, Coy gave up and tossed him over his shoulder.

He had to find the room that Amira had pulled him into before—preferably before they ran into Callas. If the place had not been so crowded, he would have been able to find it from smell alone, but there were too many people, which meant too many different smells. August's cock poked him in the chest as he walked, and he could only imagine how the two of them looked. It must have been a sight to behold.

"Who's the real toy?" a man asked as Coy walked past. He smacked August hard on the ass, and August cried out.

Coy barely kept his fire in check, but he kept walking. Still, he had gotten a good whiff of the man as he passed. He would remember it and find him later, once this was all over. He told himself that it wasn't the fact that he'd smacked August's ass, but that he'd smacked it while August was incapacitated.

It took several minutes, but he finally found their room. After stepping inside, he shut the door behind them and locked it. For a few seconds, he stood quietly, listening to make sure that no one had followed them. Satisfied, Coy walked over to the bed and unceremoniously dropped August onto the mattress.

"Maybe some fresh air will help you regain your senses."

He moved over to the patio door and opened it, letting a breeze of cool air blow into the room. Reaching behind his head, he unzipped the mask and tugged it off his head. His curly hair was matted and stuck to his scalp. The parts that weren't tangled were drenched with sweat. Still, it felt good to breathe through his nose again. Walking back over to the bed, Coy stared down at August and shook his head at the sight.

"Are you okay?"

August didn't answer. Instead, he slid off the bed onto his knees directly in front of Coy. He reached out and grabbed at Coy's unfastened pants, trying to pry them down.

"What did I tell you?" Coy gritted out, his hands smacking August's away. "Get back on the bed and go the fuck to sleep."

August stared up at him defiantly before reaching for Coy's pants again. This only earned him another smack, one harder than the last. On the third try, he hit August's hand so hard that it made his own sting.

August's look of defiance turned into a glare. He stared up at Coy, his dark eyebrows knitted close. Amira had decorated his eyelids with purple eye shadow, and even though he looked angry, he had to admit that he also looked beautiful. Even in that ridiculous dress, he looked soft and sweet. *Innocent.*

This, of course, changed when August—frustrated with not being allowed to touch Coy—reached up and pulled roughly at his pubic hair, making him shout in pain. He grabbed August's hand, snatching it away from his body, and threw it back with enough force enough to make August smack himself in the face.

Coy would have laughed if he hadn't been so pissed.

August was relentless. Coy took a few steps back, wanting to prevent any more damage, but August stood up and followed after him. His behavior was strange. The look in his eyes wasn't. August had set his eyes on something, and he was determined to get it by any means necessary.

Coy walked backward until his shoulders hit the wall. He would not hurt August. Regardless, they could not spend the entire night like this. August reached out a hand to touch him. Coy slapped it away.

"August, that's enough. Stop it." August tried again. "I said, stop it. Damn it."

Annoyed and irritated, Coy grabbed both of August's wrists and wrenched them high into the air. Moving with rapid speed, he flipped their positions, pinning August's hands against the wall. Coy glared down at him, his face hot and sweaty from having worn the mask for so long—and August's behavior was not helping his condition.

"What the hell is the matter with you?" Coy growled. "Why can't you just calm down? What the hell was in that champagne?"

August looked up at him, dazed. Coy stared back into his eyes, silently pleading with him to stop, but August's expression was so desperate, so needy and filled with want.

"Please," August begged. His voice was barely above a whisper, but Coy heard him. "Please. I... I *need* you."

"August…"

Before Coy could get out what he'd been planning to say, August pivoted, gripped Coy's arms, and slammed him against the wall.

Coy let out a growl, both frustrated and slightly turned on by the show of aggression on August's part. Something hidden deep down inside of Coy, something that he'd been pretending had not existed, reared its ugly head. It was a voice that told him that maybe he could get used to this, to August pressed against him, possessive and dominating.

But not like this.

Maybe he did want August. But, if he were to bed him, he wanted all of him. Not a drugged-up version of him. He wanted the real August—sexy, sober, and screaming his name.

Coy groaned as impatient hands explored his chest. When those same eager hands began to force their way into his already unfastened pants, he let out a surprised gasp.

"August, stop," he ordered. He reached down and gripped at August's wrists, attempting to pull his hands away. "We can't do this right now."

"Yes, we can," August purred and snatched his hands out of Coy's grip.

It became a skirmish, a dance between August's lust and Coy's desire to do the right thing. Every time Coy prevented August from reaching his goal, August responded with a stronger maneuver.

August leaned into him. Coy felt August's cock against him, hard and pressing into his thigh. As much as Coy wanted to enjoy it, he couldn't. Not when August wasn't in the right frame of mind.

"I'm serious, August." Mustering up his willpower, Coy shoved the other man away. "That's enough."

There was a second where nothing happened. Neither of them spoke or moved. They simply stared at each other.

And then August lost it.

A tussle of want became a full-on battle. August fought him, his strength and speed increasing by the second.

"What the fuck is going on with you?" Coy breathed out.

He wasn't used to other people being able to overpower him, especially someone like August. Sure, he was a Registry officer and probably was trained in some type of combat, but this? This was…

Coy cried out as the hands scrambling to force him against the wall began to dig into him. Nails as sharp as claws scratched at his sides and then gripped at his hips. No, not *as* sharp as claws. They *were* claws.

Oh, no.

This couldn't be happening. Not now.

"Damn it. Are you shifting?"

Coy grabbed August's wrists once more and then stared into his eyes. They were amber. Just like before. August's breath came out shallow, and his pupils began to dilate. There was no doubt about it. August was definitely about to shift.

Coy began to panic. He scrambled to think of what would bring August back from the brink.

"Don't fucking shift here," he half growled, half pleaded.

But, he could tell by August's gaze that he was too far gone.

"Shit, shit, shit." Coy tried to keep ahold of August's wrists.

He could handle this. He just needed to know what August's animal was. It couldn't be too bad. It was August, after all. He was probably a rabbit or something.

"What's your animal?" Coy demanded. "Tell me what your animal is."

August jerked against him with enough force to shove Coy backward into the wall. He stared in horror as the soft, honey skin of August's arm transformed, covering in fur. *Orange* fur.

"August..."

Coy jumped out of the well when August swiped at him, narrowly avoiding the sharp claws that breezed past his chest. He scrambled to put some space between himself and August, wedging himself between a writing table and an empty corner of the room.

August approached him, agile and graceful. He stared at Coy with those glittering amber eyes and licked his mouth with a long, pink tongue. Coy could not take his eyes off of him, his heart beating rapidly in fear. August stared at him curiously, sniffing him, before turning away and running out the patio door, his long, striped tail swishing behind him.

And, just like that, he was gone.

Coy could do nothing more but stay in his exact position—back against the wall, eyes wide. He couldn't believe what had just happened. He had to be dreaming. He must have still been at the prison. Beaten and drugged and hallucinating. There was no way any of this could have happened. August's animal was supposed to be something weak, something hilarious that Coy could tease him endlessly about. A squirrel, a rabbit, or a hummingbird. He could have been something—anything—else.

The last thing he was supposed to be was a *tiger*.

Time wasn't standing still, but it sure as hell felt like it. A toxic cocktail of emotions flooded him. August was a fucking *tiger*.

He balled his hands into fists.

He exhaled, smoke fanning out from his nostrils and dissipating in the air surrounding him. Anger radiated from his pores. His own nails cut into the palms of his hands. August had kept this from him—had probably run off just now because he'd sensed how much Coy wanted to strangle him for it. Wanted to, but couldn't. And now, August was out there all alone. Who knew if those Registry officers from before were still around?

As much as he wanted to murder August for all of this, he wanted more to keep him safe. He couldn't do that by standing around. He had to find August, get him to shift back, and *then* murder him. Or maybe kiss him. He hadn't quite figured that part out.

Amira was right. Somehow, through all of this, he had grown a soft spot for August. This had not been on his list. A former enemy and an associate at best, that's all that August should have been. And yet, he'd burrowed himself into Coy's thoughts and perhaps, more frighteningly, his *heart*. A parasite. That's what he was. Beautiful and soft-skinned, he'd invaded Coy's heart without permission, and now he was stuck there.

"Fuck," Coy cursed. It seemed like the only logical thing to say at the moment.

He had to track August down. He hoped that, by the time he found him, he wasn't still trotting around as a tiger. That would be unfortunate for both of them. In any case, once he shifted back, Coy would force him to explain himself and then... Well, he wasn't sure what would happen after that.

There was a commotion outside in the corridor. Fearful that August had somehow managed to find his way back into the hotel in his tiger form, Coy poked his head out of the door. He spotted Callas, red-faced and drunk, shouting for Alina to come join him in his room. Just as he was about to shut the door, Callas spotted him.

"You there," he slurred, raising the wine glass he held in his hand. "Ox man. Where is your mistress?" He began walking toward Coy, and Coy panicked. If he shut the door, there was no doubt that Callas would bang on it, drunkenly demanding that he open it, and cause an even bigger scene. Still, it didn't look like he had much of a choice.

Across the corridor, another door opened, revealing a guest undoubtedly annoyed with all the noise. Coy stared at the other person, mouth dropping open in shock when he realized who it was. He was just as beautiful and blond as the first time he'd seen him—*Elias*.

Elias met his eyes, and his own expression mirrored Coy's. For a moment, the two of them simply stared at each other. Once Coy got over his initial shock, he silently pleaded with Elias to rescue him.

"Ambassador," Elias called, stepping out of his room to distract the drunken man from his path toward Coy. "I've been looking all over for you." He was dressed in nothing more than a robe. His pale legs were bare save for the golden anklet dangling around his leg. "You absolutely must join me for a drink. I will not take no for an answer."

He reached Callas and guided him in the opposite direction of Coy, toward his own room. Glancing back, he waved Coy off, gesturing for him to go back inside. Coy watched as Elias's door closed and breathed a huge sigh of relief before closing his own. He owed Elias big time. When all this was over, he would have to find a way to thank him.

Now that the coast was clear, he rushed out the patio door and into the trees. Who knew where August was, or how far he'd gotten. Gods, he was nothing but trouble. Not a thorn in his side, but a knife in his rib cage.

Coy walked through the grove, eyes scanning the ground and lingering on trees. A slideshow of memories of his grandfather invaded his thoughts. He tried to avoid them. He didn't want to think about him at a time like this. However, remembering how he'd behaved in his tiger form could come in handy for tracking down August.

He paused, eyes wide, mouth hanging open with realization. He was a fucking moron. That's what that weird—yet familiar—smell had been. It wasn't the same, but it was just similar enough.

August smelled like a tiger.

The rustle of leaves behind him shoved him back into reality. He pivoted, one foot pressed firmly against the ground, the other swinging around, so that he was in a fighting stance by the time he faced the opposite way.

The sound he heard had definitely been August—unless there was another shifter in these woods. He stared right at Coy with piercing, amber eyes, freezing him in place.

He was still in his tiger form.

Chapter Twenty-Three

"SHIT," COY WHISPERED. His entire body trembled, his fight-or-flight response swinging into overdrive. He tried not to think about his last run-in with a tiger, about how angry and terrified he'd been, about how much he'd *hated* him. This tiger wasn't his grandfather, wasn't a mean, abusive drunk.

This was August.

Coy took a slow step backward, careful not to make any sudden moves. His entire body demanded that he shift, that he fight the big cat lurking just a few feet away. But, he wouldn't—he *couldn't*. It wouldn't be a battle. Coy would kill him. He was certain of it. A few short weeks ago, he would have given anything to destroy August. Now, he was trying to figure out how to avoid harming him. If he wasn't so damn terrified, he would have laughed at the irony.

"All right," Coy said, still whispering. "Calm down, August. It's me, okay? You remember me, don't you?"

The tiger cocked his head to the side, as if he were perplexed. Coy knew better than that, though. August wasn't confused. He was sizing him up. It seemed like he really did lose himself completely when he shifted. The animal in front of him wasn't August anymore. He was simply a tiger, a creature who acted on impulse and instinct. Coy only had one option.

He had to run.

He took another step backward, heels pressing against the soft earth. The tiger shifted his paws, wiggling his entire body and crouching down until his nose almost touched the forest floor.

He had to run *now*.

Coy pivoted and bolted forward. He heard August behind him, his paws trampling fallen leaves and twigs. There was no way he could outrun him, but maybe he could confuse him. If he zigzagged through the grove, he might be able to tire him out. If August was too tired to chase him, maybe Coy could help him shift back.

"Fuck." Coy dashed around a tree, hoping to slow August down, but August was right on his heels. If he could get enough distance between them, he could climb up. He knew tigers could scale trees, but he doubted they could scramble up as high as he could.

He kept running, cursing at how determined August was to catch him. Stubborn as always, Coy thought, as he ran deeper into the forest. Glancing back, he saw that August was farther away than he'd expected, giving him the perfect opportunity to scurry up one of the nearby trees. He'd just managed to grab onto one of the branches when it broke under his weight, sending both him and the branch itself tumbling to the ground.

August leapt forward, the picture of power and grace, his strong, fur-covered body preparing to attack Coy where he lay. In a last-ditch effort, Coy grabbed the fallen branch, held it in front of his face, and blew.

Fire burst from his mouth and caught onto the wood. Flames engulfed the tips, lighting up a small portion of the grove. Coy held up the makeshift torch, using it as his only defense against the tiger coming for him.

At the last second, August veered his heavy body and landed just a few feet away. He hissed, teeth bared, as he swiped his sharp claws through the air.

Coy panted, one eye closing from the sweat pouring down his face. The only thing standing between him and August was a rapidly burning branch. He couldn't use it to hurt August, and eventually it would go out. When it did, it was all over.

August swiped at the air again and then lunged immediately. He didn't connect with Coy, but he was close.

"Come on, August," Coy pleaded. "I don't want to hurt you." Well, that wasn't entirely true. He wanted to strangle August for not telling him that he was a tiger shifter. But, he wanted to do that to the August he knew—the one he'd journeyed across Asuda with—not this tiger before him.

August swiped at him once more, only this time Coy was too slow to react. He cried out when claws tore at the skin of his arm, creating four fresh wounds, blood gushing from each one.

He was out of time. The branch was burning too quickly, and now that he was injured, it would be impossible to outthink August. He had no choice but to fight. He had to shift, despite that there was no way he could avoid being seen if he did. Even this deep into the trees, someone would at least hear him. Dragons weren't exactly stealthy.

"Hummingbird, please. Don't do this," Coy begged, desperate.

The tiger whipped his head to the side, eyes widening and ears flicking back. His snarl began to vanish, teeth no longer bared in a show of aggression. Even his posture began to let up, not stiff and poised to attack, but more relaxed, as if he were seconds from plopping down and taking a nap.

"Is that it?" Coy asked, words soft, voice smooth and gentle. "Hummingbird. Do you remember that name?" The tiger went slack before him, practically in a trance, like someone had shot him with a tranquilizer. "That's it, hummingbird. That's it."

Coy watched as the tiger collapsed to the ground, twisting and contorting its body. Fur began to fade, giving way to soft, brown skin and dark hair. August slid to the ground, chest rising and falling in time with heavy breaths.

"C-Coy?"

He looked like a bewildered angel that had fallen from the moon right into the forest. He knelt there, nude and glowing, hair catching the wind so that it blew about his head, long and luxurious.

He was breathtakingly beautiful, to say the least.

Never in his life had Coy felt such strong desire to kiss someone— while also wanting to snatch the life right out of him.

"I'm so sorry," August said.

Now that he could be relieved that both of them were mostly okay, Coy allowed himself to feel the anger he'd kept in place after August's sudden shift. "Damn right, you are. You're the sorriest piece of shit I know."

"I wanted to tell you, but—"

"But what? Huh? Why wouldn't you tell me something like that?" It felt as if his blood were boiling, like a volcano of frustration, rage, and agony was seconds from exploding from his body.

"I did not want you to hate me."

"Hate you?" He let out an overdramatic laugh. "You, we...we almost— If not for..." Coy trailed off. If it hadn't been for the ambassador and that drugged champagne, the whole night would have been different. It would have been...special. This wasn't fair.

"I know you're upset. I just—"

"Don't." Coy shook his head. "You *lied* to me, August."

"What would you have had me do? Tell you the truth so you could have even more of a reason to want me dead? I did not want to..."

"Want to what? Make my life even worse than what it already is? Honestly, I thought that would be impossible, but fucking up people's lives must be a natural talent for you."

August glared up at him before holding his head down in defeat, and then he climbed to his feet. He began to walk off, naked and shivering, venturing in the opposite direction of the hotel.

"Where the hell are you going? You think you're just going to run away from this?" Coy reached out and grabbed August's wrist but had to dodge the swing of August's other hand to avoid it connecting with his face. Still gripping August's wrist, he shoved him backward, forcing his back against a tree and showering them both in fallen pine needles. "Who the fuck do you think you are?"

August stared up at him, defiant eyes asking him what he planned to do next. The wind blew around them, and Coy saw the slight tremble of August's body and the chatter of his teeth. The temperature had fallen. He had to be freezing. Knowing this infuriated Coy. He shouldn't have been worried about whether or not August was cold. He shouldn't have wanted to lean against him, to warm August's body with his own. He wanted to hate August, wanted to make him pay for all the trouble that found him the moment he walked into his life.

Only...he couldn't. There was something that wouldn't let him. Something that made it impossible to hate August. Something that could no longer remain dormant. It would always be there, nagging him, eating away at his thoughts, taunting him. It would never disappear.

And though he wouldn't admit it, not even to himself, he didn't want it to.

"Let's go," Coy said. He turned and began to walk back toward the hotel, not bothering to see if August was following. He knew he was. It's not like he had a choice. Coy was still gripping his wrist.

"So, you have forgiven me?" August asked tentatively.

"No."

"Will you forgive me?"

"Who knows?"

"Is there anything I can do to make this right?" August asked, eyes directed at his feet.

"Yeah," Coy answered. "For starters, you're gonna let me teach you how to shift properly. Right now, you're a fucking liability."

Thankfully, there was no one out in the hotel's garden, so they were able to enter their room through the same patio door they'd previously exited. The moment they were indoors, he let go of August's wrist. Coy took a second to listen out into the corridor, but it was silent. Elias must have coaxed Callas away. He hoped that Elias had been clever enough to ply the ambassador with more wine instead of his charms. Or, at least called security on him.

Coy cleaned up his wounds as best he could while ignoring August's apologies and offers to help. "Get some rest," he said, sinking into the bed.

August didn't reply. But, after a few moments, the bed dipped from the weight of his body climbing onto it.

They lay together, just the two of them and the enormous elephant sitting on the bed between them. The room was quiet, so much so that the silence became almost deafening—a soundless, never-ending scream shared by the two of them—until August broke it, soft and uncertain.

"I apologize for everything. About not telling you. About how I behaved when I..." Coy wasn't looking at him, but he could *hear* the blush in his words. "That drink... I was not myself."

"So, you're saying the real you didn't want to be fucked?"

"That is not... I am not..."

"It's not all your fault," Coy said, sighing. "Hell, it's not your fault at all. It's that piece of shit Callas. If anyone should be apologizing here, it should be him." Coy turned so that he could face August. "He came looking for you, you know. Well, looking for Alina. Luckily Eli—" Coy paused. Maybe bringing up Elias to August wouldn't be the best idea. "—elite security came and dragged him back to his room."

August shook his head. "He really is awful, isn't he?"

"Awful is a compliment for him," Coy replied and then shifted so that he was lying on his side with his arm propped up beneath his chin. "Can I ask you something?"

Coy knew he needed to back off, especially after a night like tonight. It wasn't him—he was still furious. It was the dragon, the greedy beast inside of him that operated purely on instinct and self-gratification.

It wanted August. It'd been denied a battle. It didn't want to be denied the chance to mate.

August looked at him with curious eyes that made the inside of Coy's stomach flutter.

"Of course," August replied and offered Coy a small, uncertain smile.

"If things hadn't been…" Coy waved his free hand through the air, at a loss for words to describe how horrible the night had turned out. "If you hadn't been drugged, would you have even wanted to…"

"I would have," August answered softly, shyly, and *eagerly.*

Coy smirked. "Interesting…"

August rolled his eyes, but the smile on his face was impossible to miss.

"Hn." Coy dropped his hand so that it grazed August's thigh. "Too bad I can't tell if that's really you or the drug talking."

"It's me," August said. "I'm certain that shifting has sobered me completely."

Coy shook his head. "Mm, that sounds like something a drugged person would say."

"I'm fine," August argued.

"Prove it," Coy replied, still smirking.

"How?"

"Answer these questions." Coy shifted again so that he was even closer to August, feeling the warmth of his skin against him. The scent of the forest was in August's hair. It took a ridiculous amount of strength to resist leaning over and taking a deep whiff of it.

"I don't see how questions will—"

"Question one. Where are you?"

August rolled his eyes again. "I'm at a hotel," he answered. "For an event, which I believe is some kind of sex party."

Coy snickered. "Question two. Which are the strongest of all the shifters?"

August tugged at a lock of his own hair. "Some would argue that dragons are the strongest, most powerful shifters, but I believe—"

"Final question," Coy interrupted. "What's your name?"

"My name is Augustus Seaton," August answered.

"Nope." Coy shook his head. "Not that name. Your *other* name. Your nickname. The one you love."

"I don't love it." August huffed. "It's childish."

"Looks like you can't answer." Coy moved his hand away from August's thigh, rolled onto his back, and stared up at the ceiling. "Too bad."

"It's *hummingbird*," August answered quickly. "And it's stupid."

"See. That wasn't so bad, was it?" Coy glanced over at August and grinned. "Good job."

"So...?" August stared at him.

"So, what?" Coy asked.

"Don't I get a—" August turned away from him. "—prize?"

"Isn't being able to answer all those tough questions prize enough for you?" Coy teased.

"There was nothing tough about—"

The rest of August's statement was cut off by his sharp gasp. August's skin was warm where Coy touched it, his fingers creeping up along his inner thighs. August whimpered when Coy wrapped his hand around his cock, the slow strokes pulling gasps from his mouth that were music to Coy's ears. August lowered his head, forehead pressed against Coy's shoulder, hips rocking slowly and evenly like the calming lull of the sea.

"C-Coy?" August whispered, the word more question than name.

"Shh, hummingbird," Coy whispered back. "You want this, right? I'll stop if you don't."

"Please don't stop," August begged, moving his hand to join Coy's own.

August's movements became erratic, jerky, and rough, a storm on the once-quiet sea. It didn't last long—a few ginger strokes, a couple of swift tugs, and August came apart against him, gasping and shuddering, fingers gripping at Coy's wrist. Coy couldn't feel surprised at how quickly it was over, too relieved that August hadn't shifted again. Besides, he knew August didn't have much—*or any*—experience. It was only to be expected.

"Thank you," August whispered.

Now, that did surprise him, and despite himself, Coy chuckled. "Don't mention it."

August fell quiet for a few seconds before speaking again. "Coy?"

"Yeah?"

"Do you want me to... I mean, I've never...but I could... Or we could...pick up where we left off from before?"

Coy recognized the hopefulness in August's words but pretended he hadn't. "Nah, don't worry about it."

"Oh," August replied, hopefulness replaced with disappointment. "I guess I'll just go to sleep. I probably wouldn't be very good at it anyway. Though, I wonder. Would it really be so horrible?" he asked softly.

"You should get some rest," Coy said. "Goodnight, hummingbird."

"Oh, um. Goodnight," August murmured back.

August hadn't probed about why Coy hadn't wanted August to reciprocate. Whether it was because he was too afraid to or because he fell asleep a few minutes afterward, Coy didn't know. Sleep was a good idea. Unfortunately, Coy remained awake, staring up at the ceiling. He wanted to deny the truth, to pretend none of this was real, that what he was feeling wasn't possible. Even as he tried to convince himself that he wasn't feeling anything at all, his heart was there to remind him of his lies.

He was falling for August. Or maybe, he'd already fallen for him.

Somehow, August had burrowed his way inside Coy's heart, and now it was impossible to get him out. Except, Coy couldn't deal with that right now—or maybe ever. He couldn't allow himself to fall in love, or be loved, when he still had a grandmother's death to avenge and a missing brother to find.

He thought about his grandparents. At one point, the two of them had been happy, before...everything. It had been a long time ago, but it was true. He'd seen it firsthand. His grandfather may have been an abusive alcoholic when Coy had killed him, but at one time, he'd been the love of his grandmother's life—and Coy had taken that away from her.

What right did he have to keep his own?

Coy wrapped a strand of August's long hair around his finger and sighed. "Nah, hummingbird," he murmured to August's slumbering body, knowing August would never hear his answer. Leaning down, he brought his lips near August's, hesitated, and then moved his head up to press a gentle kiss against his forehead.

"I don't think it'd be horrible at all. In fact, I bet it'd be the most perfect thing in the world."

About the Author

S.T. Sterlings is a university librarian, a part-time instructor, and a full-time fangirl. She is originally from Virginia but currently lives in Southern California with her two sons and her maniac of a dog.

Website: http://www.ststerlings.com/

Twitter: https://twitter.com/ststerlings

9 781947 139602